POSH

LUCY JACKSON

ST. MARTIN'S PRESS
NEW YORK

This is a work of fiction. All of the characters, organizations, and events portrayed in this novel are either products of the author's imagination or are used fictitiously.

www.stmartins.com

Book design by Gretchen Achilles

LIBRARY OF CONGRESS CATALOGING-IN-PUBLICATION DATA

Jackson, Lucy.
    Posh / Lucy Jackson.—1st ed.
        p. cm.
    ISBN-13: 978-0-312-36389-5
    ISBN-10: 0-312-36389-3
    1. Women school principals—Fiction. 2. Private schools—Fiction.
3. High school students—Fiction. 4. Parent and teenager—Fiction.
5. Teenagers and adults—Fiction. 6. Upper East Side (New York, N.Y.)—
Fiction. I. Title.
PS3610.A3535P67 2007
813'.6—dc22

                                                        2006032136

First Edition: January 2007

10 9 8 7 6 5 4 3 2 1

The greatest griefs are those we cause ourselves.
—SOPHOCLES, 430 B.C.

These shoes hurt more than life itself, but how cute *are they?*
—DAISY CAMARANO-ROSENTHAL, A.D. 2003

POSH

*E*lizabeth Goldfine is treating herself to one last manicure and pedicure before she departs from this earth. This is the final day of her life and she is high on morphine, but if there is one thing she knows for sure, it's that she wants to go out looking like a babe, or at least beautifully groomed and dressed to the nines in her silvery Dolce & Gabbana mini-dress, and, of course, her Manolo Blahniks. Two years ago, when she was about to turn forty, Elizabeth was informed that her life would be brought cruelly to a halt six months later, give or take a month. No way in hell, *she told her oncologist.* No way. *She had, after all, a loving husband, two treasured children, a duplex on Park and a house in Greenwich, a BMW 745iL, a Mercedes sports coupe, and a thriving practice as a family therapist, not to mention a law degree from Columbia that she'd never put to use. In short, she had everything; an embarrassment of riches, surely.* Screw you, you lying bastard! *she offered the doctor, who only nodded, as if he were accustomed to being addressed this way by all his terminal patients. Which surely he was not, though he understood the impulse. And now, after two years of fighting a ferocious battle that could not be won—despite a cast-iron will to live and the best medical treatment money could buy—it has come to this: lying at home in a rented hospital bed on a balmy September morning, attended by a registered nurse and a Korean manicurist from a nail salon a few blocks south of the Goldfines' apartment. Elizabeth* resembles nothing so much as a concentration camp inmate, heartbreakingly gaunt, wrists and ankles thin as a little girl's, arms and legs not much more than bone, eyes sunken and nearly defeated. Reflecting an irony almost too harsh to contemplate, Elizabeth's mother, Lil, happens to be a survivor of Auschwitz, and so, the Goldfine family knows, she cannot gaze at Elizabeth for even an instant without conjuring up her own unthinkable past.

"Well, we've all got to go sooner or later," Elizabeth says in a whispery voice to no one in particular. Hearing this, Morgan flinches and grasps the hand of her best friend, Julianne, who has taken the morning off from school to be here with her. Morgan is seventeen and not yet ready for her mother to die, despite having known, for a long while now, that this day was drawing near. Obviously, her mother won't be around for her wedding, or even for her senior prom and graduation in the spring. She won't even get to find out which college Morgan enrolls in next fall. Unbelievable. Morgan loves her mother more than she's ever loved anyone, though, as she's confided to Julianne, looking at the skeletal figure in the hospital bed sometimes makes her feel weak in the knees, as if she might keel over at any moment.

"Okay, yes?" Ki, the manicurist, asks, holding up two bottles of polish for approval.

"Sheer Moonberry for your hands and Cravin' Raisin for your toes, okay, Mom?" Morgan says.

"Fine," says Elizabeth. "Fine fine fine. And for you, too."

"You want me to have a manicure?"

"For the funeral."

"Don't say that, Mommy."

"Merrily merrily merrily merrily, life is but a dream."

"Don't," Morgan says.

"Damned if do, damned if don't," says Elizabeth, pronouncing her last words, her frail voice singsongy.

"I don't know what you're talking about," Morgan claims, but what she tries to explain to Elizabeth and Julianne is that none of *this is real to her, that it is beyond her powers of imagination to envision her mother sealed away in a casket and buried beneath the earth, gone forever and unreachable, even though Morgan needs her this very moment and will continue to need her for the million and one reasons that will arise between now and the end of her own life, an end so far off into the future that it's impossible to even think about. In the eyes of the world, she's merely a spoiled rich kid, but the agony she feels as her mother shuts her eyes and drifts toward death, well, all that money and the privilege it buys, all of that is rendered meaningless as the ache in her heart and soul is amplified beyond measure and all she feels and knows is that she is about to become motherless.*

When it is too late and her mother is already gone, she calls her father's office on her cell phone, but he can't understand a word she is saying. Not a word. "Calm down," he instructs her. "Calm. Down." If only he hadn't felt the need to go into the office for a couple of hours this morning. Just to check up on a few things.

Julianne takes the phone from Morgan. "Mister Goldfine?" she says, but then she, too, begins to sob.

The manicurist goes about her work anyway, swiftly and silently, because it is, after all, more than a little creepy to be painting the nails of a dead woman.

1

KATHRYN HOFFMAN

I t falls to Kathryn "Lazy" Hoffman, headmistress of the Griffin School (grades K–12), to notify the ninety-nine other students in Morgan's class about the funeral. (Lazy, a childhood nickname bestowed upon her by her parents when, as a three-year-old, she refused to walk and demanded to be carried everywhere, has stuck to her all these years, like a barnacle to a rock.) She sends out a mass e-mail from her office, wherein she makes clear that attendance at the service is mandatory:

> Attendance is not mandatory, but it is my hope that each and every one of you will show your support of Morgan and the entire Goldfine family during this sad time. Remember that we at the Griffin School are a caring, responsible community—a family, if you will. Tomorrow morning, three buses will be waiting outside the school at 9:45 sharp to take us to the funeral chapel. Please make every effort to join us.
> —KH
>
> P.S. Any test or quiz scheduled during these hours will, of course, be postponed.

She clicks SEND and lights up a cigarette, though of course there is no smoking allowed anywhere in the school, not even in her beautiful office with its Persian rugs and burnished mahogany furniture, its stained-glass windows and built-in floor-to-ceiling bookcases. She's the headmistress, for God's sake; if she wants to smoke one or two (well, make that three) lousy Newports in her own private office at six P.M., who's going to stop her? The truth is, most of the time she loves this job, loves being high man on the totem pole, loves the (relatively) generous salary they pay her for keeping the students and faculty in line and for stroking the swollen egos of all those superstar parents—Academy Award winners; publishing and real estate moguls; Emmy and Tony Award winners; painters whose work goes for a million dollars a pop and is part of the permanent collections of the Whitney and the Modern; Pulitzer Prize winners; authors whose books are perched at the top of the *New York Times* bestseller lists. And then there are the housewives richer than Croesus who arrive in their chauffeur-driven cars with nothing better to do than torment her with their own torment: *If Erin doesn't get into Yale, Harvard, or Princeton, I'll shoot myself, Lazy! In the head! I'll blow my brains out and that's no idle threat! Just last night I dreamed that Erin was rejected everywhere except Cornell, and I woke up drenched in sweat!* How many times had she heard this neurotic refrain sung by a designer-dressed mother with impeccably styled hair and makeup, and tears in her eyes? And how many times had Lazy reminded a parent that her very own son was a graduate of, believe it or not, the University of Michigan. And that after only three years at Michigan, he went on to Harvard Law School, where he's now a first-year student.

University of Michigan? Are you joking?

"Lunatics," Lazy murmurs, and exhales a perfectly formed smoke ring. And then two more. If these parents don't drive her to her grave, nothing will. Maybe she should quit this job she sometimes fiercely despises; take an early retirement and move to some tranquil little town in Dutchess County or Connecticut where she would grow her own vegetables and herbs and reread all of Henry James and . . . whom is she kidding? This is a dream job, at one of the very best private (or "independent," as they say in the biz) schools in all of America, filled with exceptionally bright, impassioned students; it's a privilege to be surrounded by them day after day as she walks the quiet, carpeted hallways and pops her head into a classroom or two to listen to her faculty with their Ivy League doctorates brilliantly dissecting *King Lear* or *To the Lighthouse* or *Anna Karenina*. And in one of those very classrooms, she can get a good look at Doug McNamee, WASP prince in his Cole Haan loafers and tweed jacket, his pale blue eyes alert and watchful, his graying blond hair a pleasure to her fingers as he pins her to the burgundy leather couch in her office. He's got a wife and she's got a husband, but these things, unfortunately, sometimes happen so let he or she who is without sin cast the first . . . not that she's proud of herself. Far from it. The guilt, in fact, has caused a chronic case of nocturnal teeth-grinding, for which her dentist has already prescribed a plastic mouth guard to be used at bedtime. (Fat chance she'll ever wear *that* to bed.) But if Bloomingdale's sold sackcloth and little bags of ashes, she'd be there with credit card in hand. And if she were a Catholic, she'd be first in line for confession, absolution, and penance—an act of self-abasement or mortification might very well do the trick for her, Lazy thinks.

Turning forty-three last week was, like all her birthdays after thirty-nine, no picnic, and without Doug to look forward to, she might have been too depressed to get out of bed. But he arrived at school early that morning with a large chocolate-dipped strawberry and a bottle of sparkling wine in hand, and they made love at seven A.M. in the private bathroom attached to her office, Lazy pressed against the pedestal sink, the skirt of her suit yanked above her hips, her heart thumping as she neared orgasm, heart knocking harder and harder at the thought of being caught by a member of the housekeeping staff, though of course the office door and the bathroom door were both locked and she and Doug were safe as could be. *Happy birthday, my darling Jewish princess,* Doug had murmured, as if she hadn't asked him more than once not to refer to her that way. *It's so undignified,* she told him. *Not to mention the teensiest bit anti-Semitic.*

2

JULIANNE COOPERSMITH

It was the old tall-dark-and-handsome thing that first captured her attention. That, and the exceptionally smart, articulate comments he offered up in the A.P. English class they were both taking in this, their senior year. One day during the first week of school, he'd spoken at length about Sarah Orne Jewett's *The Country of the Pointed Firs,* and not once, Julianne noted, had he used the word "like"; as in, "I think this book, like, totally rocks"—just the sort of moronic declaration you might hear in the classroom any day of the week. Now the two of them, Julianne Coopersmith and Michael Avery, are joined at the hip. Before Michael, she had never been in love, had never been attached to any guy at all for more than a few awkward kisses. She is a tiny, sweet-faced blonde, barely five feet tall, barely ninety-five pounds, and people who don't know her well might make the mistake of thinking she is shy. Which, in class, she often is, rarely saying much of anything, even about her favorite books from among the ones they are reading—*Portrait of a Lady* and *The House of Mirth.* But she has a good many friends of both sexes, and goes out Friday and Saturday nights to hear music downtown at the Knitting Factory and at the Bowery Ballroom, and then travels uptown to the Jackson Hole on Second Avenue where she sits for a couple of hours picking at a cheeseburger and talking endlessly—with her best friend, Morgan, and whoever else happens to be around—about everything in the world. She never drinks, as some of her friends do, though she smokes weed occasionally, a hit or two, just to be sociable. She and her friends are among Griffin's best students, and most of them hope to attend colleges like Yale and Harvard and Stanford when they graduate. Smaller schools like Haverford, Williams, and Amherst are more her speed, Julianne thinks, or maybe even an arty place like Sarah Lawrence. No matter what, she'll need lots of financial aid wherever she goes. Griffin has given her plenty of help to cover its $23,000 annual tuition, but who knows if the colleges will be so generous. Julianne will just have to wait until April to see how it all shakes out.

She and her mother, Dee, formerly a novelist and currently a freelance editor and part-time cab driver, live together in a rent-controlled high-rise in Chelsea. It's just the two of them—her father has relocated to Houston, Texas, with his girlfriend, who is only in her thirties and has suffered one miscarriage after another these past few years. Julianne feels sorry for her, but her mother does not. This is only one of the many things Julianne and Dee disagree on. Every night her mother kisses Julianne's forehead or cheek and tells her that she loves her more than anything on this planet, which Julianne doesn't doubt for a minute. But not a day goes by that they don't argue strenuously over something—the "disastrous" state of Julianne's room, her habit of lingering on the Internet until two-thirty or three A.M. on school nights, her refusal to drink anything except coffee and Diet Coke, her insistence on taking her cell phone everywhere, even into the bathroom. Sometimes her mother slams Julianne's bedroom door so forcefully that the framed posters of Superchunk and Modest Mouse and Ani di Franco on her wall actually tremble. *If only you would listen to me even a little, if only you would clean up that pigsty of a room, if only you would get off that damn AOL and into bed at a decent hour. . . .* Sometimes Dee loses it completely and cries, but Julianne has hardened her heart against the sound of her mother's weeping. She's a good kid and knows it—so what if she talks on her cell phone while she sits on the toilet, or uses the floor of her room as a closet, or leaves tiny orange flecks of cheddar popcorn on her pillowcase? So what? She has pointed out to her mother that, in fact, things could be infinitely worse. Think of the possibilities, she instructs Dee: she could be a druggie, high on Ecstasy or coke fifty-two weekends a year; she could be a slut, sleeping with every boy in her grade; she could be a victim of obsessive-compulsive disorder or bulimia, like some people she knows at Griffin. "Well, I'm grateful that you're not," Dee tells her, "because I just wouldn't be able to deal with it. I'm a single mother and I can deal with only so much."

3

DEE COOPERSMITH

Rolling over in her daughter's double bed where she happened to fall asleep tonight after watching a two-and-a-half-hour video, Dee resists the temptation to stroke Julianne's soft blond hair; out cold, she looks especially serene, and Dee stares and stares, entirely free to do so and still amazed, after all these years, that this beautiful child is hers. What will she do next year when Julianne goes off to college—cry herself to sleep night after night like some pathetic loser? (*Loser:* that's her daughter's word, employed to denote anyone she finds useless.) Dee ought to get back to her own bed, a perfectly good convertible couch parked in the living room of their one-bedroom apartment, but she'd rather just stay where she is. Mostly out of laziness, but also because it's sweet and cozy with her daughter beside her. The next time Dee goes to her shrink for a tune-up, she may finally raise the subject of how desperately she wishes Julianne would choose a college right here in the city and continue to live at home. She could, in fact, use a general, all-purpose adjustment from Dr. Kaye, whom she likes to think of as the chiropractor of her soul. He is also, in Dee's estimation, a full-fledged mensch, as evidenced by his willingness to look the other way when it comes to the thousands of dollars of unpaid bills with Dee's name on them. From time to time, Dee pays off a portion of what she owes, but it's clear to both her and Dr. Kaye that she is never going to catch up, not unless she writes a book that happens to hit the bestseller lists or is bought by a major studio for serious money. Neither of these possibilities seems at all likely. Not by a long shot. Dee, who is the author of a half-dozen critically praised (but otherwise ignored) novels, hasn't had a book out in eight years. And she has no plans to finish the new one she is only halfway through, because, she keeps reminding herself, she is no longer a writer. Been there, done that. Had her heart broken all too many times out there in the marketplace of public opinion, where, apparently, those with $23.95 to spend would rather spend it on anything but her books.

She is forty-nine, precariously, perilously, close to fifty, and the manuscript of her latest novel currently rests on the dust-coated surface of the Nok Hockey board she's been storing under Julianne's bed for the past five or six years. Every so often she's spotted some of her earlier efforts in a used book shop, priced to move at a humiliating $1.95. Affectionately, she strokes their covers, leafing through them tenderly, as if they were her poor, doomed, infinitely vulnerable offspring, fatally afflicted by some awful genetic disease for which there is no cure. She finds herself taking comfort in the words of countless professional critics who'd judged her "gifted," "prodigiously gifted," "abundantly gifted" throughout her career. "I may not be Dostoyevsky," Dee had been fond of saying to her husband (when they were still married and even after they weren't), "but I have to believe I'm pretty decent at what I do, right? I mean, if I'm not convinced of even that, I might as well give it all up and get a job, I don't know, driving a cab?" Not surprisingly, she'd annoyed the hell out of her ex with that kind of talk.

In addition to the money she earns as a hack, Dee gets by on child support and alimony and the freelance editing jobs frequently tossed her way. But it's always a struggle. And of the sort that Julianne's friends and their families are unacquainted with— accustomed as they are to their uniformed housekeepers and laundresses and cooks and chauffeurs, their winter vacations swimming in the Caribbean or skiing at Telluride or in the Swiss Alps, their summers in the Hamptons or on Nantucket, their seemingly charmed lives burnished by the endless flow of money-moneymoneymoneymoney . . . and oh how hard it is not to regard them with envy and maybe a smidgen of loathing, even when they're hardworking and smart and generous. Just like Dee herself.

4

LAZY

The funeral chapel is packed, standing room only, a tribute, Lazy knows, to all the money the Goldfines have given away over the years—to the Democratic Party, to Planned Parenthood, to Mount Sinai Hospital (where there is a pavilion named after them), Harvard Law School (from which Morgan's father graduated at the top of his class thirty years ago), to the Make-a-Wish Foundation, Lincoln Center, the Museum of Natural History, and to Griffin, naturally, where a science center has been named in their honor. And soon enough, Lazy bets, Griffin will be the lucky beneficiary of an extravagantly large gift dedicated to the memory of Elizabeth Goldfine. The lower school is currently in cramped quarters several blocks from the twelve-story building that houses the rest of Griffin—a new building for K through 5 might not be too much to hope for! The body's not even in the ground yet and here she is interviewing architects in her head. . . . It's more than a little unseemly, but an important part of her job is fund-raising, and surely there's nothing wrong with thinking ahead, is there?

"These shoes hurt more than life itself, but how *cute* are they?" she hears someone seated behind her say, and turns to see Daisy Camarano-Rosenthal, a transfer student from Our Lady of Holy Agony, showing off her new Jimmy Choos to Julianne Coopersmith.

"Shush!" Lazy orders, and glares at them both. "Does the word 'inappropriate' mean anything to you girls? This is a funeral, for God's sake. Show a little respect!"

"Sorry," Daisy says, and Julianne's face reddens.

"I certainly hope so," says Lazy, just as the rabbi positioned up front at a small podium begins to speak in Hebrew. He quickly switches to English, quoting Sophocles' description of man as "but breath and shadow, nothing more." The rabbi pauses, dramatically, and a single wrenching sob fills the silence.

"That's Morgan!" someone says in a stage whisper, and then Richard, Lazy's husband, who teaches neurobiology to med students all the way up at Columbia, slides into her velvet-upholstered pew.

"Well, this is a surprise," Lazy says.

"I thought you wanted me here."

Not really. "Shouldn't you be at school?"

"Actually, my first class isn't until noon today," Richard whispers in her ear. "Didn't I tell you that last night?"

"Oh."

Two rows in front of her and off to the side, a woman, pen in hand, appears to be balancing her checkbook. Talk about inappropriate! Lazy is outraged on behalf of the poor Goldfine family in their time of sorrow! This morning on the bus, she heard a rumor that Elizabeth Goldfine's dying wish was to have a pedicure. Of all the things to wish for on one's deathbed . . . well, to quote F. Scott Fitzgerald, the rich are different from you and me. Or is it "different than"? Lazy can never remember. Though she did major in English at Wellesley, and then there's her doctorate in Comp Lit from Yale. (And also that doctorate in Education from Teachers College at Columbia.) Frankly, she has more important things to be worrying about than conjunctions and prepositions. She's responsible for safely and efficiently herding nearly a hundred teenagers back on those buses and . . . look at those godawful shoes Richard is wearing! Worn down at the heels and in need of a good polishing. "Yea though I walk through the valley of the shadow of death . . ." the rabbi is saying, and Lazy can't believe who she sees sauntering down the aisle searching vainly for a seat: It's Stone Phillips, one of those guys from ABC or NBC, whichever network Morgan's father

reigns over . . . what a hunk! She hates to admit it, but Doug Mc-
Namee, who's quite the hunk himself, doesn't hold a candle to
Stone Phillips, who's even more striking in person than he is on
the tube.

She examines her husband critically. A shlump in those de-
crepit Weejuns, his sport coat wrinkled, his tie dangling limply.
He's one of the sweetest guys in the world, and very, very smart . . .
but, well, he's lacking in the charisma department, and after
twenty-two years of marriage, as much as she loves him, sweet and
smart have come to seem a little dull. And may God forgive her for
not feeling infinitely thankful for a good marriage with a good and
generous man.

"While I appreciate your taking the time to be here with me,
Rich, you certainly didn't need to come," Lazy says.

"No problem," says Richard, and takes her hand in his. And
then he leans his nearly bald head against her shoulder. Across the
aisle, Doug turns toward her and winks. It's been a while since
they've made love, almost ten days. In all the time she and Doug
have been "together," they've rarely—except during the summer
break—gone this long without sex. The thing is, it's not easy convincing him to hang around after school until six or so, when the
building has pretty much emptied out. His wife, Clarissa, teaches
at another independent school in the neighborhood, and often
they meet at Griffin's front entrance to go home together. She's a
skinny blonde with long legs and big feet, a blue blood whose
great-great-great-great-great-grandfather, John C. Calhoun, was
vice president of the U.S. starting in 1825. Lazy was supposed to
be impressed with this bit of information, but when Doug shared
it with her, her only response had been "B.F.D.," three little letters whose meaning was a mystery to him. " 'Big fucking deal,' "
Lazy explained, and the hurt look on Doug's face surprised her.
"I'm sorry, dear heart," she apologized, "it's just that I had no idea
your wife's pedigree meant so much to you." The memory of this
irks her now and so she does not respond to Doug's wink.

"I love you," Richard murmurs as the first of five eulogies begins.

"Love you, too," says Lazy absently. She tunes out the eulogist, a woman in a smart black pantsuit who is introduced as a childhood friend of the deceased; unable to finish her speech, the woman is led away in tears by the rabbi. "You climb that stairway to heaven, Elizabeth!" she cries, breaking free of the rabbi's grasp and hurling herself against the casket. "You go, girl!" A moment later, a man leaps from his seat and peels her off the gleaming walnut coffin.

The remaining eulogists do their part without a hitch, and then the rabbi announces that the Goldfine family has set up a Web site on the Internet.

"Those of you who wish to do so may post your condolences on wwwdotweloveyouelizabethdotcom," he says, frowning slightly.

"Could you repeat that, please?"

"Is the _E_ in 'Elizabeth' capitalized?"

"How long will the Web site be up?"

Stone Phillips has had enough and is already heading for the door, followed shortly thereafter by Senator Hillary Rodham Clinton and two grim-looking men who are obviously her bodyguards.

Just your typical Griffin funeral, Lazy thinks with pride. _God, I love this job,_ she nearly says out loud as she tries her hardest to catch Hillary's eye. But the senator sails past her, her posture regal, the slightest of smiles on her lips.

5

JULIANNE

It's wall-to-wall people in the Goldfines' living room the first night of their shiva, Morgan and her father and her twelve-year-old brother, Zach, all sitting on sturdy cardboard boxes instead of chairs for some religious reason Julianne knows nothing about. (Though Jewish herself, she is the child of an atheist and an agnostic and has received, every December, what her parents call "holiday gifts," but nothing else to connect her to any religion at all.) Considering the state Morgan is in—zombie-like, barely saying a word, merely nodding politely to all the people who approach to let her know how sorry they are—she looks surprisingly good, Julianne thinks. Her glossy, dyed-black hair is tucked up in some kind of complicated knot, and there's a diamond-and-gold heart on a V-shaped chain suspended delicately from her neck. She'd taken some Valium earlier and told Julianne she felt numb, which was surely preferable to feeling those waves of grief that just kept coming and coming—"tidal waves," she'd called them—the day her mother died. In Julianne's opinion, it's nearly impossible to know how to make someone feel better about something this huge, and so all she can do is sit there on the floor beside Morgan, patting her best friend's knee or rubbing her shoulder, asking in a quiet voice if Morgan is hungry or thirsty or needs tissues for the tears that leak from the corners of her eyes every few minutes. The Valium may have numbed her, but not entirely.

And then Julianne asks their friend Luke Zucker-Johnsen, seated on one of the folding chairs arranged for the crush of visitors, to accompany her to the kitchen to get some ice and Diet Coke for Morgan. "Losing your mother is the worst, obviously, but I sometimes wish my own mother would take a hike and come back in twenty years or so when she'll have no authority over me whatsoever," Julianne confides in a whisper. Whenever Dee is really getting on her nerves, Julianne thinks enviously of Luke. He lives in the garden apartment of a townhouse owned by his parents, who have the three upper floors to themselves. Now and then he comes up for dinner, and there are phone calls back and forth every other day; sometimes he and his parents actually run into each other in the vestibule and have time for a quick exchange. The housekeeper does Luke's laundry, but he's usually on his own when it comes to meals, which suits him fine. He can make macaroni and cheese with the best of them, grill soy burgers on his George Foreman grill, or get take-out sushi or Chinese or Thai from any one of a half-dozen Asian restaurants in the neighborhood. His allowance is three hundred dollars a week and that's more than enough, really.

The love of Luke's mother's life is three-year-old Ashley, born when Grace, his mom, was fifty-two. Grace is some famous feminist writer and when Ashley was born, there was something about it in the "Public Lives" column in the *Times*. And then later, an article in the paper's "Style" section, with a picture of Luke's mother and all these intimate details about how she'd been in menopause and had it reversed somehow, with hormone treatments maybe, to jump-start her ovaries back into business so she could get pregnant again at the unbelievably embarrassing age of fifty-one. Who would willingly reveal that kind of totally personal history to a newspaper? And who would ask their son while he was still a junior in high school if he preferred to have his own apartment instead of living with his family? Luke is cool with it, happy to be pretty much living on his own. But do his parents even love him?

Sending him downstairs to live in the garden apartment doesn't exactly strike Julianne as a loving gesture. She doesn't get it, doesn't get any of it, but especially why an old woman like Grace had to prove to herself that she was still young enough to bring another child into the world. Though Julianne has heard that Ashley is a cute little kid, good-natured and talkative, a three-year-old who has already figured out how to read. Not long ago, Ashley leaned over and read aloud from the *New Yorker* open in Luke's lap; he nearly fainted, he told Julianne. His three-year-old sister is, apparently, a genius of some sort. Or maybe just precocious, as Luke insists. In any case, it seems pretty clear she won't ever be in need of the $595-an-hour SAT tutor Luke and Morgan and some of their other friends have used. Srikanth, the tutor, is an Indian dude with a photographic memory: he'll take the SAT along with you on the very same day, and afterward you go over the test together with a copy he somehow manages to have in his possession. If you and Srikanth determine that in all likelihood you haven't done well enough, you have forty-eight hours to cancel your scores so that whatever colleges you applied to won't have access to them. Luke has already taken the test six times. Because he's got some sort of OCD problem and can't stop himself from painstakingly filling in the ovals on the answer sheet until they are done to perfection, like a porterhouse at Peter Luger's, he is allowed unlimited time—seven, eight, nine hours, whatever it takes to get the job done. A special arrangement that hardly seems fair to the rest of the seniors, most of whom, Julianne included, would have been more than happy with a deal like that.

She and Morgan have been to Luke's apartment plenty of times since he moved in, and once they all did a line or two of coke in his living room. A super, really fast high, but then, afterward, Julianne felt incredibly bored and in a bad mood and took a cab straight home. She never told Dee, who would have been worried and upset, but Morgan confessed to Elizabeth the very next night, and her mother hadn't been too alarmed, which was one of the things that was so wonderful about her. *Now that you've tried it once and satisfied your curiosity, just promise me you won't do it again,* she'd told Morgan, and that was the end of it. Elizabeth was *such* an incredibly cool person, Julianne thinks; Morgan could tell her anything at all, *anything,* and still be able to count on her sympathy. So how unfair is it that she'd had the best mother in the world and lost her? Maybe, Julianne muses, the fate of every human being is actually decided before birth, and on the day Elizabeth was born, it was already predetermined that she would die forty-one years later of liver cancer and nothing could have saved her. On the other hand, since Julianne doesn't believe in a god of any kind, who's the one doing all that predetermining? *Can't answer that one,* she thinks. *Haven't a clue.*

"You didn't know Morgan's mother, did you?" she asks Luke. "She was a really, truly nice person, someone who didn't deserve to get horribly sick and die the way she did, weighing maybe seventy pounds and looking like someone in a horror movie, her face this waxy yellow, her eyes huge in their sockets, staring out at you in this unbearably sad way that made you feel sick yourself, you know what I mean?"

"Um, maybe," Luke says. Taking the ice-filled glass from Julianne, he slowly pours in soda almost to the top and then advances carefully to the living room, where, on bended knee, he presents the drink to Morgan. Perched on a mourner's cardboard box imprinted with brown-and-white swirls to mimic wood grain, she looks, with her perfectly straight back and shoulders and pitch-black knot of gleaming hair, like royalty.

"Morgan?" he says, uttering her name with such sweetness, Julianne believes that she herself will never forget the sound of it.

6

JULIANNE

J ulianne isn't, to be honest, much of a cook, but one Friday afternoon, she impulsively invites Michael over for dinner. They're hanging out on Madison Avenue after school with Morgan and Daisy, lounging on a wooden bench outside a favorite bakery-café, all of them except Julianne smoking Marlboro Lights from the pack Michael forked over nearly nine dollars to buy a couple of minutes ago. (Like any of the shopkeepers care whether or not you're actually eighteen and legally old enough to buy a pack of smokes.)

"Cool!" says Michael, clearly pleased with Julianne's invitation.

It feels like a big step to Julianne; in fact, she's never asked a boy to dinner before. And she is, actually, sort of excited at the prospect of having her mother meet this super-smart, head-turningly handsome guy, who seems to adore her as much as Julianne adores him. Sitting here on the bench with his arm around her shoulders, Michael ditches his cigarette after a couple of drags and plays with her hair, twirling a hank of it lightly around his index finger and then draping it across his mouth. "You're like a little doll," he murmurs, and reaches for her hand. "Your hands are doll-sized!" he says, as if he's never noticed before, and he just has to kiss her diminutive fingertip with its candy apple–red nail polish that's already beginning to flake away.

She smiles, self-conscious in front of Daisy and Morgan, but only fleetingly, because there's nothing terrible, is there, about her friends getting the picture—she and Michael aren't merely dating; they are a bona fide couple. Linked as they are, by the obvious sexual attraction thing, plus admiration for the quickness of each other's minds, and, of course, a mutual respect for the same books and movies. Because how into a guy can you be if he's someone who likes, for example, *Harry Potter* (Julianne just doesn't get that whole fantasy bit and never will) or the stupid movies of, say, Adam Sandler?

"Those two look so fucking cute together, don't they?" Daisy says, nudging Morgan, who smiles vaguely in Julianne and Michael's direction.

"Hey, want to help me shop for the dinner I'm cooking tonight?" says Julianne. She hopes that Morgan will say yes, poor Morgan, who could obviously use the distraction, even if it's just a trip to the supermarket. Julianne's already decided on chicken *masala* because she knows Michael likes Indian food and she saw someone make this dish on the Food Network on a show called "30-Minute Meals" or maybe it was "Emeril Live."

Morgan is shaking her head, saying, "You two go. You and Michael, okay?"

"Yeah," Daisy agrees. "Morgan and I are gonna catch a cab and check out some stuff at Sephora, right?"

"What stuff?" says Julianne.

"Um, there's this new lip gloss called 'Orgasm' that I saw on their Web site."

"Whoa!" Michael says, and Julianne blushes, but she's laughing, too, burying her face under Michael's arm, inhaling the fragrance of his deodorant, which smells like kiwi or maybe lime, she thinks. It's the intimacy of it that she savors, the smallest details about him that are now hers to be recollected whenever she likes.

"See ya, guys," Daisy sings out.

Julianne and Michael head for the subway downtown, but then he suggests that they might as well stop first at the Food

Emporium right there on Madison, then bring the groceries back to her apartment in Chelsea.

Holding hands, they meander up and down the supermarket's glaring, fluorescent-lit aisles, and, in front of a beautifully arranged display of polished-looking peppers in yellow, red, orange, and green, exchange the sort of kiss that makes Julianne shut her eyes and causes her to sway slightly, as if the granite tiles underfoot have somehow shifted. The store is like an igloo, its air-conditioning turned up too high, but the back of Julianne's neck is damp now, and the waist of her jeans is stuck to her spine. Who would have guessed that a kiss in the Food Emporium's vegetable aisle could have generated all that heat?

"Whoa," Michael says again, just as a woman with short, spiky hair reaches into the rows of peppers and grabs one yellow and one orange, no bargain at $5.99 a pound. "Monet's a cubist?" she says into her cell phone. "Haven't we been through this already? He's an *Impressionist*, you numbskull!"

"Can you imagine thinking Monet was a cubist?" Michael says after the woman has walked away. "How funny is *that!*"

Julianne laughs.

"Bet you didn't know he once tried to kill himself."

They're in the meat and poultry section now; Julianne is examining packages of chicken cutlets, trying to find one no larger than a pound. "Who?" she says.

"When Monet was in his twenties, he was the father of an illegitimate kid and so impoverished, so at a loss to earn a living, he saw no way out but suicide. Lucky for the art world, he didn't succeed. In fact, he managed to live to the age of eighty-six. Good story, right?"

"Good story," Julianne says, impressed, but more by the fact that Michael knows these things than by the facts of the story itself. She's beginning to think he knows just about everything.

After tossing a package of chicken into the wire shopping basket he's carting around for her, and then a box of rice, they make their way to an aisle stocked with what appears to be condiments for every type of cuisine. "Hey, it's like the UN of sauces here," Julianne says, counting off Malaysian, Vietnamese, Japanese, and Mexican before Michael calls out, "Got it!" and, triumphantly, snatches up a bottle of *masala* sauce.

"Actually," Julianne confesses at the checkout counter, "I'm not exactly what you'd call a great cook. So don't get your hopes up, okay?"

"Hey, my hopes are always up when it comes to you and me, Jules."

"So who gave you permission to call me 'Jules'?" she teases, and does not argue when he takes out his wallet to pay for their groceries.

By the time Dee shows up, the chicken has been cut into one-inch cubes and is simmering in *masala* sauce in a skillet on the stove. Julianne and Michael are foraging through the pantry in a futile search for a bag of chips to tide them over until dinner is ready.

"Call me crazy, but I could swear it smells like an Indian restaurant in here," Dee announces from the foyer, just outside the kitchen, then falls silent when she sees that Julianne isn't alone.

"Hey, good to meet you," Michael says. He introduces himself, and, like an adult, extends his right hand politely to Dee as she walks toward him.

"Ah," she says, nodding, then smiling. She looks dead tired, the way she almost always does when she's been out in the cab, but Julianne suspects her mother isn't too tired to take note of the obvious—that, no kidding around, Michael could probably pass for a model in one of those Ralph Lauren magazine ads you see in the Sunday paper every week. Dee must be entertaining similar thoughts because she's still smiling, even as she gestures toward the kitchen counters and the mess Julianne has made of them, and says, "'Clean as you go'—do those little words of wisdom make any sense to you?"

"Yeah, sorry," says Julianne.

Michael has already gone to the sink for a sponge, which he uses to mop up the orangey-red sauce that has somehow trickled down one of the white cabinet doors all the way to the floor.

"That's a start," Dee says. "Thank you." And to Julianne, "What's with the rice cooker? I haven't taken that thing down from the shelf in years."

"Basmati rice," says Michael. He pitches the sponge gracefully into the sink.

"We thought plain white rice just didn't seem special enough," Julianne explains. Michael is standing behind her now, and his arms are crossed around her waist. His sneakers are under the table where he abandoned them and there's a large hole in his sock that exposes the tip of his big toe. Only rich people can walk around like that without embarrassment, Julianne knows. But there's something endearing about Michael's lack of self-consciousness, about the way he's hanging out in his torn socks in her kitchen, entirely comfortable here with her and her mother, offering now to wash the dishes after they're finished with dinner.

"Guests don't do dishes," Dee says, staring at Michael admiringly, just as Julianne knew she would. And, later, after dessert, when he's scouring a pot at the kitchen sink and telling Dee why he's decided to apply early to Harvard, it's as if he has her eating right out of his hand.

Another night, when Dee is at the movies with two of her closest friends—a couple of other divorced, single mothers—Julianne jumps at the opportunity to do exactly what her mother has specifically told her not to do. *We do NOT entertain in the boudoir, you got that? Stay out of the bedroom!* Dee has said more than once. More than twice, come to think of it.

Hearing, in her head, her mother's strident words, Julianne has to laugh. Her mother is neither stupid nor naive, so how can she possibly expect Julianne to comply with this bullshit rule of hers?

"What's so hilarious?" Michael says. Both of them are sprawled on her bed; Michael's chest is bare, but Julianne is still wearing her bra. The halogen lamp standing in the corner by the window is at its dimmest setting and she has to struggle to distinguish the features of his face.

She starts to say, *My mother,* but those are the wrong words and instead she says, as his fingers slide shyly under her bra, "You can take it off if you want to."

He murmurs "Thank you" as she turns on her side so he can unhook her bra, which he does with such delicacy, it's as if he's afraid he might hurt her. And then he breathes in sharply at the sight of her breasts and lowers his face into them.

She is a virgin, but so is he, she learns to her surprise. It's too soon, she tells him, just too soon for them to go any farther than they already have. And—another surprise—he agrees that they may as well take it slow. What's the rush, really, he says. They have all the time in the world to get it right.

7

DEE

Out for dinner on a blind date arranged by her eighty-two-year-old mother, Dee is surprised to find that she is actually enjoying herself. Which is a shame, really, since her date, an amiable businessman named Jack Newman, lives in Hawaii and is only here for the week visiting his parents. Dee wonders why her mother neglected to pass along this crucial piece of information, and she looks ruefully at Jack Newman and his remarkably warm smile. It's a smile that makes her think that under other circumstances, he would probably be worth a second date. Maybe even a third. To be honest, Dee has gotten out of the habit of dating; after splitting up, a year or so ago, with her boyfriend (who, wouldn't you know it, went back to his wife after a two-year separation), she just can't be bothered making room for anyone new in her life. Her shrink doesn't like hearing this and has tried to get her to explain what, exactly, she means by "just can't be bothered." Well, she's busy with two jobs and a teenage daughter, isn't that enough of an explanation? Dr. Kaye thinks she's depressed about her abandoned writing career, but Dee doesn't want to go there. She has nothing to say on the subject. Nothing.

"So," Jack says as he offers her the plate of carpaccio with grilled trumpet mushrooms that has just been delivered to their table, "I hear you're a writer."

"I'm a freelance editor who also happens to drive a cab, but trust me, I'm no writer," Dee says. "And I don't mean to be rude, but can we talk about something else?"

"I don't understand. Your mother told my mother you had a bunch of books published. Novels, right?"

A bunch of books? The carpaccio is excellent—moist and delicate and without the slightest trace of fat—but her appetite is gone. "I really can't talk about this."

"Okay," Jack says. "But I want to ask one question. Were they fictional novels?"

Fictional? You betcha! "Not a word of truth in 'em," Dee says. And as Jack reaches for a piece of garlic toast, she thinks she notices, in the dim light of this high-end Italian restaurant, a clear coat of polish on his nails. Something both she and Julianne agree is completely unacceptable on a straight guy.

She can't wait to get home to tell her. And to hear her daughter's good-natured squeal of disapproval. *Ewwww!* In any case, Dee couldn't possibly be interested in a man who keeps his nails polished. And then there are those "fictional novels," a phrase whose very sound makes her teeth hurt.

"The temperature in Maui," Jack Newman is saying, "never goes below . . ."

So many things to discuss with Dr. Kaye and her next appointment isn't for another five days. Perhaps she should cut this date short and call him. They could have a phone session, which might prove almost as satisfying as a face-to-face appointment. She's never had the nerve to call him after hours, but there's a first time for everything.

"If you'll excuse me," she tells Jack Newman.

Never mind that when her mother finds out, Dee will never hear the end of it. But if you can't stand up to your mother when you're nearly half a century old, you really are a first-class loser.

8

JULIANNE

several hours before Julianne and her boyfriend Michael Avery make love for the first time, they take the subway downtown from his apartment to see a Broadway play. They are sitting in orchestra seats Dee picked up at half-price; resting her head against Michael's shoulder, Julianne tries her best to pay attention. It's very compelling theater up there on the stage and she is aware of that, but even so, she has to struggle to concentrate. After a couple of weeks of vigorous discussion, she and Michael have decided that this will be the night they will lose their virginity. *It's now or never,* Michael had said; they are, after all, definitely in love, and the world being the uncertain place that it is these days, well, who can blame them for wanting to experience the most awesome thing two people in love can possibly share with each other? Julianne reviews all of this in her mind as the elderly actor taking center stage now begins his descent into madness. The truth is, she is already worrying that her mother will somehow sense a change in her after tonight, will somehow know exactly what she and Michael have been up to. There are plenty of mothers out there who are oblivious, or close to it, but Dee isn't like that. She wants to know every detail of everything Julianne does from one day to the next; she hungers for details. Occasionally, when Julianne is feeling generous, and she and her mother are hanging out on Julianne's bed late at night, she will tell Dee some of what she wants to know. Like all about the enormous apartment Michael lives in on Central Park West; how his next-door neighbor, a junior at Griffin, sometimes babysits for Jerry Seinfeld's kids; how the cook Michael's parents hired actually wears a white uniform and a chef's hat even when he's only making Julianne and Michael a couple of grilled cheese sandwiches on English muffins. Dee loves hearing this stuff, and Julianne remembers how her mother's face was lit with gratitude and pleasure one night a few weeks ago as Julianne herself talked on and on, feeling a little guilty that most of the time she is so stingy, refusing to let her mother into her life in the way that Dee so obviously craves. But her mother is forty-nine years old, a middle-aged woman who can't possibly see things the way Julianne does. The two of them are mother and daughter roommates, but they aren't—as Dee would like them to be—friends. *Give it up, Mom,* Julianne always wants to say. *No way are we buds. No way!* Besides, she already has enough friends as it is. And, more important, she has Michael, that tall-dark-and-handsome smart guy in her English class, smart enough to end up at Harvard, no question. But next fall is a long way off, Julianne thinks, and who can tell what will happen between now and then?

As the theater lets out, the audience spilling companionably onto the sidewalk on this cool October night, Michael fires up a cigarette with a sterling silver lighter engraved with his grandfather's initials. He'd swiped it from his father's desk, Julianne knows, and she hopes that he will return it. And also that he will quit smoking. Not for health reasons necessarily, but because it makes his hair and clothing smell dirty. At one of the entrances to the subway on Forty-second Street, a homeless man calls out, rather jauntily, "Hey, wanna donate to the United Negro Pizza Fund?" Michael finds this hilarious and gives the man a ten-dollar bill from his wallet. What's saddest, Julianne thinks, is the eagerness with which the guy snatches the money from Michael's hand. The homeless guy's wearing woolen gloves with the fingertips snipped off; his exposed fingers look horrible, purple and swollen, and Julianne has to turn away. When she mentions this a minute later to Michael, he offers her only a noncommittal "huh," a response that annoys her. But she lets it go because this is the person she loves, and she can't expect him to be perfect, can she? On the train, heading homeward, she sees a couple of women sending admiring glances in Michael's direction. They are women in their twenties, well-dressed in high heels and dark overcoats, laptop cases propped on their knees, and they are lusting after her boyfriend—how cool is *that*? she thinks to herself.

The coast is clear, as Julianne knew it would be, when they arrive at her apartment. Dee is in New Jersey visiting old friends from college and isn't expected back until after one A.M. Michael goes straight to the refrigerator and helps himself to a glass of water, and then to a package of apple-cinnamon mini-muffins, which he wolfs down standing at the counter. Although she is hungry, Julianne is a little too jittery to eat, and instead looks, or pretends to look, through the junk mail piled on top of the microwave. Sonia, a plump black cat with a white ruff like a Victorian collar, is sprawled flat on her back on the dining table, hind legs spread apart, looking like a lazy sunbather on the beach. Approaching her, Michael lets her lick muffin crumbs from his fingertips.

"Don't," Julianne says. "She doesn't need all that cholesterol and fat."

"They're crumbs," says Michael. "*Crumbs.*" But, obediently, he leaves Sonia and goes to the sink to wash the cat spit from his hands. His shoes are off, and his shirt is untucked from his jeans. He takes Julianne's hand and escorts her down the uncarpeted hallway to her bedroom. Inside, there are a couple of bras flung over the back of the desk chair, but she isn't embarrassed in the least—it's not, after all, as if Michael has never seen a bra before. Last night's pajamas are on the floor, along with a fake cashmere scarf, three dirty socks, a slide rule, a calculator, a paperback copy of Plato's *The Last Days of Socrates*, an uncapped Hi-Liter, pens and pencils, a nonfunctioning cell phone, a cordless phone, a stick of Arrid Extra Dry, a bottle of nail polish remover, and a half-finished milkshake in a tall paper cup. Lying face down, its head resting despondently on a video tape, is a plush pink teddy bear. So face it, she's a slob. Big deal. *Big deal.* Michael's room would be a disaster, too, except that he's got Pearl, his live-in housekeeper, to pick up after him.

Julianne pops an Indigo Girls CD into the player on her bookcase, lowers the halogen light halfway, and then she and Michael stretch themselves out on her unmade bed. "I love you," Michael murmurs into her ear, and even though he's told her this at least once a day for weeks now, it's still good to hear, good to know, especially tonight. "Love you *aussi*," she whispers back. They're both taking A.P. French, and Michael is taking Latin as well. He's unbelievably brilliant, and it's not as if he studies all day and all night like some kind of geek. In fact, he's the very antithesis of a geek; instead, he reads a lot on his own, contemporary poetry, all six-hundred-odd pages of *Don Quixote,* the short stories of F. Scott Fitzgerald and Ring Lardner, Don DeLillo stuff, Sinclair Lewis, D. H. Lawrence, Vladimir Nabokov. You name it, he's read it. You can't help but be impressed with him. And then there's his face—those pretty, bright blue eyes and silky dark hair, the slender, perfect nose, the squarish chin. Sometimes Julianne just can't get over how lucky she is.

He's unbuttoning her shirt now, slipping her bra over her head, unzipping her jeans and his, humming along with the Indigo Girls. And then they're naked and she can tell he's trying to go slow and sweet and gentle, but it hurts and she's moaning, almost inaudibly, because she doesn't want him to suspect that there's no pleasure in it for her; the only pleasure, really, is in knowing that they are, at this very moment, as intimate as a couple can ever be. Afterward, she cries a little, tears of relief that it's over; probably, she tells herself, it will be a lot better next time around. Certainly it can't be much worse. Michael is kissing her tenderly on the lips, behind her ear, at the corners of her eyes, and then, in a heartbeat, he falls asleep on top of her, the heavy, dead weight of him such a burden that she can barely breathe. A moment or two later, she pushes him off; the Indigo Girls are still singing, harmonizing so beautifully that Julianne is all teary-eyed again.

While Michael sleeps, she gets dressed, locks herself in the bathroom, and calls Morgan on her cell phone. "Well, we did it," she confesses to Morgan, and examines herself in the mirror above the sink to see if there is any evidence of her altered status. There is none—nothing in her eyes that says she is no longer a girl, that she has crossed the border into womanhood and there is no turning back. Morgan shrieks at the news, screaming, "I'm SO happy for you! I am SO SO happy for you!" and it's good to hear her sounding this way a month or so after her mother's death—not that she has recovered yet, of course, but this is the first time since the funeral that Julianne has heard her sound so full of life.

"Are you okay?" Morgan asks.

"Michael's sleeping," says Julianne. "I've got to get him up before my mother comes home."

"I'm really happy for you guys," Morgan says.

"No big deal," says Julianne.

"Did it hurt?"

"I don't want to talk about it."

"I'm your best friend—you HAVE to talk about it!" Morgan squeals.

"I need to go wake up Michael," Julianne says, and clicks off. She brushes her teeth and puts on some flavored lip gloss and plucks a few errant hairs from each eyebrow. She smiles at herself in the mirror and says, "You're *such* an idiot."

She phones Morgan again, but there is only an answering machine this time. She doesn't blame Morgan for not picking up, but leaves a message asking her to call back tomorrow morning. Michael is still sound asleep in her bed and it takes some doing to awaken him—some tickling, a little stroking, a couple of kisses here and there. "We've got to flush the condom down the toilet," she says. "Right now."

"I love you to pieces," he says with his eyes closed. "More than anything."

"Uh-huh," she says. Then adds, *"Moi aussi."*

Propped up on one elbow, Michael yawns and says, "Want to go out to a diner or something?"

"Sure. Fine. Whatever," says Julianne. She sniffs the air around her bed, wondering if the room smells like sex. Just to be extra careful, she darts back into the bathroom, grabs a can of melon-scented deodorizer, and sprays the bedroom as Michael begins to dress in a dilatory, lazy-ass way that immediately grates on her nerves. "Could you please get a move on?" she says.

"'I loafe and invite my soul/I lean and loafe at my ease,'" Michael says, smiling. "Walt Whitman, for those of you who might be curious."

"Get dressed and then you can lean and loaf all you want," says Julianne, returning his smile, no longer annoyed but still a little impatient to have all incriminating evidence cleared away before her mother gets back. Why go looking for trouble when you can just as easily avoid it?

"Seen my wallet?" Michael asks. His jeans are back on but he's still shirtless and his big pinkish feet are bare.

"Did you check your pants pockets?" Scooping up some ball-point pens from the floor—a quick, cursory clean-up just for the hell of it while she waits for Michael—she flings them across the desk, then dips back down for her pajamas and that trio of dirty socks, all of which she shoves into a dresser drawer. One of these days she's going to make her mother happy and really whip this room into shape. But not tonight.

"It's not there," says Michael. "And it's not in my jacket either."

She must be mistaken, but she could swear he's close to tears. "Well, it's got to be here somewhere, right?" she says warily. "I mean, obviously."

Michael has already ripped the comforter from her bed, the sheet from the mattress; grunting, he pulls the mattress onto the floor. He turns toward her, and his face is crimson, sweaty, terror-struck. She watches, in utter astonishment, as he goes for the drawers of her desk and yanks them out, turns them upside down and shakes them so that papers and notebooks, a stapler, a plastic container filled with colorful paperclips, a twelve-inch wooden ruler, an open miniature sampler of four ancient, whitish chocolates, litter the floor. "What are you *doing*?" Julianne says, thoroughly alarmed as he leaps onto the box springs of her bed and beats his fists against the wall, over and over again, wailing in a high-pitched voice she would never, in a million years, recognize as his. She calls his name but is afraid to approach him and so she stops where she is, her back against a bookcase jammed with paperbacks and stuffed animals. The sounds coming from Michael aren't quite human, she thinks—they're the wordless cries of an animal in the worst sort of pain and despair. *Over a wallet?* Surely there's more to it than that, and surely she can't and won't keep her cowardly distance all night as his fists slam endlessly against the pink-painted walls of the room that has always been her sanctuary.

"Baby," she says, though she has never called him this in all the time they have been together, and then she climbs up onto the box springs. "Stop, okay?" She grabs his flailing fists, one and then the other, and sees those bruised and bleeding knuckles of his, and lets out a cry of her own. "What are you *doing*?" she asks him again and again, as if he has an inkling, as if he can tell her just what she needs to know. And his battered hands that she's holding remind her of the homeless man at the entrance to the subway; effortlessly, she imagines Michael in his expensive jacket from Abercrombie standing out there on that very street corner, his hair filthy and ragged, his teeth half rotted away, his affect one of utter hopelessness as he begs for quarters, dimes, pennies, even, anything at all so he can buy himself a lousy cup of coffee and a sandwich because he hasn't eaten in who knows how long and has nowhere to go, nothing to sustain him, not hope or love or confidence in his own ability to survive another day. He breaks free of her now and flies from the room and out the door of the apartment, and she flies after him. Later he will confess that over the years he's broken every one of his knuckles, all ten of them, some of them more than once. And his father will say to Julianne over the phone, in an oddly detached, clinical sort of way, *He's a very angry young man indeed.* His voice so chilly and distant, it's as if Michael really isn't his son, which, for all Julianne knows, is precisely what his father wishes *were* the case. Catching up with him now at the bank of elevators, she watches as he paces frantically back and forth, still keening like a banshee, someone who knows for sure that the end is near for one of them. Or maybe even both of them. She sees, to her surprise, that *she* is the one blessed with strength and authority, that it is within her power to lead him back to the apartment, to say quietly but firmly that they will find his wallet but that first he has to call a halt to this, this heartrending display of fear and desperation that, hard as she tries, she can't even begin to understand.

She grabs him by the crook of his arm and tells him that he's going to wake the neighbors and for that reason alone he has to quiet down. "We'll go look around in my bedroom again and I'll find your wallet for you, okay? But first you're going to calm down and take it easy, okay, baby?" He is sobbing now, though without much noise, and suddenly he's gone docile and slack, and she feels hopeful that, at the very least, she can get him back into her apartment. She's never seen a guy cry before, except, perhaps, in a movie or on stage, and it kills her to witness her six-foot-tall, 165-pound boyfriend weeping, his nose leaking, his shoulders trembling as she and Michael navigate their way down the hall. *Kills* her. Nothing in her ordinary little life has prepared her for this, she reflects. Her life *is* thoroughly ordinary, no doubt about it. There's school and friends and Michael, and of course, her loving but annoying mother (forget her father, he's way in the background); it's one day pretty much like the next, the texture basically unchanging, the same feel to her life day in and day out. The steadiness of it something to be grateful for, though until a few minutes ago she would never have noticed. And the truth is, she doesn't care about Michael's damn wallet, but she will pretend that she does, that finding it is the single most important task she's ever set for herself. And she needs to get Michael's shirt back on and his socks and sneakers on his feet and then hustle him out of here and into a cab that will take him home to Central Park West. Because if her mother sees that pockmarked wall above her bed, not to mention Michael's damaged hands, she will flip out and just naturally conclude that he is a dangerous psycho and that no daughter of hers will ever be a hundred percent safe in his presence. But Julianne knows she is safe, that Michael would never, not in this lifetime or any other, lift even a finger against her.

Too late: there's her mother's key in the lock as Julianne is bent over tying the laces of Michael's Pumas in the living room. At least the two of them are fully dressed, Julianne thinks. At least there's that. She sprints down the hallway and shuts her bedroom door, then hightails it back to the living room. *I lost my wallet,* Michael is explaining to her mother and begins to sob again, and then he's up from the couch, and wild-eyed with that unaccountable grief and terror, circling the coffee table and tearing at his hair with both hands. And Julianne suspects that forgiveness will not be forthcoming from her mother, that she will be unmoved in the face of any and all explanations and entreaties, and that she and Michael—Julianne-and-Michael who made love less than an hour ago—are history. In her mother's eyes, anyway. These few moments when Dee stands nearly spellbound, a witness drinking it all in, committing to memory the sight of Michael as he is right now, cannot be undone, Julianne knows. And the knowledge makes her heartsick. She figures that by her mother's lights, the smart, articulate, handsome, and well-mannered Michael no longer exists—he's been permanently replaced by this frantic, howling figure in her living room, a seventeen-year-old boy unstrung by a missing wallet. It's not too hard to understand why her mother or any mother would feel this way, Julianne thinks, not hard at all. But as *she* sees it, you don't abandon the boy you love simply because he's had a meltdown right there in front of you, revealed a part of himself you wish you'd never had even a momentary glimpse of. No way: you stick with him and watch over him as, slowly, his old self reemerges in all its beauty. This is the argument she will offer her mother; unsurprisingly, Dee won't buy it. Because, as she will say once, twice, perhaps a thousand and one times, *My only concern is* you—your *safety, your well-being. Not his*—yours. *And my job as a parent is to keep you safe. End. Of. Story.*

9

SUSAN AVERY

Like her son, Michael, Susan reads a lot. Waiting for the elevator, in line at the post office, the Korean market, the drug store, there's always a book in her hands. She's currently enrolled in a course in Russian lit at the New School—Dostoyevsky, Tolstoy, Gogol, Turgenev—and although she's not taking it for credit and therefore has no obligation to write a paper or study for the final, she wrote the paper anyway. Title: "The Dual Nature of Dmitry Karamazov." Grade: B++. Really, would it have killed the instructor to be a little less stingy? And what's the difference between B++ and A– except two-tenths of a point? Couldn't the guy have given her a break? In any case, she knows a great deal about the dual nature of certain personalities and it's not just Dmitry K. she's thinking of.

She never longed for a child the way so many women do. Felt no biological imperative to reproduce and all that. She kept this thought to herself because you never know how people are going to regard you when you say a thing like that, conventional thinking holding that only a peculiar sort of woman wouldn't want a sweet little infant of her own nesting in her arms at 2:30 A.M., soaked in baby pee and shrieking, but still the flesh of your flesh and the very best part of your life. As things turned out, after a dozen years of marriage, Susan and her husband found themselves awaiting the birth of their son and figuring, *What the hell, let's go for it.*

And here they are seventeen years later, not quite the family they might have hoped. Hindsight, they say, is twenty-twenty.

They say, as well, that a beloved pet can go a long way toward filling a void in one's life, and Boyfriend, Susan's Chinese crested hairless, is living proof. He's a dear, gentle soul who wears his heart on his sleeve. Literally. Well, almost. The breed is a mistake of nature, and so Boyfriend has hair covering only his head, paws, and tail; from October through April, and during the summer months when the air-conditioning is turned on, he trembles with cold unless he's dressed accordingly. (Susan may not have been the best of all possible mothers to her son, but when it comes to Boyfriend, she has to acknowledge she's done a first-rate job.) On her sewing machine, she's whipped up a closet full of clothes for her little man, including the following: three pairs of pajamas (one of them silk), a military uniform (complete with gold braid at the shoulders), and what Michael contemptuously and mistakenly calls Boyfriend's "gay outfit"—a black leather jumpsuit. And, too, Susan has knit him countless sweaters in a variety of colors and styles, among them cardigan, V-neck, boat neck, and turtleneck.

She's never quite warmed to her son and she suspects he knows this; he is, after all, a highly intelligent kid. And the guilt she bears would be crippling if she allowed it. But here's something she finds oddly comforting: not long ago she happened to stroll past Woody Allen, who was walking along Lexington Avenue, hand in hand with his two youngest children. There was a tennis hat squashed down over his head and his shoulders were slumped as if the proverbial weight of the world were upon them. *Hey, Woody,* she wanted to call out to him, *I know just how it feels.* She's not a fan of his, actually—his shtick doesn't do much for her. But catching a glimpse of him that moment on Lex and Ninety-second, she couldn't deny that what she felt was a genuine kinship with the man.

We take our consolations anywhere we can get them.

10

The missing wallet is never found, though Michael suspects it was the homeless man, who, with sleight of hand, somehow managed to make it disappear along with the ten-dollar bill he'd pocketed so swiftly. Julianne doesn't know *what* to think. That night, she and her mother fell asleep together in Julianne's bed with Dee rubbing the small of Julianne's back, stroking her hair, her shoulder blades, as Julianne wept unceasingly, begging her mother to understand just how much she loves Michael, how she couldn't desert him just when he needs her most. *Understand?* Dee said. *What I understand is that he's one sick kid and that he'll set foot in this house again over my dead body.*

According to the shrink Michael's now seeing (and there have been others, five or six of them over the years, Julianne has learned), he is bipolar, afflicted with a disorder that can never be cured but can be controlled with medication—medication which he will take faithfully every single day, he assures Julianne. A few weeks later and he's pretty much back to his old self, but this isn't good enough for Dee. When it comes to Michael, nothing will ever be good enough, not an official letter from his shrink, not a single article from medical journals that Julianne has printed out for her on the Internet, not Julianne's promises that he would never hurt her, that the only person he has ever hurt is himself.

As a matter of fact, no one can stop them from seeing each other. This isn't, after all, Afghanistan or Pakistan or Saudi Arabia, where horrific things can happen to a teenage girl who doesn't obey her elders. This is New York City, where people do as they damn please. Sneaking out to Michael's apartment every weekend, telling Dee she's off to Morgan's or Daisy Camarano-Rosenthal's or a concert, Julianne doesn't feel much more than a scintilla of guilt over deceiving her mother. If her mother were a reasonable person, which she is not—on the subject of Michael anyway, Julianne wouldn't have to lie. But her mother leaves her no choice. Actually, Dee has made her see a therapist several times a week, a very tall, skinny woman with a punked-out orange hairdo and a trace of a German accent. Dr. Schuster is a psychologist (not a psychiatrist like the shrink Michael goes to), but she's a cool person with a tiny ruby embedded below her lower lip and an array of small gold studs lining the curve of one ear. She nods her head sympathetically when Julianne talks about love and loyalty, and how you don't just take off at the first sign of trouble because that, obviously, would be incredibly selfish, not to mention just plain cruel.

"And what do your friends think you should do, hmm?" Dr. Schuster asks during their third session together. She offers Julianne a brandy snifter filled with Tootsie Rolls and cellophane-wrapped mints that look like M&M's.

Julianne shrugs and helps herself to a turquoise mint but only to be polite. *It's a total no-brainer, sweetie; the guy is totally bad news.* This was Morgan, who, never having had an actual boyfriend, can't possibly understand. And from Daisy the verdict was the same, though Daisy, frankly, is in no position to be giving advice to anyone; she had an abortion only days ago and has no one to blame but her own careless self.

"I don't know," Julianne says.

"Okay," Dr. Schuster says with a sigh. "But you do know that Michael will never be cured, that eventually the medication will cease to be effective and they'll have to try something else, and something else after that . . ."

"He cries sometimes," Julianne confides. "We fight about stupid things, he gets angry, and then he cries."

"It's a mood disorder, this illness of his, and the meds can only do so much. And, too," Dr. Schuster says delicately, her voice softening, "I have to warn you that he's at a much higher risk for suicide than the average person his age."

Julianne sees herself last week in Michael's bedroom, his head in her lap after an argument, weeping because he was afraid she would leave him, Michael saying, *I have no future, I have no future without you,* over and over again, this big strong guy with practically a 4.0 GPA, A's in every subject, Harvard material, believing there was nothing for him out there, nothing but misery. Remembering this now, Julianne is suddenly overcome by a wave of nausea. "I think I'm going to be sick," she announces, and slumps back against Dr. Schuster's couch and closes her eyes, which only makes things worse. If Michael kills himself, her life would be over. Period. Because how could you go on after something like that? Not long ago she saw part of a Holocaust documentary on PBS; one of the survivors interviewed, a white-haired old woman, said, *When I remember what I lost, everything—friends, the parents, the brother, a child—my heart cannot bear it.* Julianne had run for a piece of paper and a pen and written the woman's words down because it was the saddest thing she'd ever heard in her whole life, and she didn't want to forget it. Not to compare herself to that Holocaust survivor, but *her* heart would not be able to bear it. No way.

"Michael is *not* going to kill himself," she tells Dr. Schuster. "He wants to go to Harvard and then to graduate school to get his PhD in literature or something."

"And you?" Dr. Schuster asks. "What do *you* want, hmm?"

"I'm definitely going to be sick," Julianne says, and Dr. Schuster leaps from her seat behind the desk and runs toward her with a wastepaper basket, just in the nick of time.

11

LAZY

azy's mother, Charlotte, has been asked a hundred times not to call her at work, not unless it's an emergency, and a life-threatening one at that. But Charlotte's definition of life-threatening is different from her own, Lazy has discovered, and those calls just keep coming, like all that spam that so relentlessly fills her mailbox in cyberspace.

"What's wrong, Mom?" Lazy says, suddenly desperate, at the sound of her mother's voice, for a cigarette, though it's only nine in the morning and of course she can't have one. Can't smoke at home because Richard won't allow it, can't smoke at school until after six when the building has emptied out. What's the point in being the queen bee if you can't even light up a lousy cigarette when you need one? Whenever and wherever you want. Everyone in this city is on Ativan or Prozac or Zoloft or Paxil or Wellbutrin; at Griffin, teachers and students alike can calm themselves down or cheer themselves up and it's all perfectly legal. But if *she* wants one little cigarette to help her through another phone call from her mother . . . well, tough luck.

"I'll tell you," Charlotte says, and Lazy tries her best to pay attention. Ever since her father's death a few years ago and her mother's subsequent move to the Fairhaven Residence for Seniors, Charlotte has become increasingly plaintive, helpless, and insecure, depending on Lazy to pay her bills, balance her checkbook, organize her pantry, her mini-fridge, her linen closet, her life. Fairhaven, a mere eighteen-minute car trip from Lazy's apartment, is staffed by exceptionally patient and good-humored people and provides all sorts of programs for its residents, bringing in lecturers, physical fitness instructors, musicians, and art therapists week after week. According to Charlotte, however, things at Fairhaven are nearly intolerable—the food tasteless and overcooked, the elevators and movie lounge too noisy and crowded, and, most important of all, her fellow residents so selfish, petty, and gossipy that Charlotte can barely stand a single one of them. Her life—what's left of it anyway—is bad news. Not that she expects Lazy, at the tender age of forty-three, to really understand, she says. Sometimes, after hearing the endless litany of her mother's grievances over the phone, Lazy shuts herself away in her study at home, slides some Laura Nyro or Joni Mitchell into the CD player, and—never mind about Richard—smokes a joint. And all is right with the world again. In truth, she loves her mother (who is, in her experience, no better or worse than anyone else's mother), but occasionally, in her darkest moments, she finds herself fearing that Charlotte's incessant complaining is going to send her, Lazy, straight to her own private suite at Payne Whitney.

"... and so there I am minding my own business in my living room, when the door opens and some crazy old woman I've seen in the lobby and the dining room comes right in and tries to sit down on my couch and make herself at home. And I say to her, 'What are you *doing*? You can't just come in here uninvited like that.' And she says, 'What are you so worried about? I promise I won't hurt you.' And when I heard that, I'll tell you, a chill went down my spine."

"But why?" says Lazy.

"It was terrifying," Charlotte says. "A nightmare."

"She's what, eighty-five years old and you're afraid of her? What's she going to do to you?"

"She's ninety if she's a day and who knows, if I hadn't called Security right then and there, she might have gone into my bedroom and into my jewelry box and taken who-knows-what, my pearls or my gold bangle bracelets, maybe, or one of my Hummels on the dresser. Those Hummels are worth a fortune."

"What can I say to make you feel better, Mom? Tell me," Lazy says, seizing her reading glasses by the tip of the earpiece and twirling them so violently, the glasses go flying across the room.

"I want to go home. Take me home, bubbeleh."

To Lazy's astonishment, her eyes fill. "You *are* home," she says gently. "Fairhaven *is* your home, you know that, Mom."

"Yes I do and every time I think about that, I want to kill myself."

"No you don't," Lazy says, horrified. And a little resentful as well—for being made to feel a sickening guilt that heats her now like one of those hot flashes her gynecologist has warned her to be on the lookout for now that she's peri-menopausal and hasn't seen hide nor hair of her period in over two months. "Of course you don't," she tells her mother.

"Fine. Have it your way. If *you* say I don't want to kill myself, then I don't want to kill myself."

"That's better," says Lazy. "Thank you. And I don't want to hear you talking like that again."

"Fine. They're having broccoli-and-turkey omelets for lunch today," Charlotte reports. "Who ever heard of such a disgusting meal?"

Just when Lazy has begun to think there's no graceful way out of this conversation, her assistant, Brooke, buzzes her. "Your nine fifteen is here, sir," she says. "Can I send her in?"

"God, yes," says Lazy. "Immediately." And to her mother: "I'm sorry, but I've got to go, Mom. Just tell me you're all right."

"You want me to say I'm all right, then I'm all right."

"Okay, then. Great!"

"And I love you with a full heart."

"Um, me too," says Lazy. "Me too."

12

DEE

Parking her cab a couple of blocks from the school, Dee arrives at Griffin exactly on time for her once-a-year tour of duty with the safety patrol. Every Griffin family is assigned their two-hour slot; equipped with walkie-talkies, silver whistles to wear around their necks, and fluorescent-orange vests stamped with the words "Safety First," parents from each of two families are paired and sent on their way to police the immediate vicinity, as if they could, unarmed, possibly halt a robbery or assault in progress. (On the coldest winter afternoons, Dee knows, you can see mothers on patrol wearing their official vests over full-length mink coats, Prada bags slung across their shoulders.) It may all very well be nothing more than a big joke, but the program has been in place for over twenty years and no Griffin family is exempt: whether you're in Hollywood receiving your Best Supporting Actor award or at the White House lunching with Laura, at least one parent in your household is required to show up for duty. And if your spouse has joined you in Hollywood to share in the excitement, you must, at least twenty-four hours in advance, find another Griffin parent to take your place.

Dee signs in, slips on her orange vest and whistle, and picks up her walkie-talkie from the security guard in the lobby. She's been arbitrarily paired with Paul Conway, a wildly successful writer who has earned millions from his screenplays though he's a best-selling novelist as well. And formerly a big cokehead, not that it ever detracted from his celebrity status at Griffin. "Shit shit shit," Dee murmurs, which is exactly what being in Conway's presence at various school functions has always made her feel like. Just what she needs—to spend two endless hours patrolling the same few streets over and over again while listening to him talk about his newest project, set to begin shooting next month, she's heard, with Ralph Fiennes playing the lead. Conway's already ten minutes late; perhaps Dee's going to be spared after all. But no such luck: here comes a small, dark-skinned woman about Dee's age dressed in a shabby brown leather jacket; clearly it's not Conway's glamorous wife walking toward her. It is, in fact, his housekeeper. Isn't there a directive issued every year by Lazy Hoffman that specifically says "You may NOT use your housekeeper, secretary, or assistant as a substitute. We are a community of caring, responsible parents. Please do your best to remember that!"

"Safety?" the woman says breathlessly.

"Yeah, hi," says Dee, and introduces herself.

"Evita."

"*Habla inglés?*" Dee asks, though she suspects it's hopeless.

"*Un poco,*" says the housekeeper sweetly, shaking her head. "A little."

"Well, *hablo español un poco,*" Dee says. She actually remembers a few sentences from her three years of high school Spanish. What she can't remember, however, is exactly what the words themselves mean.

"*Bueno,*" says Evita. "We go now, *sí?*"

"*Vamos,*" Dee says, determined to keep up her end of the conversation for the next two hours. She and Evita walk in silence three blocks down and then up Madison, and finally Dee feels compelled to say something, anything, as long as it's in Spanish. "*Me estoy matando estudiando para este curso de literatura española,"* she says. (I'm killing myself studying for this Spanish literature course.)

"*Bueno,*" Evita says. She touches Dee's shoulder. "*Bueno.*"

Emboldened, Dee says, "*Cada día que pasaba, la pila de basura afuera del garage crecia cada vez mas en altura y profundidad.*" (The pile of garbage outside her front door grew higher and deeper with each passing day.)

"If you say so, missus."

So far so good. "*Señor Goldstein, yo estoy acostumbrado a cenar en los mejores restaurantes de Madrid.*" (I am accustomed to dining in Madrid's finest restaurants, Mr. Goldstein.)

"And who is this Goldstein you speak of?"

Dee shrugs. "*El se veia totalmente ridiculo vestido con brassiere y panty hose.*" (He stuck out like a sore thumb in his bra and panty hose.)

"You loco, missus. But okay."

"*No dejes de dar vuelta hasta la ultima piedra, en tu conquista del perfecto par de jean.*" (Leave no stone unturned in your quest for the perfect pair of jeans.)

"Okay, missus, you like Spanish in school?"

"Oh, *mucho,*" Dee lies. "*Pobre Reinaldo estiro la pata.*" (Poor Reinaldo has kicked the bucket.)

"Reinaldo who? You tell me about him?"

"That's basically all the Spanish I know," Dee confesses. "I'm sorry. *Lo siento mucho.*"

"Okay. We walk, and we say nothing, and is okay."

Dee checks her watch and can't help but sigh. "We've got a long, long way to go, señora."

"Mister Conway home sleeping, very very tired, he say."

"I'll bet."

"Missus Conway in Palm Springs until weekend."

"My heart goes out to them both," Dee says, and fantasizes a couple of quick phone calls, one to Conway in his Fifth Avenue penthouse, and one to the missus in the desert. *Just who the hell do you think you are?* she wants to say. As if she doesn't know. Because, of course, it's all too obvious who they are. And who *she* is—someone who would probably trade her life for theirs at a moment's notice.

13

JULIANNE

Julianne is worried enough about Morgan, who failed to show up in homeroom this morning, that she rushes the few blocks over to Park Avenue to check on her during her first free period of the day. She finds Morgan coiled into a fetal position, unwilling or unable to move from her bed. Reaching under her pillow, Morgan extracts her cell phone and calls the Griffin Attendance Hotline to report herself absent. Today is her mother's birthday—what would have been her forty-second—she tells Julianne, and Morgan will commemorate it by staying at home, under the covers, and thinking about Elizabeth every minute.

"Every minute?" Julianne says. She thinks of Morgan's glamorous mother who always smelled faintly of Obsession, whose earlobes were ornamented with three diamonds apiece, whose hands and feet were so perfect that she had once, long ago in college, earned extra money as a model, though the clients weren't interested in her face, only in those hands and feet of hers.

"I want my mommy," Morgan murmurs, and Julianne winces. What an embarrassing thing for a seventeen-year-old to admit, though of course Julianne knows Morgan's never wanted anything more in her entire life; she would give up everything in it, *everything*—all her hard-earned A's in school, all her designer jeans and bags, all those vacations in Europe and the Caribbean— just to get her mother back. *It ain't gonna happen,* Julianne thinks, not that she would ever say the words aloud. And now she listens patiently as Morgan tells her, once again, how much she hates every one of those doctors who treated her mother and had nothing but pessimism to offer, hates every inch of Sloan-Kettering and especially the main waiting room where she and her father and her grandmother and Julianne, too, waited for sixteen hours that endless Saturday as the surgeon and his assistants tried, but not hard enough, Morgan insists, to set things permanently right.

She doesn't have to tell Julianne, who has her own memories of those sixteen hours in the waiting room, during which all four of them sat in their floral-patterned cushioned seats, Morgan the only one who refused to eat or drink or go to the ladies' room or even stretch her legs for a few minutes while her father and her grandma Lil walked over to First Avenue to Wok 'n' Roll and returned with cartons of chicken-and-broccoli and pork lo mein and plastic forks and spoons. But Morgan wouldn't touch the stuff, couldn't, the look and smell of it sickening to her even though it was perfectly decent food and Julianne tried so hard to get her to eat, twirling lo mein on a flimsy plastic fork and raising it to Morgan's lips only to have Morgan shove her hand away, so violently that Julianne dropped the fork in her own lap and ended up with a permanent grease stain on her favorite jeans. And at eleven that night, after having worked on Elizabeth since seven A.M., the oncologist finally emerged to talk with them, explaining in a weary voice, *Well, we got everything we could see.* And Morgan's father had said, *I'm not sure I understand precisely what you're telling me.* The doctor looked down toward the tips of his green paper booties, a bad sign, Julianne suspected, and so she had grabbed Morgan's hand and held it tightly. *In all likelihood,* the doctor began and went on to inform them that microscopic bits of the tumors would, *in all likelihood,* eventually travel through Elizabeth's bloodstream and kill her, though he certainly didn't use the word "kill" and his voice trailed off when he got to that final part of his horrible little speech, the speech that he knew they, the three mourners-in-waiting plus one family friend, didn't want to hear even a syllable of. And Morgan could only wail, *It's not fair!* like a ten-year-old who's been told she's too young to wear eye shadow or shave her legs, her plaintive voice grating on everyone's frazzled nerves, even Julianne's, until, at last, Grandma Lil, her bare, plumpish forearm imprinted with a string of blue numbers, said, *Fair? Vat's fair in this vorld, darling?* And who knew better than Morgan's grandmother the answer to that? *Nichts,* she said, *nothing,* swallowing Morgan in an embrace so close that Morgan looked as if she could barely breathe. Her father, Jeff, thanked the doctor and took off, heading down the escalator and out the door, where they found him smoking a cigarette after they'd caught up with him. The four of them got into a dark blue service car and rode up Park Avenue in shocked silence; Morgan's father, a tall, wide-shouldered man with perfect posture, seemed, in his grief, stooped and shrunken. Julianne hated it that he was no help to Morgan; he had nothing much to give her then, or any other night of the crisis, maybe an occasional kiss on the forehead or a few soft words here and there. Mostly, it turned out, Morgan would have to fend for herself during the two years between the surgery and her mother's death. Her grandmother stayed on for a couple of weeks and then returned home to Boca Raton, and except for Julianne, the rest of their friends were too bummed out by the whole subject to listen for long when Morgan felt the urge to unburden herself.

It's Julianne alone who has the patience to sit and listen, to hear this very instant how much it hurts Morgan just to go on breathing.

But Julianne has to get back to school now in time for Philosophy, and she can't convince Morgan to come with her.

"Go," Morgan says. "I'll get up in a minute and brush my teeth, maybe, and have breakfast, okay?"

Julianne, who doesn't believe her, says, "And then what?"

Morgan shrugs. "I'll call you on your cell after Philosophy."

She doesn't call, though, and when Julianne returns at two forty-five, she finds her sitting on the carpeted floor of Elizabeth's enormous walk-in closet, a closet big as a small boutique, where Elizabeth's things are perfectly aligned on endless rows of fancy, satin-covered hangers, and where, burying her face in a silk blouse still scented with Obsession, Morgan claims she can conjure her mother simply by invoking her name over and over and over again.

"Mommy," Julianne hears her say for the second time today.

"You couldn't *possibly* believe that," Julianne says. And then, more gently, "I *know* you don't believe that."

Okay, she doesn't, not really, Morgan admits, but then she is explaining all about that ache she carries with her from one day to the next, how it waxes and wanes but is always there, like the perpetual ringing in his ears a friend of her father's endures but cannot get rid of, no matter how many doctors he consults.

And Julianne finds herself nodding her head, thinking *this* is something she understands completely.

14

DEE

honing Will, her ex-husband, isn't something Dee looks forward to; even after so many years, the sound of his voice gets to her in all the wrong ways, and so she tries to keep her calls to a minimum. Once every few months, only when absolutely necessary. It's humiliating to admit to herself that in the unlikely event that Will were ever to dump his longtime girlfriend and come to Dee with the news that he wanted nothing more than a fresh start with *her*, she wouldn't need to consider his offer for more than two seconds. This little fantasy of a fresh start with the one and only man she's ever deeply loved is, in Dee's eyes, so pathetic, she wouldn't dream of sharing it with anyone, not even her shrink. (The history of their breakup is a tired story, utterly pedestrian, and it makes the artist in her cringe. If she were to write the story herself, she would punch it up with quirky details, remake Will as a cross-dresser, perhaps, or a man who needed a partner to join him in S&M games in the bedroom.) What her shrink *does* know is the unvarnished truth; how Will left her for Laura, a fellow attorney in his office, after fifteen years of what Dee had mistakenly assumed was generally a good, stable marriage; how she was so despondent after the divorce that she stopped walking their Pekingese and, instead, allowed him to poop on the floor of the guest bathroom for days; how she had lost so much weight in the aftermath of Will's departure that her internist insisted she drink three cans of Ensure a day and threatened to hospitalize her if she didn't comply. But this was half a dozen years ago and she's pulled herself together, admirably, she sometimes believes. If only she could think of Will and think, *hateful bastard.* At least she's willing to concede that he's an uncommonly selfish man and that's a start, isn't it? That she continues to love him isn't *his* fault; there's no one to blame but herself for that particular folly.

She picks up the phone in the kitchen, dials his number in Houston, and it's Laura who answers, Laura who is thirty-six years old and always perfectly pleasant, friendly even, always trying to make the best of what can only be one more awkward conversation in what feels, to Dee, like an endless series of them.

"So how *are* you?" Laura asks.

"How are *you*?" Dee says.

"Good. Great . . . Actually, I'm pregnant again. At the end of my fourth month, farther along than I've ever gotten before. And feeling pretty terrific this time around, no morning sickness, which is fantastic. My boobs, though, are killing me. They're huge all of a sudden and really painful to the touch. Did that happen to you? When you were pregnant with Julianne?"

A *boob*, Dee would like to say, *is a boor, a crude, insensitive person, someone who cheerfully discusses the size of her breasts with her husband's ex-wife.* "Speaking of Julianne," she says, "I need to talk to Will about her."

"Everything all right?"

"I just want to talk to him for a couple of minutes, that's all."

"Is it about the boyfriend?"

"I'm afraid so," Dee says. "So if you could get Will to come to the phone . . ."

"No problem," Laura says. "And Dee? Great talking with you. As always."

"Sure," says Dee, and rolls her eyes, even though there's no one in the room to take note of it except Sonia, the cat, who's lounging on the stove holding a crumpled tissue between her front paws, contemplating a sneeze, Dee imagines.

"Talk to me," Will says into the phone, not even bothering to say her name.

And so she talks, for a long while, about Julianne and Michael, and Will listens silently. "Sounds like an adolescent soap opera to me," he says at last, and not wanting to jeopardize the smooth flow of child support and alimony checks from one month to the next, Dee ignores the casual cruelty of his remark.

Bastard, she thinks, and it feels like real progress.

15

LAZY

igning the visitors' log at the security desk in Fairhaven's lobby, Lazy can't help but notice the uninspired Halloween decorations taped everywhere, cardboard cutouts of ghosts, witches, and jack-o'-lanterns, all of which would look appropriate hanging in the hallways of Griffin's lower school. As if the residents of Fairhaven were no more sophisticated than seven-year-olds.

"Are those depressing or what?" she tells Richard, who has driven her out here to Queens, knowing just how little Lazy enjoys making these visits on her own.

Richard shrugs. He smiles at the elevator operator, a dainty young Korean woman wearing an extravagantly tall witch's hat. "Happy Halloween," he says, and guides Lazy into the elevator, nearly filled to capacity with several grim old ladies gripping the metal bars of their walkers, a white-haired gent in furry bedroom slippers, and two attendants, both Haitian, chatting in Creole.

"Will there be a Catholic mass today?" asks one of the old women. She's clutching a banana in one hand and leaning on her walker, its bars encrusted here and there with unidentifiable bits of food.

"Already was," the elevator operator says. "You'll have to wait until next Sunday, Mrs. Barrone."

"Goddamnit," Mrs. Barrone says.

At the eleventh floor, as Richard and Lazy are exiting the elevator, Mrs. Barrone taps the sleeve of Richard's jean jacket with her banana and says expectantly, "Will there be a Catholic mass today?"

"Next Sunday, Mrs. Barrone. You'll only have to wait seven days," he soothes her.

"Do you *know* her?" Lazy says in surprise. They're dragging their feet toward Charlotte's apartment now, waving to a 101-year-old man who, inexplicably, doesn't look a day over eighty-five. He strolls down the hallway, dapper in his navy blue three-piece suit, gold-tipped walking stick in hand.

"Nope, never saw her before."

"You're such a sweetheart, Richie," Lazy says. "I mean it." And to the 101-year-old man, "So how've you been, Mr. Tannenbaum?"

"Are you aware that I received a citation, suitable for framing, from both the mayor of New York City and the President of the United States, in honor of my one-hundredth birthday last year?"

"What, nothing from Governor Pataki?" Lazy says, her standard reply each of the three dozen times she's heard this from Mr. Tannenbaum.

"The governor? May he rot in hell, the bastard."

Lazy's mother is poised at her partially opened door, staring out into the hallway. "I thought I heard a familiar voice!" she says, elated. "Come in, come in!" Closing the door behind Richard and Lazy, she whispers, "Did Mr. Tannenbaum say anything about me?"

"Like what?" says Lazy. In accordance with her customary routine, she shuts off the TV, lowers the heat, and raises the Venetian blinds.

"Truthfully, I'd have to say he's in love with me. But what can I give you two to eat?"

Lazy and Richard take seats at the edge of the living room couch, rejecting, as they usually do, Charlotte's dubious offerings, which have been dumped onto a ceramic platter and today include two bruised McIntosh apples left over from lunch; one whole-wheat donut left over from last night's dinner; and one dented Kaiser roll left over from yesterday's breakfast.

"Some cookies, maybe?" Charlotte says hopefully. "Half an English muffin?"

"So what makes you think he's in love with you?" Richard reluctantly helps himself to the better-looking of the apples, an act of kindness that Lazy will try not to forget.

"Some ice cream to go with that apple?" Charlotte suggests.

"He's twenty-five years older than you, Mom," says Lazy. "Don't you think you're a little too young to be dating a 101-year-old man?"

Charlotte has finally sat down, casting her heels onto a bronze-colored vinyl ottoman. On her feet are white Reeboks and white anklets, worn over panty hose whose color is inaccurately described by the manufacturer as "nude." (Lazy knows this because it's she who buys handfuls of them for her mother at a discount drugstore every other month.) "Twenty-*four* years older," says Charlotte. "Not twenty-five."

"What is he, a great-great-grandfather by now? And how old are his children?"

"His children are *my* age," Charlotte admits. "They're elderly. But your husband's not doing a very good job on that apple, I see."

Dutifully, Richard takes another bite.

"You're dating a man old enough to be your father!" Lazy exclaims.

"Did I say I was dating him? I merely said he's in love with me. The whole thing's a little mystifying, really. Almost every day, he follows me in here from the dining room after lunch, kisses me on the lips for a while, then lies down on my bed and takes a nice long nap. After the nap he gets up, uses the bathroom, and out the door he goes."

In an effort to disguise his laughter, Richard is pretending to choke on a piece of apple, Lazy sees. She slaps him on the back a few times, trying to make his choking look legitimate and also to keep her own laughter in check.

"What's wrong with you two?" Charlotte says. "You think I

don't know you're making fun of me? So I let a 101-year-old man kiss me on the lips; what's so terrible?"

"Nothing!" Lazy and Richard cry in unison.

"He was a music professor at Brooklyn College for many years, a distinguished man, what's so terrible about *that*?"

Still laughing, Lazy delivers several more slaps to her husband's back.

"Get out of here, both of you, if you're not going to behave like adults!" says Charlotte.

Adults? Well, her mother may have a point there, Lazy thinks, and feels herself beginning to sober up.

But Richard has beaten her to it—he's up and running, approaching Charlotte sheepishly, sinking to his knees at the ottoman, assuring Lazy's mother that they weren't mocking her, they would *never* mock her, because, in fact, *they love her with a full heart,* just as she loves them.

Thank God for Richard, who doesn't yet know, as Lazy surely does, that there's already a place reserved for him in kingdom come. And as he rises to his feet now, she cannot stop herself from flying toward him and girlishly draping her arms around his neck. "You can't imagine how much I adore you at this moment!" she says.

"Yeah yeah yeah," he says, smiling, "I'm pretty terrific, aren't I? Like I don't hear this from my med students every day of the week."

"Your modesty becomes you, sir."

"In that case, I might as well break the news to you: they're going to"—he lowers his voice to a whisper—"fucking canonize me!"

Well, maybe. "All right, let's not get carried away here," Lazy says.

"You'll have to excuse me, please," says Charlotte, and goes off to the bathroom.

Richard pulls Lazy's hands from behind his back and takes them in his own. "Listen, this may sound a little weird," he says, still whispering, "but sometimes when we're together, even just sitting at the dinner table, I could swear it's like you're there, but not entirely. And I keep wondering how to reel you back from wherever it is you've gone."

The tips of Lazy's fingers have turned a grayish blue; it's nothing serious, just poor circulation, the doctor has told her. *Just rub your hands together to get the blood flowing.*

"Don't be silly," Lazy reassures Richard. Now she's whispering too. "I haven't gone anywhere."

He smiles faintly; still, it's a smile of sorts. "If you say so."

"What's going on with you two?" Charlotte says when she returns. "What are you people *talking* about?"

"*Nothing!*" Lazy says. And then she shows off her blue fingers, a sight you don't, after all, see every day.

16

JULIANNE

One night Julianne and Michael cruise down to Soho to a party thrown by a school friend named Ethan Rinehart, whose parents are away in St. Bart's for the weekend. There's plenty of beer and hard stuff, too, which Michael eyes longingly. But of course, for him, drinking is out of the question. He smokes a little weed instead, which Julianne thinks isn't such a great idea either, though maybe it will help to mellow him out. She stays completely sober, just in case. She hates parties like this one, with music thumping and a couple of dozen Griffin kids crowding the 2.3- or 3.2-million-dollar loft filled with expensive furnishings, like the original Warhol given to Ethan's parents by Andy himself in honor of the birth of their eldest child. There's booze but no food, not even a bowl of chips, and some of the guests look pretty wasted even though it's only nine o'clock and the night is surely young. *What's the point?* Julianne wants to say. She and Michael are seated at one end of a huge L-shaped black leather couch, holding hands, as Kurt Cobain's voice, hoarse and damaged sounding, sings, *I want to eat your cancer,* and a couple at the other end of the couch slip their hands down the front of each other's jeans. They're both in Julianne's forensic science class, and she knows that the guy's father is a famous artist who won one of those genius awards and that the girl's mother used to be a regular on *Saturday Night Live.* If they want to have sex, they should go into one of the bathrooms, the one with the hot tub, and screw each other's brains out, Julianne thinks. But why should *she* have to witness them writhing around as they are now, in full view of everyone? "Let's go," she says to Michael suddenly. "I want to go home. Back to your house, I mean."

"What for?" says Michael. His grip on her hand tightens. "I'm not drinking, everything's cool."

"I hate being here," Julianne confesses, and then one of her wishes comes true and the couple at the other end of the couch vamoose, the guy's pants so tight she can see the outline of his hard-on as he leaves. "Let's go back to your apartment and rent a movie or something."

"We just got here," Michael says, "I'm just getting comfortable."

"Then I'll go home myself," says Julianne, surprised at how determined, how unyielding, she sounds. "No problem."

"Fuck . . . you," Michael says, enunciating crisply, making sure she hears him loud and clear over Kurt Cobain's wailing and the buzz of drunken conversation.

Julianne has turned to ice, except for her face, which feels as if it is on fire. No one has ever spoken to her this way—*no one*—and she is truly shaken. "Now I'm *really* leaving," she says. She frees her fingers from Michael's, rises up from the couch. Her throat is parched and, when she opens her mouth to speak, she hears, *It's got a much better cheese-to-sauce ratio and a very thin crust.* This can't be her; it's a girl nearby with ironed hair, speaking earnestly into a cell phone.

"All right all right all right," Michael says. "I'll go with you."

He sounds put upon and pissed off, and she'd just as soon take the subway alone than spend another minute in his company. "Fine," she says, because she doesn't know how to stay angry, seriously angry, the way Michael does; even with the meds he's taking, sometimes you can see how he has one of those short fuses that when lit might just send him out of control. Frankly, if she didn't love him so much, she would have taken a hike long ago and never once looked back. Recently he's been sending her e-mails that scream "I LOVE YOU!!" in huge letters, 36-point type—once in the morning before she leaves for school and once at night when they instant message each other immediately before logging off their computers. They communicate a lot on the Internet because Julianne is pretty sure her mother's convinced they've broken up, and so it's too risky to have Michael call her at home. But sometimes they just *have to* hear each other's voice so he calls on her cell phone, which her mother would never pick up. In a way, it's all very romantic, like *Romeo and Juliet,* except that Michael's parents couldn't care less about her. Those parents of his are unaccountably chilly people; whenever Julianne encounters them lounging around in their apartment, all they offer her is a nod and a half-smile or a clipped "Hi there." Julianne has trained herself not to take it personally, but of course it's hard not to.

As she and Michael drift across lower Broadway, not holding hands, not talking, Michael suddenly speeds up, taking swift, long-legged strides she can't possibly match. "Wait up!" she calls out, but he pretends not to hear and keeps going, a man on a mission. Hurrying to catch up, her feet nearly collide with a basset hound, its droopy ears skimming the sidewalk. "Take it easy," the dog's owner cautions; Julianne murmurs "sorry" as she rushes by. "Sorry" is a word that is missing from Michael's vocabulary—he may very well feel it, but he can't say it. Whatever the reason, he just can't.

He's gone, or at least out of sight for the moment. The street is safe, full of people going in and out of restaurants, boutiques, chic places selling things you would never need but still might like to have—small Japanese fountains of brass or stone, Zen gardens, rubber flipflops studded with rhinestones, spray cans with chemicals that will turn your hair green or purple or royal blue for the evening. The street is safe, but why should she be out alone on a Saturday night, wondering where her boyfriend is? Her boyfriend who cursed at her when all she wanted was to leave a party that was deadly anyway.

Slowing down, catching her breath, she falls in line behind a long-haired guy and a woman making their way down the flight of steep stairs into the Spring Street station. "We, as U.S. Americans, have got to watch our backs," the guy announces when they reach the bottom of the stairs. "You think?" the woman says, and links her arm in his. How could you love someone who says "U.S. Americans"? Julianne wonders. Then again, how could you love someone who says "Fuck you," not in the jokey way that she and her friends often do, but in a way meant to sting? So if you're in love, your self-respect goes straight out the window, is that it? She wishes, not for the first time, that she were twenty-five or so and knew what to do, what to say to Michael now as he comes toward her.

"Give me your MetroCard," he orders.

"Don't be mad," she says, handing over the card, though she would like to ask why he never seems to have his own, why she's the one who is always paying for their trips around town. She realizes that she's afraid to ask this simple question, the slightest bit afraid of him at this moment, and she shivers in her peacoat.

Michael sweeps through the turnstile and, without saying a word, gives her back the card so she can use it.

"What's wrong?" she says, and, as expected, doesn't get an answer. Then the train pulls in and as she sinks into a seat in the nearly empty car, she watches Michael claim a place for himself at the opposite end. He's miles away and that's the way he wants it.

Humiliated, she stays where she is, staring for a while at a family of three, a couple and their toddler, the parents speaking too loudly to be ignored.

"Wanna sit next to Daddy?" the man asks.

"Shut up, will you?" the woman says. She and the little girl are in matching soiled pink quilted jackets.

"Shut up yourself, *dearie.*"

"I'm trying to fuckin' sleep," the woman announces, pokes a cigarette in her mouth, and then shuts her eyes. "And change her diaper while you're at it."

"Stinky!" the little girl says.

Julianne's not staying around for a diaper change, that's for sure. Rising, gazing down the length of the car, she sees Michael, his head bowed, weeping quietly into the small bowl he's made of his hands. Something—compassion or love, she can't tell them apart—fills her chest and throat. She navigates down to his end of the car, alternating hands as she grips one steel pole after another for balance until she is standing in front of him. And it hits her then that he's stopped taking his meds, that he cannot be trusted to tell the truth about this, cannot be relied upon to take care of himself in the ways that he must. Sitting down beside him, wrapping her arm across his quivering shoulders, the litany she hears is her mother's: *You're not a psychiatrist, you're not a psychologist, you're not a social worker; you're just a seventeen-year-old girl who deserves to be happy.*

The truth is, she doesn't even remember what it's like to be happy anymore, what it's like to awaken in the morning without this heavy weight bearing down upon her, like the weight of Michael himself when he fell asleep on top of her the first time they'd made love. In the beginning, when she and Michael first evolved into Michael-and-Julianne, she awakened every day buoyant with expectation: the warmth of his lips upon hers, the easy glide of his fingers threading through hers, his beautiful face illuminated at the very sight of her as she sauntered down the carpeted hallway toward their English class—all of this awaited her and suddenly her life became something she would have envied had it belonged to someone else. And now? What she feels like is a passenger in an elevator that has plunged a dozen floors in an instant and is sure to crash in the next. If Michael were simply a friend and not the guy she loves, would she abandon him, leave him to his shrink and his inexplicably stony parents? She's asked herself this a thousand times and the answer is always the same: no way. But in fact, Michael is someone to whom she is bound by both love and obligation—a moral obligation, as she sees it—and there is no question of her taking flight. None whatsoever.

"He's sick," she'd told Dr. Schuster, who didn't need to be told. "What if he had cancer? Would you want me to leave him then?"

Hearing this, Dr. Schuster had frowned. "But he *doesn't* have cancer. And what about your obligation to yourself, hmm?"

"What obligation?"

"To keep yourself out of harm's way? And I don't necessarily mean physical harm."

"I've told you fifty times," said Julianne irritably, "the only person he's ever hurt is himself."

Another frown from Dr. Schuster.

What a total waste of money, paying for her to sit there behind her desk scowling and handing out crappy advice that no one wants to hear anyway. She, Dr. Schuster, just doesn't get it, doesn't get what it's like to be Julianne, to be seventeen and have your one and only boyfriend ever sitting in a subway car, hunched over and sobbing uncontrollably into his cupped, trembling hands.

The smell of cigarette smoke drifts from the other end of the car where the toddler is on her back now, legs in the air, looking like a trussed bird as her father clamps her ankles together and cleans her with wipes and her mother smokes away, despite the eighty-dollar fine she will have to pay if caught in the act.

"Tell me why you're crying," Julianne says softly, her voice barely above a whisper because it's the best approach when Michael gets like this.

"I wouldn't treat my worst enemy like you treated me tonight," he says bitterly.

"Excuse me?" She's at a loss; sometimes his mind works in ways she simply can't fathom. And this, too, is frightening.

Michael's nose is dripping; he wipes it with the cuff of the gray cashmere sweater that sticks out from his jacket sleeve. But at least he's stopped crying, something to be grateful for.

"You have no regard for what *I* want," he says. "What *I* want means *nothing* to you, *nada*. You don't love me anymore, do you?"

"What?" says Julianne. "You think I don't love you?"

"You think I don't love you?" he mimics in a cruel falsetto. "Yeah, that's exactly what I think."

"If you'd been taking your meds, you wouldn't be talking like this."

"Bitch."

Her eyes burn; there's a twinge of self-pity and then it's gone. She reminds herself that he's sick, that he cannot be held accountable for the confused, mistaken notions that fill his head. But it's not much of a consolation, not when you're the one who's being spoken to with such disdain.

I cannot do this anymore. These are the words that come to her now, but they're not hers, they're Dr. Schuster's, who instructed her to say them aloud, to try them on for size, over and over again, until they were a comfortable fit.

Well, thanks anyway, Doc, but you're clueless. Clue-less.

Down at the far end of the car, the little girl's father is wrapping the dirty diaper in a couple of sheets of newspaper and stowing it under the seat.

"You know what I wish?" his wife says in her big voice. "I wish I had nails and a hammer so I could nail you into your coffin."

"Eff-you, dearie," the man says, amused. "Without me, you got nothin'."

"Even if you don't love me anymore," Michael begins, "I'll always love *you.*" His lashes are shellacked with tears, the tip of his nose blush-colored. Clamped around one wrist is the flat, unadorned silver bracelet—the kind that's open-ended and can never be fastened securely—that Julianne gave him on their one-month anniversary. His gift to Julianne was a CD he'd burned just for her with all his old favorites—Dylan, the Beatles, the Kinks, the Lovin' Spoonful. She listens to it at night as she struggles to fall asleep, wondering what will happen and whether she is strong enough to hold on to what is dear to her and ignore all the rest. And the following week, when Michael's parents have him discreetly sent away to Evergreen, a private residential facility in Connecticut where he will be evaluated and reevaluated and spend unproductive hours every day in group therapy, she will talk to him on her cell phone in that quiet way of hers, soothing him with one lie after another.

"I know you will," she tells him now, but can only think of the pure sadness of all of it, the sadness that pierces her raw, teenage heart like a razor.

17

SUSAN

Visiting Michael at Evergreen, Susan finds the facility itself lovely; it's an imposing pale-stone building that resembles the Palace of Versailles, meticulously maintained, not a scrap of litter nor inch of soiled carpeting in sight. Michael, Sr., otherwise known as Mickey, is also nowhere in sight; as luck would have it, he had to leave for Zurich on business immediately after depositing Michael at Evergreen and won't be able to make it back in time to visit. Her first time here, Susan had hired a driver and brought her dog, Boyfriend, along for company, but when she tried to get him through the front door, a security guard stopped her and very politely explained that there were no animals allowed; Boyfriend would have to wait in the car. A shame, really, since he'd been wearing a new turtleneck and a crisp pair of khakis, both of which Susan had whipped up for him without much trouble. He was, in fact, better dressed than Michael, who materializes in the lobby this afternoon in droopy jeans, a rag of a T-shirt, and those awful clunky Birkenstocks. He looks bleary-eyed and his hair needs a shampoo, he turns away from her when she moves closer to kiss his cheek.

They ride the elevator up to the rooftop "lounge," which overlooks nine acres of nothing but lifeless brown grass. There is a pool table and a large-screen TV, and the walls are lined with upholstered chaise longues. It is the middle of the afternoon and the place is utterly deserted, except for a boy of twelve or so playing a hand-held video game while an attendant all in white stands nearby looking bored.

"Your father and I are very, very concerned," Susan offers, as she and Michael choose their seats.

Michael shuts his eyes. "I'll bet," he says. Sitting there, stretched out on the chaise with his eyes closed, he might have been sunning himself around the pool on a summer day at their beach house on Nantucket. But this is the funny farm and it is only November.

The heat is turned up too high; Susan shrugs off her cardigan and starts over. "So . . . how are you?"

"Take a guess."

"Can't you open your eyes when you're speaking to me?" she asks.

"What for?"

"Your father and I raised you to be respectful, didn't we?"

"Fuck you," Michael says, shockingly matter-of-fact.

"I see."

"You don't see anything," Michael tells her, and opens his eyes. "All you see is yourself. It's all you ever see."

This isn't, she has to admit (though only to herself), entirely unfair. And she knows it sounds terrible, but to be honest, she doesn't much like spending time with other people, has never really seen the need for more than a friend or two, or for spilling her soul to them all night like some self-dramatizing schoolgirl. She takes pleasure in being alone, reading or working at her sewing machine on Boyfriend's ever-expanding wardrobe. Mickey is often away on business and that suits her fine. When he's home, they have dinner together and attend the theater or a performance at Lincoln Center or the opera, but that's *all* they do together. They're seldom intimate and that, too, suits her fine. (Whether it suits Mickey or not is *his* business, she thinks.) Intimacy, physical or emotional, just doesn't come naturally to her. As she sees it, people are entitled to their privacy and you have to respect that. As for those who might accuse her of a certain frostiness, well, it's undeniably painful to be regarded that way, but what can she do? She is who she is, as much as she may sometimes regret it. Though certainly she's not heartless; hasn't she visited Michael twice over the five days he's been away at Evergreen?

"So what can I do to help you?" she asks him, and reaches over and tries to pat his poor bruised hand, making him scowl.

"Leave me the fuck alone."

She remembers him then—in that wistful way that mothers of adolescents do—as a white-haired toddler, one who for some unknown reason called her "ma'am" instead of "mom" and who adored his Legos, spending hours lying on his little potbelly building bridges and tunnels and apartment buildings. He was so beautiful that a photographer actually stopped Susan on the street one day and gave her his business card. Which led to a succession of modeling jobs—the magazine covers of *Child* and *Working Mother* and *Children's Vogue* and also to enormous posters of Michael that hung from the ceilings of one of those discount stores all over the country—perhaps it was Walmart, she thinks. So when she says Michael was a beautiful child, it's no exaggeration.

In her eyes, these days, his beauty has been tarnished, and you can believe that, too. But most people would consider him rather strikingly handsome, especially his little girlfriend (whose mother drives a cab, of all things, though apparently she's the author of several books as well, Susan has heard). It's long been apparent to her that Julianne is no good for her son; the two of them linger on the phone at ungodly hours and from her bedroom late at night Susan can hear him weeping and shouting, cursing Julianne and then proclaiming his undying love and then cursing her all over again. It makes Susan heartsick to hear this, to know that Julianne is only adding to the misery that seems to have engulfed Michael like a furious wave of dark, dirty water.

"I *said*, leave . . . me . . . the . . . fuck . . . alone."

"I'm sorry, were you talking to me?" Susan asks.

"Don't come here anymore."

"You're my child," Susan says. She longs to touch some part of him—his face, his shoulder, his knee—but knows enough not to.

"That's a laugh and a half. Next thing you know, you'll be telling me how much you love me."

Love. Now there's something she isn't much good at; like tennis or bridge, she has no gift for it. Even a discussion of the subject renders her thick and clumsy. Oafish.

"I *do* love you," she hears herself telling Michael, and they are unfamiliar words on her tongue.

"Never kid a kidder," Michael advises.

The shame she feels burns a hole right through her.

18

LAZY

Rising from her desk, Lazy greets her 11:00 appointment with a hug. "Always a pleasure to see you, Emma," she says, and wishes this weren't a lie. Emma Hughes, president of Griffin's board of trustees, is a near-anorexic with a perpetual tan and a seventeen-million-dollar home in the Hamptons. She is also the mother of a set of big-boned, ill-tempered twin girls, Jade and Palmer, both of whom have demonstrated an unfortunate inability to negotiate even halfway decent scores on the SATs despite endless hours of high-priced tutoring. They will, nevertheless, go to Princeton like their father before them, driving down in their matching Porsche Boxsters next fall to New Jersey, where happiness will elude them, just as it continues to elude their mother.

"I'm a basket case," Emma confesses.

"Have a seat," Lazy says. "May I offer you something to drink?"

"A Diet Coke with lots of ice and a twist of lime," says Emma, as if she were addressing a waitress. "On second thought, I'd prefer to have the ice on the side, in a separate glass."

"Pardon me for just a moment," Lazy says, and rushes out to Brooke. "Run down the street for me, will you, sweets?" she says. "Emma Hughes needs a Diet Coke, ice on the side, twist of lime."

"May I take this opportunity to remind you that I have an MFA from Columbia," Brooke says. "What am I, an errand boy all of a sudden?"

"And I have a doctorate from Yale," Lazy sighs, "but I still have to take Emma Hughes' drink orders, okay?"

"Let's tell her to get her fucking Diet Coke herself," Brooke suggests amiably.

"Would that I could," says Lazy. "Perhaps in some other lifetime."

"Hmm . . . I think I know why she's here," Brooke says, and lowers her voice. "I heard a while back that Tweedle Dum and Tweedle Dee lost their respective cherries at some Griffin orgy last month."

"You mean Emma's daughters?"

"Yeah, Tweedle Dum and Tweedle Dee; the 'b' is silent in 'Dum.'"

"Don't be mean," says Lazy. "They're, um, large-boned girls, but I wouldn't really call them overweight, and let's not forget the unassailable fact that the Hughes family has been uncommonly generous to this school."

"True, but if I get that Diet Coke for her I won't be able to live with myself."

"I wish you had a choice, sweets, but you don't," Lazy says regretfully. She and Brooke get along famously; the kid is bright and efficient and, at twenty-four, young and hip enough to occasionally serve as a confidante to students. If Brooke's heard about an orgy, odds are it's no idle rumor.

Back in her inner sanctum, Lazy steels herself for what she knows is about to come her way.

"My throat is terribly dry," Emma Hughes complains. "Will that Diet Coke I ordered be here soon?"

"Any minute," Lazy soothes her. "Even as we speak."

"That's good. What's not good, however, is the reason I'm here."

"Oh?" Oh for a hit of nicotine! *How about the two of us stand outside in the courtyard while I have a quick cigarette and you tell me what this is all about,* Lazy would like to say.

"Not good at all," says Emma. "My daughters know the difference between right and wrong, of that you can be sure. They know, as well, that the threat of AIDS and other sexually transmitted diseases is something we're forced to take very, very seriously these days."

"Of course." Her eyes on Emma, Lazy pulls open a desk drawer, feels around blindly for her pack of Newports.

"So I'm sure you can imagine that I almost died when they finally came to me last night and confessed that they, along with three of their friends, invited five seniors to you know . . . deflower them, have sex with them, you might say. This was at Ethan Rinehart's apartment, and my question to you is, WHERE WERE HIS PARENTS?" Emma finishes with a shriek.

"Away for the weekend?" Lazy guesses.

"Correct," says Emma, one hand open against her throat. "The Rineharts go away for the weekend and my daughters lose their virginity. Does that seem right to you?"

Rolling a cigarette between her palms now, Lazy says, "While I can certainly understand how distressed you are, Emma, surely you understand that I have no control over what—"

"While the Rineharts were sunning themselves in the Caribbean, my children were having sex with FIVE DIFFERENT PARTNERS! Five girls and five boys swapping partners all night long, you get the picture?"

"All too vividly," Lazy says. The cigarette has been crushed between her perspiring palms, and she busies herself brushing flecks of tobacco to the floor. "I'm so sorry," she says, "but lamentable as all this may be, the fact is, this is what teenagers do, what they dream about . . . and really, there's no stopping them. Or the Rineharts, who have every right to go to the Caribbean any weekend they please. Unfortunately," she adds.

"You're not upset enough!" Emma says accusingly. "You should be livid! You should want to kill the Rineharts with your bare hands, tear them limb from limb! What's wrong with you? Why are you sitting there so calmly? You're unfit to lead the school in this new century! And where's my damn Diet Coke?"

"Let me check on that," says Lazy, about to flee just as Brooke walks through the door, two plastic cups in hand.

"Bless you," says Emma. She grabs the cups from Brooke, plunks some ice chips into her drink, takes a sip. "This is Diet *Pepsi,*" she announces. "Did you think I wouldn't notice? I specifically asked for Diet Coke and instead you bring me *this*? I'd rather have *nothing* than Diet Pepsi. Nothing!"

And nothing is what you deserve. "Forget it," Lazy mouths to Brooke, who rolls her eyes and backs out of the room, insisting that Diet Coke is what she ordered at the deli down the street. "I'm sorry," says Lazy.

"This school seems to be falling short in so many ways," Emma Hughes observes. "It has, after all these years, suddenly come to seem low-rent."

"I beg to differ," Lazy says, and, with pride, offers that one crucial statistic that every Griffin parent longs to hear: "Last year over fifty percent of our graduates went on to Ivy League schools, and I can assure you that this year, once again, we'll match those numbers."

"Oh that," says Emma, dismissing that all-important fifty percent in a couple of syllables. "That's a given." Taking another sip of her unsatisfactory soda, she says, "I want the Rineharts crucified. Not here in your office behind closed doors, but publicly."

Lazy instantly envisions Mr. and Mrs. R on their own calvary, matching his and hers crowns of thorns adorning their heads, Emma Hughes dressed in a fashionable Roman toga and leather sandals and adding to the Rineharts' anguish with sticks and stones and anything else available to her.

"What I want," Emma continues, "what I *demand,* is that you send a letter notifying every Griffin parent that the Rineharts allowed an orgy to take place in their loft, and, in doing so, sullied the reputations of five lovely young girls. The boys I don't care about. They can rot in hell for all I care."

Lazy's first response is to clear her throat. And then: "I'll try my best to get the message across, Emma, but I really don't think that mentioning the Rineharts by name is the right way to go. It's purely vindictive and it's only going to humiliate them. Let me find a better way to deal with this."

"Then you'll have to excuse me for raising the subject of a close, personal friend who happens to write lengthy op-ed pieces for the *Times* every other week. He's a Griffin parent, as I'm sure you're aware, and the father of a darling little girl who happens to have been present at the orgy, though she wasn't one of the players. So I'm sure you can connect the dots here, can't you?"

"Is that a threat?"

"Don't be silly!" Emma says cheerfully. "And by the way, when you send out that memo crucifying the Rineharts, please make sure to put their names in boldface."

Lazy feels a hot flash, her very first, working its way through her worn, middle-aged body. Her temperature has shot up to 212 degrees; in a single instant, she's sweat through her silk suit, her blouse, her bra and matching thong underwear. And her brain is on fire as well. "Get out of my office," she tells Emma Hughes. "OUT!"

Chalk it up to a hormone-induced fury or, perhaps, a reckless courage; whatever it is, it just may have cost Lazy her corner office, not to mention the somewhat impressive title and salary that go with it. And at this moment, she cares not a whit.

19

It's been almost three months now since her mother's death, but Morgan continues to log on daily to www.weloveyou elizabeth.com. She never knows what she might find there. Sometimes days pass and there's nothing new, and it's a little disappointing. But every now and then something takes her by surprise, she tells Julianne, like a very sweet message from Lazy Hoffman saying how much her mother's generosity meant to the school, and how she, Ms. Hoffman, is available 24/7 to talk to Morgan should the need ever arise.

"Can you believe she signed it 'with affection'?" Morgan says, and Julianne snickers, since everyone at Griffin is aware that Ms. Hoffman has plenty of that for Mr. McNamee, who's actually quite a hottie, at least if you're into big blond preppy old men who think that F. Scott Fitzgerald is the greatest writer who ever lived. Julianne and Morgan have heard rumors of Hoffman and McNamee rubbing up against each other in the hallway near her office one night; everyone suspects that those two have been hooking up and nobody really cares. Why should they?

"What could be more boring and unimportant than the private lives of teachers?" Julianne says. "Honestly!"

Logging on to the Web site in her bedroom, with Julianne standing right beside her, Morgan discovers a message from Luke Zucker-Johnsen that says he remembered something about her mother from years ago: one time, in kindergarten or first grade, she'd accompanied their class on a trip upstate to a pumpkin farm. Luke had had to take a whiz urgently but there were no bathrooms around anywhere. So Elizabeth had led him to a secluded spot just beyond the pumpkins and stood guard while he peed.

And afterward she tucked my shirt in for me and smoothed my hair back with her hands, as if I were hers and not someone else's child. Her hands were warm against my back when she fixed my shirt but maybe I'm making that part up, I don't know. But I don't think so. I think I'm remembering it all because I have so few memories of anyone paying attention to me like that . . . Well, whatever.

Reading this, Morgan just has to share it with her mother, she says. She retypes it in her own words, then adds a few other things she and Julianne agree might be of interest, like the A– she got on a philosophy paper she'd slaved over, and how amazing Vanessa Redgrave was as Mary Tyrone in *Long Day's Journey,* which she saw with Luke last week. It wasn't, strictly speaking, an actual date, Julianne muses, or maybe it was, because Morgan and Luke went to a late dinner afterward at Chanterelle, one of the best restaurants in the city, and he paid for all of it, the theater tickets, too. They never got beyond hand-holding and a good-night kiss, according to Morgan, but if something more were to develop, she said she'd probably welcome it. Julianne hopes so; it would be good for her to be dating someone, even someone who took twice as long as everyone else on the SATs because of that OCD problem of his. And she can't help smiling, remembering the way Luke knelt to give Morgan her drink that first night of the shiva, the endearing way he said her name aloud, hiding nothing.

The thing is, Morgan's mother is dead and won't be reading this latest message, or any of the others Morgan occasionally leaves for her on the Web site. But who knows what goes on out there in cyberspace, Julianne thinks. Suspending her disbelief (a concept she's learned about in A.P. English this year), she tells herself that Elizabeth could be anywhere, tuned in to Morgan this very instant, happy to hear about that A−. And relieved to know she hasn't been forgotten.

These messages of Morgan's are posted late at night and deleted by her early the next morning to minimize the possibility of anyone other than her mother seeing them on the Web site.

"If anyone besides my mom—and you, of course—were ever to read them, I would be so totally mortified," Morgan confides. "Because I know how it would look to other people; like I've gone off the deep end into a very weird place."

"But you haven't," Julianne says, and she is pretty sure of that. Morgan misses her mother and that's allowed, isn't it, even if she's clearly old enough to fend for herself every minute of every day, from the moment she awakens until the moment she finally lets herself be carried off into a dream-riddled sleep. Hey, if people don't think that's allowed, well then, who needs them?

Julianne finds herself thinking—as she so rarely does—of her father, of how little she misses him, really. They talk on the phone from time to time, but it's no big deal. Funny how fathers can seem sort of irrelevant, almost, not like mothers, who, no matter how annoying they might be, are still indispensable. You just can't live without the warmth of that unconditional love.

Poor Morgan. How can she bear to live without it?

20

DEE

Even if Julianne hadn't confessed that she and Michael Avery are still very much a couple, Dee would have known anyway. For one thing, Julianne is always, day and night, whispering into that tiny silvery cell phone. And for another, Dee discovered, just yesterday, a pair of plaid boxer shorts carelessly thrown into an old wicker laundry hamper that hadn't seen a single article of men's clothing since her ex left a lifetime ago.

"The question 'how stupid do you think I am?' comes to mind," she'd told Julianne, dangling the boxers by their waistband from her thumb. "Or did you *want* me to find these, is that it?"

"I don't want you to do anything except leave me alone."

"Nothing good can come of this relationship," Dee had said, sighing, pretending this was some brilliant revelation she was offering up now for the very first time. "Nothing! Why can't you see that?" They were in the bedroom she'd long ago given over to Julianne, where both their dressers were hidden away in the closet and where almost everything Julianne owned somehow managed to find its way to the floor. Was there anything about their lives that was in order, anything at all? Well, at least Will sent his child support and alimony checks on time every month. She had to be grateful for *that,* at least. But now that his girlfriend was finally enjoying a normal, healthy pregnancy, he seemed to have less interest than usual in Julianne and her "adolescent soap opera," as he'd labeled her relationship with Michael, though, on the positive side, he was actually willing to kick in some extra money to pay for her sessions with Dr. Schuster. Dee had been a single parent for years, and had never, in all that time, encountered anything she couldn't handle reasonably well on her own. But Michael Avery? Who could possibly be prepared for the appearance of someone like that in her life? The kid was a force of nature, a brutally destructive storm that left a trail of broken spirits in its wake. His own parents, according to Julianne, hadn't a clue about how to mend all that needed fixing there. It wasn't, as Will insisted, a soap opera, but a tragedy, really. In truth, Dee was filled with pity for the poor kid. But sometimes she fantasized about disappearing in the middle of the night, scooping up Julianne as if she were a baby she could carry away in her arms, the two of them leaving everything behind and boarding a train that would whisk them away toward the middle of the country, Chicago, perhaps, where they would find a comfortable place for themselves to start anew, hundreds of miles from Michael and his poisonous misery. But Julianne would be off to college in a matter of months and if they could only get from here to there safely . . . was this too much to hope for?

"Where are you going?" Dee asks her now.

Barefoot, dressed in an ankle-length turquoise bathrobe, a bar of outrageously expensive scented soap in hand, Julianne rolls her eyes. "Uh, the shower?" she says, and grabs her cell phone.

"And why do you need to take the phone into the shower with you?"

"Not *into* the shower. Just into the bathroom. In case it rings."

"Like the world would come to an end if you missed one of his calls." Now it's Dee's turn for eye-rolling.

"He gets upset if he can't reach me," Julianne explains. "These little things upset him and then it just snowballs into something really big and all of a sudden he's out of control."

This information is a precious gift; usually Dee gets next to nothing. Like a lover who rarely has the upper hand, she knows enough to play it cool, not to appear too needy, too fearful. "Is he taking his meds?" she asks, feigning, as best she can, nonchalance.

"I think so," Julianne murmurs, and lowers her head.

"What?"

"I mean I hope so."

"You *hope* so?"

"Could we not have this conversation, please? I have to get into the shower. I'm meeting him in fifteen minutes."

"Well, that's great news."

"Just give him a chance," Julianne says. "Please."

"A chance to what?"

"To get better, okay?"

"How's he ever going to get better if he doesn't take his medication?"

Down goes Julianne's head again. "Well, he does most of the time, I think. You know, since he was released from Evergreen."

"Most of the time isn't good enough."

"It makes him dizzy and a little nauseous. And really, really tired. So it's a choice between sick and tired, or manic . . ."

Sick and tired? Well, *she's* sick and tired of her beloved pipsqueak of a daughter playing nursemaid to a boy who can't control his impulses, who's broken every one of his knuckles smashing them into walls, doors, and God knows what else.

"I'm begging you," Dee is saying. "Begging you . . . Just let me do my job as a mother and keep you safe. . . ." It's the wrong thing to say and she knows it. That kind of talk gets her nowhere, just like telling Julianne how much she loves her gets her nowhere. But somewhere out there are all the right words, which, when arranged in just the right order and delivered in just the right voice, will do the trick. She's a writer. Or was a writer. Arranging words to do her bidding is the one and only talent she possesses. So why has she failed, again and again, to get this right?

"Sorry, but no," the pip-squeak tells her. Four feet eleven and a half inches tall, ninety-something pounds, and she's the victor here. "I just can't, okay?" she insists.

Okay? It's so far from okay that Dee can't even begin to calculate the distance.

21

LAZY

ate in the afternoon, as Lazy is revising the ninety-seventh draft of what she refers to as "The Orgy Papers," Brooke appears in the doorway and, reading off a business card, announces, "Prince Abdullah bin Fawwaz al-Aziz to see you, sir."

"Pardon me?"

"The transfer student from Eton?"

"Oh, right," Lazy says. "Send him on in."

"He's with his, well, handler, I think. Okay?"

"Fine. And let me take a look at that business card, would you?"

"It's a calling card," says Brooke. "You know, like in all those Edith Wharton novels?"

"How utterly civilized," says Lazy, impressed.

"So this guy is the real deal? Real live royalty?"

"Yes, though apparently he's not in the direct line of succession to the throne. And even if he were, we're not going to go around calling him 'Prince' here. This is America, sweets."

"Whatever you say, your majesty," Brooke says, and bows low.

Lazy does a lipstick check and powders her nose. "Ready," she tells Brooke and gets up from her seat as two young men, the older one bearded and ordinary-looking, the other clean-shaven and darkly handsome, set foot in her office. Both are in blue blazers and gray flannel pants.

"I am Mr. Ahmed al-Salan," the bearded one says, his accent

impeccably British. "And may I present Prince Abdullah bin Fawwaz al-Aziz.""

"Welcome to Griffin," Lazy says, shaking hands with each of them. *And may I ask what you two were doing on the morning of 9/11? Nothing untoward, one hopes.*

"Prince Abdullah will be ready to begin his classes on Monday, Headmistress."

"And please call me 'Jimmy,'" the prince says in his lovely Brit accent. "That's what all my chums at Eton called me."

Chums. Indeed! Lazy has been disarmed by his accent, his graciousness, his perfectly tailored blue blazer and burnished penny loafers, and also by his pretty green eyes. His father, she knows, is the head of a publishing empire of newspapers and magazines, in both England and Saudi Arabia. Worth billions, no doubt, some of which, if she plays her cards right, might just find their way into Griffin's coffers where they could help build a new theater for the drama department, add a pool to the gym, and improve the faculty's health benefits.

"Just call me 'Ms. Hoffman,'" she says. "We're delighted to count you a member of our student body."

"Thank you, Headmistress."

"Ms. Hoffman," she corrects him.

Prince Jimmy smiles, revealing beautifully aligned, shockingly white teeth. "If you insist, Headmistress," he says.

It's Prince Jimmy's emerald eyes Lazy finds herself thinking of as Doug McNamee cries "Oh, sweet Jesus" for the third and final time and then pulls out. Her rear end sticks unpleasantly to the leather couch in her office and she shifts herself around trying to get comfortable. Faking an orgasm with your lover can't be a good sign, she reflects, and wonders if there is cause for concern. Maybe it's just the damn couch, which used to seem sexy and now seems merely annoying, way too narrow and confining for two fully grown adults.

"You know what I would love?" she says, as Doug scoops the condom into his monogrammed handkerchief—which later will be properly disposed of in a Department of Sanitation garbage pail on a Park Avenue street corner.

"A nightcap?"

"Silk sheets on a nice king-size bed, a long, steamy shower with you afterward, and then maybe room service."

"That does sound awfully inviting." Sitting up at the edge of the couch, Doug pulls on his tattersall boxers and then his khakis.

"But why *can't* we ever go to a hotel?"

"Number one, it's not safe for us to be out and about, and number two, it's too damn expensive in this town—five, six hundred dollars for a few hours in a good hotel. You know it, honeybunny; we're better off staying right here."

"Just one time," Lazy persists. "Let me indulge my fantasy. And I'll pay for it, of course, since . . ." Since her salary is more than triple Doug's and they both know it.

"We'll see," Doug says. "Maybe." Running his fingertip slowly from the crook of her arm all the way down to her wrist, he says, "Tell me some more of your fantasies."

"Not a good idea," says Lazy.

"Try me," Doug murmurs, and reaches for her other arm.

"Well," Lazy begins, closing her eyes so she doesn't have to see the expression on Doug's face, "sometimes I wonder what it would have been like for us if we'd met under other circumstances, if we'd both been single, I mean. Would we have wanted to spend the rest of our lives together, do you think?"

Doug's finger is traveling now along the inside of her thigh, very, very languorously. "Would you still be my boss?" he says. "Because one doesn't marry one's boss, not if one is a man, that is, and the boss is a woman. It's just not done."

"That sounds like sexist bullshit," Lazy says. "And while we're on the subject, I may not be your boss for too much longer. Emma Hughes is probably going to make sure the board of trustees shows me the door once she sees the memo I'm planning to send out about the orgy. She's called me twice already trying to hurry me along, but I'm having such a hard time getting the tone just right."

Hesitating a moment or two before he speaks, Doug offers, "One might say she's rather an odious woman. And I guarantee you those dopey daughters of hers will be off to Princeton, never mind that each of them is dumb as a post. Or dumber. It's disgraceful, really."

"I threw her out of my office, can you believe it? What was I *thinking*?"

Again Doug hesitates. "I say you're to be commended for refusing to allow her to intimidate you."

"Pride goeth before a you-know-what," Lazy says ruefully. "I should have at least made a concentrated effort to appease her, but instead I lost my temper and . . ." And there's another one of those hot flashes. Why didn't she appreciate all that lovely estrogen while she had it—that wonderful hormone doing its job so efficiently, working overtime to monitor her body temperature, maintain the elasticity of her skin and the sexual heat that allowed her to keep the two men in her life happy between the sheets, or couch cushions.

"You're burning!" Doug says, but inside she's already cooling down. "Are you all right?"

Actually, she's not. She's afraid of growing impossibly old, of her skin turning slack, her breasts droopy, of her mind turning obsessively fearful and her demeanor pathetic and helpless, just like her poor mother; she's afraid of Doug leaving her and Richard never forgiving her if he ever discovers she's been unfaithful; she's afraid of being middle-aged and on her own. And most of all, she's afraid of Emma Hughes. Because without this job of hers, she can't imagine who she will be.

22

JULIANNE

Shopping at Barneys with Morgan and Daisy Camarano-Rosenthal, who always seem to have money to burn, Julianne imagines her mother's voice filled with a mixture of astonishment and contempt, saying, *Two HUNDRED and twenty-five dollars for a pair of JEANS? What are they, studded with DIAMONDS? Lined in MINK? What kind of PARENTS do these girls have? What kind of VALUES are they teaching them? What is WRONG with these people?* Well, it's not their fault they're rich, Julianne thinks. Or that they have generous parents. Her mother would flip out if she saw those Y-3 sneakers Morgan bought a few minutes ago—two hundred and ninety bucks for a simple pair of black-and-white sneakers. And then there's the two-hundred-and-seventy-eight-dollar long-sleeved T-shirt Daisy picked out for herself. Nothing special, just a nice lavender T-shirt to wear to school. Daisy squealed when she saw it; she had to have it. And didn't even have to call her mother to ask for permission first. Julianne has to ask for permission if she's going to buy anything that costs over fifty dollars; it's one of Dee's hard-and-fast rules and it has to be obeyed. Julianne's friends play by different rules, as does almost everyone else she knows at Griffin. It's never really bothered her. Honestly. Her Pumas only cost seventy-five dollars, her Mavi jeans just fifty, so what? Morgan's walking around with six hundred dollars in cash stuffed into the pockets of her jeans, but who cares? Morgan's beloved mother is dead. Not only that, but her father's never around, her grandmother's in Florida, her brother's twelve and kind of a geek; in other words, she has no one in the world to pay attention to her, to give a damn if she has, for example, terrible cramps and needs a couple of Aleve and a heating pad. If she needs those things she has to drag herself out of bed and get them herself, no matter how awful she's feeling; even worse, there's no one to put his or her lips to Morgan's forehead to see if she's running a fever, no one to arrange her satin comforter for her in a nice cozy way as she lies on her stomach, toes kneading into her mattress, waiting for the cramps to subside. Julianne's mother does all of that for her. She's an annoying pain in the ass much of the time, but she's devoted and loving, too, and there's a lot to be said for that. Daisy's mother—a total loser—didn't speak to her for over a week after Daisy's abortion a few months ago, and when she finally started talking to her again, the first thing she said was that Daisy had committed a mortal sin that deprived her soul of sanctifying grace. In other words, when the time comes, Daisy will be going straight to hell. Her father went crazy after hearing that, and he insisted Daisy's mother apologize, and then she and Daisy went out shopping together and Daisy came back with a Marc Jacobs bag that cost over three thousand dollars. *Like a three-thousand-dollar pocketbook is going to repair the damage,* Julianne's mother said when she heard about it. *The kid's soul has theoretically been deprived of grace and an obscenely expensive handbag is supposed to take the edge off things? Poor Daisy! Imagine having a mother like that!* Julianne couldn't. Nor could she imagine a mother like Michael's, who named her dog "Boyfriend" and spends half her useless life designing outfits for him, as if he were some kind of flesh-and-blood doll. Michael despises Boyfriend and his ridiculous wardrobe, and he's told Julianne, more than once, that he would love to see the pooch come to a sorry end. He hates his mother as well and isn't too crazy about his father either. Not that he doesn't have his reasons.

Her cell phone rings and it's him. "Hey," he says.

Things have been pretty good between them lately—he's been taking his Depakote and Effexor again and staying away from weed—but even so, her stomach tightens at the sound of his voice. "Hey," she tells him.

"So what do you think of these Juicy jeans? Should I get them, too?" Morgan asks, holding them up to her waist. They're jeans with a double seam stitched in yellow down the length of each leg—nothing special for a hundred and eighty-five bucks. "Well, let me tell you what I don't like about them—when I tried them on, they almost made me look like I've got some kind of J-Lo thing going on—a big butt, you know?"

"Forget about 'em," Daisy advises.

Julianne nods in agreement though she has no opinion about the J-Lo thing. "So what's up?" she asks Michael.

"Where are you?"

"Shopping with Morgan and Daisy. They're waiting in line to pay. This place is insane. Wool socks for ninety-five dollars, can you believe it? And a pair of panties for two hundred and thirty— amazing, right? They were silk and lace but give me a break—over two hundred bucks?" She laughs, a little nervously, hoping he'll laugh, too.

He doesn't.

"Why do you always have to be with them?" he says. "I'll meet you downtown and we can go CD shopping."

This is his new complaint—that she spends too much time hanging with her friends. He doesn't have any really close friends himself, doesn't understand what it's like to routinely take pleasure in the company of other people.

"We're seeing each other tonight," she points out. "Can we go to the movies?" She tries to keep her voice neutral, tries to pretend that they're just two ordinary people having a phone conversation about nothing of any consequence. Nearby there's a large fish tank dominated by a huge white piece of coral shaped like an open hand; she stares at the half-dozen or so privileged fish gliding by at their leisure. "The Quad Cinema has some really great movies. Want to do that?" she asks.

"You're my girlfriend," Michael reminds her. He sounds impatient. "If I ask you to go CD shopping with me on a Saturday afternoon, you should be more than happy to do so. If you're not more than happy to do so, maybe we should reevaluate our relationship."

She can hear him exhaling cigarette smoke, hear him drumming his fingers against something hard, a book cover, she guesses. "Are you threatening to break up with me over this?" She looks down at the squared-off tips of her boots, then up at a toddler strapped into a stroller parked a few yards away on the shining cream-colored marble floor. He's wearing a plain gray sweatshirt and, oddly, a single strand of pearls, and is drinking from a red Sippy cup molded into Elmo's face. She smiles at him.

"I'm not threatening you," Michael says. "I'm merely suggesting you think twice before blowing me off like that."

"Let's not fight about this," Julianne says. "Meet me in the lobby of my building around seven, okay?" She looks again at the little boy, who's nibbling on his pearls now. Someday, she predicts, in about fifteen years or so, he, too, can make some girl miserable if he chooses. This is what Michael does—he chooses to make things difficult whenever possible. On his meds or not, he generally rejects the easy way, the path of least resistance. Her mother says that they—Julianne and Michael—are like a bad marriage. Get a divorce, she says, before it's too late.

"I love you," Michael says gravely, joylessly. "Without you, I'm nothing, I have nothing. Don't ever forget that."

She hates the way her throat burns, the way her eyes fill, at the sound of these words he uses all too often. "Don't say that to me," she whispers. "Please." But he's already hung up and she's broken out in a sweat in this overheated, overpriced store filled with people who look as if they're accustomed to getting everything they want in this world, but who may, in fact, be no happier than she.

23

Subject: our children
Date: 12/09/2003 9:04:45 AM Eastern Standard Time
From: savery@wazoo.com
To: coop@xmail.com

Dear Mrs. Coopersmith,

I would truly appreciate it if you would do everything in your power to keep your daughter away from my son. He has, as you're no doubt aware, a serious mood disorder, and it would be best if your daughter refrained from complicating his already complicated life. I urge you to monitor her phone calls and e-mail correspondence, and also to forbid my son to enter your home. The less these two see of each other, the better; in the long run, this will prove the wisest course of action, of that you can be sure.

Thanks,
Susan Avery
(Michael's mother)

Subject: Re: our children
Date: 12/10/2003 11:31:18 PM Eastern Standard Time
From: coop@xmail.com
To: savery@wazoo.com

Dear Susan (if I may),

First things first: please call me Dee. And let me say that while the thought of our children's relationship deeply disturbs me as well, I don't think we can, at this late date, do much to keep them apart. Michael is indeed a troubled kid—God knows, I witnessed first-hand one of his "episodes" a while ago, and I find myself haunted by it still. And I've talked myself blue in the face trying to convince Julianne that she and Michael should have nothing further to do with each other. But she's an adolescent and she's in love, and it's clear to me that she will go her own way despite my advice. So what I'm hoping is that this relationship will die a natural death as soon as possible. And I cannot forbid Michael to come over here. (What will that do except add fuel to the fire?) That's your job—if you don't want him here with Julianne, feel free to tell him so yourself. Perhaps he'll listen to you; anything's possible. As for monitoring Julianne's phone calls and e-mails, I'm afraid that's not a possibility. I'm not the FBI!

If you'd like to meet for coffee to discuss any of this further, I'm sure we could find a mutually convenient time and place.

My best to you,
Dee

Subject: RE: RE: our children
   Date: 12/11/2003 7:59:04 AM Eastern Standard Time
   From: savery@wazoo.com
      To: coop@xmail.com

Dear Mrs. Coopersmith,

Your unwillingness to cooperate grievously disappoints me. At the very least, I would appreciate it if you would get your daughter to stop calling here at 2:00 in the morning. I hear the phone ring and then Michael yelling and weeping; this has got to stop. And this happens on school nights, no less. He needs his sleep, as do I. These late-night phone calls are unacceptable!

As for your suggestion that we meet for coffee, I'm afraid I have an awfully busy schedule these days. But thanks for offering.

Yours,
Susan Avery

Subject: your busy schedule
 Date: 12/12/2003 12:17:46 AM Eastern Standard Time
From: coop@xmail.com
  To: savery@wazoo.com

Dear Susan,

Well, I'm sorry to hear you're too busy to have coffee with me. I'm sorry, too, that Michael's yelling and crying have kept you up at night. Perhaps if he were more punctilious about taking his meds, he wouldn't find himself reduced to tears at 2:00 in the morning. I've spoken to Julianne about the late-night phone calls, and she's explained to me that Michael is always the one to initiate these calls—often he becomes angry and upset about something and hangs up on her. She only calls back in an attempt to smooth things over. None of this makes me happy, of that you can be sure. And forgive me for saying so, but I wish to God they'd never met—as far as I can see, he's brought her more grief than anything else. He's an exceptionally bright and handsome young man, and I wish him well as he makes his way in the world. But his illness is a terrible weight for my daughter to bear. The fact is, she shouldn't have to. Have you thought about sending him away to boarding school for his final semester before college?

Dee

Subject: my son/your daughter
Date: 12/12/2003 7:23:16 AM Eastern Standard Time
From: savery@wazoo.com
To: coop@xmail.com

Dee:

Thank you for letting me know that you find my son bright and handsome. He is indeed both of those, though sometimes it's easy to overlook these gifts of beauty and intelligence and focus instead on that dark shadow he so often seems to cast. Did you know that the lowest grade on his high school transcript is an A–? And that he's taking 7 courses this term instead of the usual 5? His teachers at Griffin have raved about him, year after year. So you see that he's a boy one could love. And be proud of. His illness, however, is the heaviest of burdens for me. And so I can well imagine that, on the worst days, Julianne must feel as if she's being crushed by the very weight of it. But time will pass and soon enough Michael will be at Harvard. (If we're lucky, that is.) And Julianne will be somewhere else. And some of us, at least, will be able to rest easier.

Yours,
Susan

P.S. Perhaps we'll run into each other at a Griffin function sometime this school year.

Subject: that elusive cup of coffee
Date: 12/12/2003 11:59:51 PM Eastern Standard Time
From: coop@xmail.com
To: savery@wazoo.com

Are you absolutely <u>sure</u> you don't want to meet for coffee?

D.

Subject: Starbucks on the corner of Columbus and 76th
   Date: 12/13/2003 7:11:28 AM Eastern Standard Time
   From: savery@wazoo.com
      To: coop@xmail.com

Putting it that way, as you do, makes me think a cup of coffee won't do either of us any harm.

S.

24

LAZY

A full-blown joyous smile wrapped across her face, Lazy scans the lengthy list of names for the third time, just to make sure the news is as good as she thinks it is. The results are in: eleven Griffin students have been accepted early at Yale, nine at Harvard, six at Princeton, and three or four each at most of the other Ivies. Not to mention Stanford, Amherst, Swarthmore, Northwestern, Georgetown, Duke . . . "Yesss!" Lazy whoops, and thrusts her arm into the air triumphantly. "Yes yes yes!" She puts in a call to Kat Hemenway, Griffin's Director of College Counseling. "Kat, love of my life! Twenty-six at the Big Three! Good work, my darling! May I kiss the nethermost hem of your garment? Or, perhaps, the sacred ground you walk upon?"

"Hey, Lazy!" Kat says in her friendly, good-humored way. But there's something in her voice that suggests she's not quite as thrilled as Lazy is, goddamnit.

"Don't do this to me, Kat."

"Pardon?"

"Here I am dancing around my office, thrilled to death at these spectacular results of yours, of ours, but you're not dancing with me. . . . You're sitting at your desk with your feet flat on the ground and I want to know why. Talk to me, Kat."

"Well . . . as always, there are some disappointments. We didn't, for example, get a single student into Penn. Not a one. Three deferrals until the spring but not a single acceptance."

"But there's always hope for more acceptances in the spring. So come on, Kat, cheer up. We've done terrifically well and you know it."

"The disturbing thing is, one of those who's been deferred is Chase Greenglass. That family has major real estate holdings all over town, their net worth is something like half a billion, plus Chase is a double legacy—both parents are Penn alumni."

"Forgive me, but the girl's hardly the sharpest crayon in the box, is she?" Lazy says quietly. Just in case her phone's being tapped.

"Sadly, her SATs were below sea level and her transcript is littered with an ugly assortment of Ds."

"She should have been tossed out of here years ago," Lazy muses. "For her own good. It seems to me I threw a few gentle hints in that direction, but the parents were adamant that she stay. It's my fault, really. I should have insisted that she take a hike to some other school more suited to her limited abilities. Clearly she would have been much better off. What was I thinking?"

"That the family's worth five hundred mil? And that their generosity to Griffin is unparalled? So don't be so hard on yourself, Laze. You had no choice here, really."

"I suppose so. But I blame myself anyway. Who was it who said the lack of money is the root of all evil?"

"If the lack of money is the root of all evil then what's money?"

"The vile thing itself *and* the lack of it . . . yup, let's blame them both," Lazy concludes, pleased with herself.

"Regarding Chase Greenglass . . ."

"There's more?"

"The parents gave a hundred thousand bucks to Penn's economics department maybe two months before Chase's application was sent in."

"Whaddaya know!" Lazy says. "So a hundred grand doesn't buy you much these days, does it."

"Apparently not."

"Not that the kid actually deserves to go to Penn with those abysmal grades of hers."

"'Deserves' has nothing to do with it," Kat points out. "As you well know."

She does indeed. And finds it, at this moment anyway, more than a little sickening. Utterly repellent, really. And utterly disheartening. So what's she going to do about it? What *can* she do about it? Nothing. What she *must* do, what she knows she has to do, is soothe the Greenglasses' ruffled feathers and suggest, as tactfully as possible, that maybe a more generous gift to their distinguished alma mater will do the trick.

"So just how ticked off were the Greenglasses?"

"Apoplectic. The mom especially. You'd think no one had ever said the word no to her before."

"No one has. Sounds like a touch of Emma Hughes Syndrome," Lazy sighs. (But she'd diffused *that* distinctly ticking bomb just the other day with a sitdown between the accused and the accuser. Miraculously, she'd managed to get Emma the apology she wanted from the Rineharts, who were horrified to learn that their beautiful loft had been turned into Plato's Retreat in their absence.) Extracting a cigarette from the middle drawer of her desk, she fondles it lovingly. She thinks of an adjunct teaching job at Columbia that was offered to her many years ago before she'd finished up her doctoral thesis at Yale. Why hadn't she taken the job? Because Matt, her son, was a toddler; she was still breastfeeding him and he wasn't sleeping through the night and she herself was beyond exhaustion, engulfed in lethargy and indifference, craving sleep and little else. It was, perhaps, a huge mistake to have turned down the job. If she hadn't, who knows where she'd be today. Chairman of Columbia's Comp Lit department? Teaching a few classes a semester, beloved by students, respected by her colleagues for her scholarly essays published in a host of distinguished journals. A darling of the lit crit scene. Instead, she's a handmaiden to the rich and entitled, all of them believing their children to be the best and brightest. And who is she to tell them otherwise? She is no one, really. Just a well-educated, relatively well-paid, well-dressed flunky. Lazy never imagined she'd be so disappointed in herself. Never! And what she needs right now to help assuage some of that disappointment, she realizes, is a little affection from her WASP prince. Who, unfortunately, is otherwise engaged, standing at the blackboard in his classroom three floors above her, artfully interpreting some literary masterpiece for the benefit of a dozen grade-obsessed seniors and maybe a slacker or two dozing in the back row. She wants to cry on Doug McNamee's tweedy shoulder for a couple of minutes. Let those bitter tears of hers flow onto that expensive sport jacket as he seals her in his loving, adulterous embrace.

25

JULIANNE

I'm a fucking mess," Morgan concedes as she and Julianne slide into a booth at the Three Guys coffee shop on Madison, a couple of blocks from Griffin.

Julianne nods sadly. "I know how much the idea of getting into Yale meant to you, sweetie."

"Not even deferred until the spring, just flat-out rejected! I'm telling you, everything hurts, Jules—my heart, my soul, my ego, even my clenched fists," Morgan says, throwing up her hands, then lowering them so Julianne can see the crescent-shaped grooves her nails have left in her palms.

Morgan may have been rejected by Yale but, thankfully, Michael has been offered early acceptance at Harvard. If he hadn't been, well, Julianne can just imagine what might have followed in the wake of a disaster like that. She can imagine it, but doesn't want to, not even for an instant. Fortunately, the only one requiring solace today is Morgan, who, despite her stellar SATs and A− GPA— not to mention all those summers she spent as a camp counselor for homeless kids in Kosovo—has been bounced into Yale's reject pile like some loser with mediocre SATs and a transcript full of B's. Eleven people from Griffin were accepted, not all of whom had credentials as impressive as Morgan's. Some of these were students who were legacies or double legacies, whose parents gave vast sums of money to endow this or that chair or department, but Julianne knows that at least some of those who were accepted are truly smart, fiercely smart, so smart your mouth drops open when you hear them speak in class. These people are geniuses, fucking brilliant, and you have to admire them. Morgan, on the other hand, is no genius, obviously, she's merely (like Julianne herself) a smart person in a school awash in smart people, and maybe that's the problem. Maybe she should have gone to some fifth-rate private school or even public school—someplace where she would have been the kind of shining star that lit up a classroom. Or else she should have had her father fork over the money to endow the Elizabeth Goldfine Memorial Chair in Whatever. But Morgan wanted to do it on her own and Julianne has to love her for that.

"Eleven!" Morgan is saying. "And I'm not one of them." The waitress approaches but Morgan shoos her away.

"Wait," calls Julianne. "Two coffees, please."

"And?" the waitress says.

"And nothing," Morgan snaps.

"So you booked an emergency appointment with Dr. Schuster?" Julianne says.

"Yeah, I went right from Ms. Hemenway's office to Dr. Schuster's. And you know what, as soon as Hemenway shut the door behind us so that no one would hear a word of our conversation, well, that's what telegraphed the bad news to me loud and clear. I've never cried in school before, not even once all that time my mother was sick. But this time, the minute Hemenway opened her mouth, I flooded the place." It was, she tells Julianne, disappointment, humiliation, bitterness, jealousy—a combination of a lot of things, each of which, on its own, stung keenly. Ms. Hemenway had looked genuinely stricken at the sight of her. Morgan could tell she hated her job at that moment; Ms. Hemenway probably wished she hadn't come to school today or didn't have to deal with the likes of *her*. "She put a box of tissues into my lap, which was nice of her, I guess."

"She'll get you into a school where you'll be happy," Julianne promises.

"Yale was where I was supposed to be happy," Morgan says, "but screw that. If they don't want *me,* I don't want *them.*" And then she and Julianne have to laugh because both of them know that this is the most outrageous lie ever to escape Morgan's lips.

"Look!" Julianne says, and points to a guy shrugging off his jacket to reveal a T-shirt that reads, "you are SO off my buddy list!" "Cute!" she says, but Morgan has stopped laughing and is looking bereft again.

"Oh yeah, so Dr. Schuster? You know, she was generally sympathetic, but only up to a point. Then she's like, 'Suck it up and get your act together,' which might be good advice but only if you're in the right mood to hear it. Which I wasn't. So after my fifty minutes were up, I said to her, 'Just renew my prescription for Zoloft and let's call it a day.' And then instead of going back to school I went home and smoked some weed. And then Luke called, all happy about getting into Amherst and wanting me to come over for dinner."

"Did you say yes?" Julianne tears open six packets of sugar and pours them into her coffee one by one. She thinks of how this always annoys Michael, who can't understand why someone who insists on drinking Diet Coke needs all that sugar in a single cup of coffee. There's a lot he doesn't understand, and those six teaspoons of sugar are only the tip of the iceberg.

"Well," Morgan says, "the Zoloft plus the joint I smoked were a nice soothing chemical mix that put me in just the right mood to say yes to anything Luke had to offer."

So she'll be at Luke's townhouse tonight and Julianne will be on Central Park West at Michael's. Luke's parents merely upstairs and out of sight, Michael's parents safely out of the country. And sex and dinner, in that order, Julianne bets, will be on the menu on both sides of town tonight.

Michael's parents are, in fact, in Budapest; his father is on a business trip and his mother, most uncharacteristically, decided to go along with him. And Michael and Julianne have taken over his parents' king-sized bed, where they've just made love for the third time in a single night. In celebration, Julianne tells herself, of both the Averys' absence and Michael's acceptance to Harvard.

"I'm up for sushi," she announces, delicately planting a kiss on Michael's broad, hairless chest. "Maybe a spider roll, spicy yellow-tail, and maybe some gyoza for an appetizer, but do you think they're pan fried?"

"I don't know, I'm not even hungry, really."

With both hands, Julianne seizes the clock radio on his mother's side of the bed. "It's 9:47 and you're not hungry? How could you not be hungry?" Leaning over him, she whispers, "You're feeling guilty because we made it in your parents' bed, is that it? Is that what took your appetite away?"

"Fuck no," Michael says. "I could care less about that."

"Isn't it funny how 'I could care less' and 'I couldn't care less' mean the same thing?"

"Hilarious."

"What's wrong, baby?" she says automatically.

"I don't know . . ."

"Yes you do. And I'm calling to order that food anyway, okay? I'm starving, even if you're not."

"All the take-out menus are in the kitchen, near the phone, but I'm too tired to get them."

"I'll go," Julianne offers. She puts her clothes back on carefully, buttoning buttons, zipping up her pants, combing her hair with her fingers, even though she and Michael are entirely alone. Pearl, the housekeeper, and Ian, the cook, are both off for the whole week; Boyfriend is in a kennel, his wardrobe packed in an overnight bag. Along her way to the kitchen, Julianne peeks into the library, the den, Michael's father's office, a couple of guest bedrooms, the living room with a grand piano and a generous view of Central Park. So many rooms for a family of three, big rooms with twelve-foot-high ceilings and fancy moldings, built-in bookcases, Persian rugs. And no clutter anywhere. Too many rooms, really—she and her mother could move right in and no one would even notice them. It's hard to envision living with all this space, as nearly every one of her friends do. Someone at Griffin actually has a mansion in the city with a swimming pool and a ballroom (a *ballroom!*), though Julianne has never been inside. (What do you *do* in a ballroom in the twenty-first century, she wonders—waltz?) And what does *she* care, anyway? She and her mother live in eight hundred square feet and it's a little too small for them, but they're not complaining. They're ordinary, middle-class people and it's nothing to be ashamed of. Once, last year, someone in her physics class came over after school to work on a project with her, took a quick look around and said, confused, *If that's your bedroom then where does your mother sleep?* Julianne pointed to the living room couch and the girl nodded, as if she understood. Though probably she didn't. Julianne wasn't embarrassed in the least. They used to live in a bigger, nicer apartment before her father left, but they weren't rich then, either. Her father has a law degree from Yale but chose to work in the D.A.'s office. Everyone makes their choices, as her mother has said more than once. Her mother chose to be a writer. And then chose not to be. Julianne has yet to decide on anything, even which of the seven colleges she's applied to is actually her first choice. All she knows at this particular moment is that she's hungry. And proud to be the girlfriend of someone who will be going to Harvard next year.

In the kitchen, there's an enormous stone-gray stove, a Viking Professional that must have cost a fortune, and a glass-fronted, temperature-controlled wine cooler made of cherry wood with about forty bottles inside. Julianne stares out the window at a panoramic view of the city. It's a window that is positioned directly over the sink—a shame, really, since Pearl and occasionally Ian are the only ones in the Averys' apartment who ever wash dishes, and thus the only ones who spend much time gazing out at the breathtaking view of the Park and the Reservoir and the whole Upper East Side. Forcing herself to turn away from the window, Julianne finds a stack of folders filled with restaurant menus, each folder devoted to a different kind of food: Japanese, Thai, Vietnamese, Chinese, Indian, Italian, Middle Eastern. Michael's mother is very well-organized, very efficient. Not having to earn a living, she has plenty of time to organize her take-out menus. And to sew costumes for her little freak of a dog. Julianne's mother barely has time to breathe, as she is fond of saying. But she has six kick-ass books to her name, all of which Julianne has read. The critics called them "bitterly funny" and "darkly comic," but Julianne finds them sad. They're mostly about women who have been betrayed and disappointed by the men they love. Even before her own marriage was circling the drain, her books were like that. So maybe she'd had a premonition that things would not go her way, that she would end up like one of her characters, sharing eight hundred square feet with her daughter, without even a bedroom to call her own.

"The food will be here in twenty minutes," Julianne reports to Michael, who is still lying in bed naked when she returns. "Maybe you'll be hungry by then," she says hopefully.

"I don't think so."

"Are you going to tell me what's wrong? Are you going to tell me why getting into Harvard isn't the greatest thing that's ever happened to you?" He's not going to tell her, he's not going to talk to her at all but, instead, turns on his side and away from her. And so she clicks on the TV with the remote, goes to HBO on Demand, and finds an episode of *Curb Your Enthusiasm*, her all-time favorite show. *Get out of my house, Larry, you four-eyed fuck!* a fiery woman with dark curly hair screams and Julianne cracks up, as if she hasn't already seen this episode at least twice before. She loves the way the characters shriek at each other, she loves their selfishness, their stubbornness, their refusal to give an inch. In real life, she knows, none of this would be the least bit amusing, but on the show it's hilarious. Sometimes she and her mother watch the show together and Dee says, *I could write this stuff, no question. I should have moved to L.A. after college and taken an entry-level job working for the writers on some show. Sharpening their pencils, et cetera, et cetera, until I worked my way up. But instead I had these big stupid ideas about being a novelist. If only I hadn't been so stupid . . . If only.* If only Michael knew how to really savor the moment, to pat himself on the back and admit that he deserves to go to Harvard, that he's earned it. Without an ounce of help from anyone. Julianne happens to know that not even his parents saw the essay on Jacques Derrida and Deconstruction that he turned in with his application; he wrote every word of it himself and sent it off and that was that. Unlike so many other Griffin students, whose parents hired professionals to the tune of five hundred dollars an hour to help with those all-important essays. He and Julianne were both outraged at the very thought, but he never knew that Dee had critiqued Julianne's essays, had checked over her grammar and spelling, had helped her whip those essays into shape. He might have flown into a rage if he'd known about it, or he might have just sulked, letting Julianne see how disappointed he was in her.

On TV now, Larry is being chastised by his gentile in-laws for eating the Christmas cookies that were supposed to be part of a nativity scene. He thought they were animal crackers, he explains; he's Jewish, what does he know about nativity scenes? The Jews and gentiles don't get along too well on this show; each looks ridiculous in the eyes of the other. This subject has never been raised between Michael and Julianne, except once, when Julianne had the flu and missed a few days of school. Michael brought her a get-well card, a color photograph of a bowl of matzoh ball soup, and, on the inside, the words *You should live and be well.* Michael, it turned out, had no idea what the photograph illustrated—he'd neither seen nor heard of matzoh ball soup and couldn't explain what had drawn him to the card. And he was insulted when Julianne laughed at him. *I'm an Episcopalian, give me a break,* he said, and the discussion went no farther than that. When she thinks of the differences between them, religion (not that she really has any herself) doesn't enter into it. What it's all about, she reflects, is Michael's overwhelming pessimism and her optimism, now guarded; his illness and her vigorous mental health. Though she has to admit that in the few months she and Michael have been together, her sense of well-being has taken a beating.

"I'm so proud of you," she tells him now, and clicks off the TV. "Please tell me *you're* proud of you."

"For what? The Harvard thing?"

"Yeah, the Harvard thing. And look at me when I talk to you, okay?" She tries, playfully, to roll him over onto his back but he won't budge. "Come on, baby. Don't be like this."

"Fine!" Sitting up against the headboard, he yanks the sheet up to his neck. "You obviously don't understand, okay?"

"I hate it when you say I don't understand—all I ever do is try to understand."

"Well, understand this," Michael says. "Getting into Harvard doesn't change a thing."

"What do you mean?" She lays her head across his chest, strokes his prickly jaw with her smooth fingertip. And pretends she doesn't know him well enough to guess what is coming.

"Here or there," he begins, "at Griffin or at Harvard, I'm still me. There's no getting away from me, no matter how much I want to. I'm stuck with me." His voice breaks slightly, and she's afraid he's going to cry and then he does, dampening his parents' expensive satiny sheets, which he will use as a handkerchief in a few moments when the doorman buzzes from downstairs to announce the arrival of their food from Kyoto Garden. "Don't leave me," Michael says, as she starts to rise from the bed to answer the door. "Whatever you do, don't leave me."

26

MORGAN

ven if it's an exercise in futility (and Morgan still isn't convinced that it is), she just wants to leave word for her mother that she'd been rejected by the one school she truly wanted to go to. Logging on to Elizabeth's memorial Web site, which is empty of new postings, she types in the bad news:

It's 3:12 in the morning and I know you're probably thinking I should be in bed, but I wanted to tell you I didn't get into Yale. Harsh! The truth is, until recently, I wasn't doing too great—I was crying too much, especially late at night, and feeling this loneliness that doesn't seem, even now, as if it's ever going to go away. Not entirely. Even when I'm with my friends I miss you. Especially when we're out shopping and I get all excited thinking I'm going to show you these great Jimmy Choos I bought, just like the ones I saw on *Sex and the City*. And then I remember that I'm not ever going to show you anything ever again. Unless, of course, you happen to be looking over my shoulder now and then, like some kind of guardian angel. Don't laugh, but that's the kind of pathetic thought that goes through my head from time to time. You know me: I'm one of the faithless. Can't bring myself to believe in the whole God thing no matter how hard I try. But if anyone UP THERE wants to send me a guardian angel, whose earthly name happens to be Elizabeth Goldfine, I'm not complaining. So listen, I wrote about you in my Yale essay—maybe the people on the admissions committee who read it thought I was a pathetic loser and that's at least part of the reason I didn't get in. Maybe I'm just making excuses but anything's possible, right? Even my falling sort of in love with Luke, believe it or not. And I probably shouldn't be telling you this but I did actually sleep with him. If you're disappointed in me I don't want to hear about it. Just keep it to yourself. You're the only one I've told so far—it's nobody's business, really. And it wasn't at all what I expected to happen. We were in his bedroom listening to music, lying on his bed, not even touching, and then this really sweet Beatles song came on, "Here, There, and Everywhere"—do you know it?—and, I don't know, everything sort of fell into place in just the right way. It wouldn't be right for me to fill in any more details—they're private, obviously. Whatever happened, I don't regret it. If you'd been here, there's no way I would have told you about it. No way. See—there are actually advantages to being, well, no longer among the living. I never use the word "dead" or "died" in thinking or talking about you. They're ugly words—the sound of them is ugly and brittle. Hard. Just like the concept itself. "And sweet is death who puts an end to pain." That's Tennyson, actually. Well, death may have put an end to *your* pain, but it only made mine worse. I'm trying to kick the habit, to stop thinking about you first thing in the morning every day when I get up. You'd be surprised how hard it is, how my mind just keeps going there. It's like picking at a scab even though you know that you'll only start bleeding again if you keep at it. There's fresh, bright red blood under there. Fresh pain. So don't go there—that's what you're thinking, right? Easy for you to say. . . . But listen, I just want you to throw your arms around me and say, *You didn't get into your first-choice school but you're going to survive, kiddo.*

I'd really like to hear you say that, Mommy.

27

LAZY

In the middle of a conference with Prince Jimmy and his English teacher, Ms. Rushton, who has accused the prince of plagiarism and has the stolen goods right there in her hands, Lazy is interrupted by a phone call from the Fairhaven Residence for Seniors.

"I'll only be a moment," she says, and Ms. Rushton, a dry, starchy woman in her sixties with zero tolerance for human failings of any sort, purses her pale lips. "This is Kathryn Hoffman," Lazy says into the phone. "Who's this?" Just last week, right after Christmas, her mother was banished from her assigned table in Fairhaven's dining room for squeezing the wrist of one of her seatmates who, Charlotte claimed, "had used the F word" once too often during lunch. So *now* what has her mother done? Talked too loudly in the TV lounge? Failed to obey elevator etiquette and pushed herself ahead of the wheelchair contingent? Lazy looks sadly at the handsome prince, sitting there so silently and impassively, having disgraced himself, the royal family, his handler Mr. Ahmed al-Salan, and the entire Muslim world by buying a fifteen-page paper on the Internet and trying to pass it off as his own. Compared to this ugly act of arrogance and deceit, whatever her mother may have done is small potatoes.

"This is Carla? One of the security guards in the lobby at Fairhaven?" a young woman's voice says.

Security guard? Lazy instantly pictures her mother in shackles and handcuffs, carted off to the local precinct house, but for what? "Yes?" she says. "What's happened? Is my mother all right?"

"Your mom? Charlotte Hoffman? She's in the ER at Queens Memorial?"

"She is? What for?"

"We called the paramedics because she'd deliberately taken an overdose of some of her medication? But she's fine?"

A simple declarative sentence! Lazy wants to scream. *Is that too much to ask for?* "You're telling me she's fine, is that correct?"

"They, like, pumped her stomach? But they're keeping her for a while for, like, observation?"

"I'm leaving right now," Lazy says. "Thanks for your help, Carla."

"Excuse me," says Ms. Rushton. "Before you dash off to attend to your personal affairs, I'd like some assurance from you that Jimmy will pay the price for committing what is clearly an act of academic fraud." She waves the paper—"Virginia Woolf's Contributions to the Political Movements of Her Day" By Prince Abdullah bin Fawwaz al-Aziz—in Lazy's face, and glares at her. "According to Griffin's Honor Code, this calls for immediate expulsion."

"That may be," Lazy concedes, "but my mother apparently just tried to kill herself. We'll have to continue this conversation at another time."

"I'm terribly sorry for your troubles, Headmistress," Prince Jimmy says solemnly, speaking now for the first time. "And I apologize for this unfortunate misunderstanding."

"Yes, well, thank you," says Lazy. She's ushering the prince and his accuser to the door now, wondering if she can get someone to give her a lift to the hospital or whether she'll have to take a cab all the way out to Queens.

" 'Thank you'?" says Ms. Rushton. "You're thanking him? What about the Honor Code? Does he have diplomatic immunity or something? Because if he does, I'm going to, well, I don't know *what* I'm going to do."

"I will pray for your mother to regain her strength and for you as well, Headmistress," Jimmy offers.

"Thank you," Lazy repeats, stuck on that phrase and unable to come up with anything better.

Lying on a bed in the overcrowded ER, her wispy white hair flattened against a pillow, her glasses perched unevenly on her face, Charlotte says, "They tell me I'm here because I took too many of my antidepressant pills, what-do-you-call-them, Paxil, but apparently I didn't take enough. Because if I had, I'd be dead right now."

Lazy readjusts Charlotte's glasses for her. She picks up her mother's right hand and caresses it; the other hand, the one with an IV taped to it, is bruised and blackened and Lazy shudders at the sight of it. "So why did you take all those pills, Mom?" she says. "Why would you do a thing like that?"

The man in the next bed, only inches away, says, "One shot of testerone from the urologist and you're guaranteed to get it up every day. And I mean guaranteed."

"I think that's testosterone, Arnold," the friend standing over him says. "Right?"

"It's like Grand Central Station in here," Charlotte complains. "The doctor came to see me a few minutes ago and then he disappeared into the crowd. He told me as soon as he had a real bed for me, they'd put me in a room upstairs. Just overnight. And also that it would be a good idea for me to start seeing my psychiatrist a couple of times a week instead of just twice a month."

"A *very* good idea," Lazy says. "But are you going to answer my question, Mom?"

"Can I have a drink of water first? My throat feels very, very dry. And they emptied my stomach, you know, they put a tube in my mouth and sent it all the way down there and then salt water and then some charcoal and . . ."

"All right, let me see if I can find you some water," Lazy says. She barks questions at three different orderlies, one after the other, each of whom points her in a different direction. Out in the hallway, beyond the ER, she discovers a soda machine and brings her mother a can of iced tea.

"How am I going to drink it without a straw?"

"Back in a minute," Lazy says. This time she positions herself in front of a pair of nurses seated at adjacent steel desks and waits politely for them to acknowledge her.

"That was some baaad shit that happened on 9/11," one of the nurses says.

"Real bad. I got home that day and poured me a nice big bottle of wine, one glass at a time. And I said to myself, 'You got a looong fucking way to go, girl!' but seems like I polished it off in no time."

The straw, when Lazy finally gets it, comes from one of those desk drawers and is patterned with Burger King's logo.

"Did you go all the way to Burger King to get that?" Charlotte says crossly. "No wonder it took you so long."

Lazy holds the iced tea up to her mother's cracked lips. "Better?" she asks. "Are you ready to talk to me now?"

"The thing is," Charlotte begins, "I made a mistake. I took eight or nine of those antidepressant pills and then I realized that even if my life is a living hell because of those yentas I have to spend my time with all day long, well, it's still a gift and I shouldn't squander it. So I dragged myself over to that chain hanging on the living room wall by the light switch, the one I have to pull in an emergency to get their attention downstairs, and I pulled it and pulled it and pulled it until finally some people in uniforms came to rescue me. And all I could think as I was riding in the ambulance to the hospital was that my daughter was going to be very, very angry with me. Because she's a busy woman with a busy life and now she's going to have to worry about me every minute of every day for as long as I live, am I right? You're angry, aren't you?"

Every minute of every day for as long as I live. Lazy's stomach churns with guilt and love, love and guilt; she feels the uneasy mixture rising in her throat like bile. "Of course I'm not angry," she lies. It's her brother she's angry with, really, her one and only sibling who lives in San Diego with his life partner and graces "the family" with his presence once a year, in time for Charlotte's birthday. When he arrives with prettily wrapped gifts, takes his mother out to a dinner or two, and spends just enough time with her to convince her once again that he's the son of her dreams—generous, attentive, and loving, albeit for a measly seven days a year. He doesn't know the meaning of the word guilt, Lazy thinks enviously. Or else he's somehow managed to persuade himself that he truly is the über-son, perfection itself. *Think again, you selfish prick,* Lazy would like to say to him. *Get your tush on a plane and come out here and do a little hand-holding with me.* No chance of that happening and they all know it. She might as well resign herself to being the good daughter because she's already memorized the script. She's a stock character in a crappy, all-too-predictable, made-for-TV movie. Oh, and an adulteress on the side.

"Hey, look," Charlotte says, "there's my doctor."

"Where?" says Lazy. "I need to talk with him."

"Right there—the little man with funny hair. Yoo-hoo, Dr. Toussaint!" she calls out gaily.

"Those are dreadlocks," Lazy explains. "There's nothing funny about them."

"Well, I think there is," Charlotte insists, and then she laughs. Only three hours after her suicide attempt.

Three hours. Must be some kind of record. And something to be grateful for as well.

28

She's got to get out of this business. Got to. One of these days a Griffin parent is going to climb right into the back seat of her cab and Dee is going to die a thousand deaths. Cruising along the Upper East Side for fares now, she thinks of one of Julianne's Harvard-bound classmates whose father is a custodian at Griffin. At least the custodian has a valid excuse—he's an immigrant from the Dominican Republic and barely speaks a word of English. She, on the other hand, has no excuse whatsoever. Although you *could* say that she's a middle-aged single mother who has spent the better part of her life in pursuit of a career that's led nowhere. (Nowhere except behind the wheel of a screaming yellow Ford Crown Victoria with a temperamental heater and a poor excuse for a radio.) And what kind of example is she setting for her daughter? A lousy one, plainly. Women are reputed to be able to do anything in the world; there's no one stopping them from running huge conglomerates, movie studios, Ivy League institutions, from saving lives in ERs all over town, from rescuing the innocent from death row, from helping the vulnerable and the disenfranchised. So what's stopping *her*? She's a disgrace to *Ms.* magazine and everything it has stood for so proudly these past thirty years.

Stopped at a red light at the corner of Park and Ninetieth, she watches a smiling man walk down the street patting his big belly affectionately. What's *he* so happy about? And here's what appears to be an angel with broad, black velvet wings dressed in a pure white, floor-length wedding gown, a cell phone pressed to his ear. Rolling down her window for a better look, Dee takes note of his five o'clock shadow. It's thirty-three degrees outside and the angel is coatless. A few pedestrians stare as he shrieks into his phone, but this is, of course, New York, and if a man wants to wear a wedding gown and black velvet wings, well, that's *his* business. "Light a candle or curse the darkness, I don't give a shit *what* you do, Rico!" the angel howls. If she were still a writer, Dee muses nostalgically, she'd whip out the little notebook she always carried with her and write it all down.

Just as the light changes, the back door of her cab is flung open and a man says urgently, "Can you take me downtown to Hudson Street?"

"No problem," says Dee. "Hudson and what?"

"Hudson and Franklin. It's a restaurant. Nobu."

Ah, Nobu. Home of the three-hundred-dollar lunch for three. "No problem," Dee repeats. Curious to get a look at this guy who lunches so luxuriously, she glances into the rearview mirror and almost has a heart attack. It's Buster, her former agent. They haven't been in touch in years, and she notes, not without a bit of schadenfreude, that he's put on weight and lost most of his hair, which was the palest blond and dangerously thinning when she'd seen him last. The final time they'd spoken, in fact, was one of the most mortifying occasions of her life.

"We need to talk, my darling," Buster had said ominously over the phone.

"I'm listening." She'd slipped from her bed—where she'd been at work on her novel—down to the floor, and it seemed best to stay there, low to the ground, the better to absorb whatever blow was about to come her way.

"Look, darling," Buster went on, "it's not as if I don't believe in you and your magnificent work, it's merely that this magnificent work of yours has been rejected by thirty-seven publishers.

Thir-tee sev-en," he repeated loudly, as if Dee were hard of hearing. Or, perhaps, an imbecile. "So you see it's not as if we haven't tried. *Au contraire,* we've tried our best and it seems we're shit out of luck, darling."

"You mean *I'm* shit out of luck," Dee corrected him.

"Sad to say, I'm afraid I can no longer keep supporting you like this, darling. I'm deeply sorry but no can do. Not anymore."

"Excuse me?"

"Emotional support, darling. Hand-holding, ego-massaging, and the like. And so, much as it pains me, I find myself no longer able to count you among my clients."

"You're firing me?" Dee said incredulously, and fantasized delivering a good one right to his solar plexus, imagined Buster's weak brown eyes watering behind those preposterous Philip Johnson specs of his. Never mind his roster of utterly distinguished clients, the Nobel Prize–winning authors, and even one or two with fatwas on their famous heads, best-selling novelists one and all. Never mind any of that. "Aren't I the one who's supposed to fire *you*?" Dee heard herself say.

To his credit, Buster's laugh had been gentle, almost kindly.

And that had been the end of that.

Dee grips the steering wheel hard now to stop her hands from trembling. That he doesn't recognize her is a blessing, of course. But also, perhaps, an insult. Sliding the Plexiglas partition shut, which she rarely does, she seals herself away. She turns on the radio, finds herself a Bach string concerto that she happens to love— it's a beauty, even on this crappy radio. In the rearview she sees that Buster is busy on his cell phone. Good. Let him ignore her all the way down to Hudson Street as he conducts his very important business. She's close to tears: even ferrying a Griffin parent, the mother or father of one of Julianne's friends, couldn't make her feel this awful, this diminished.

Pulling up in front of Nobu, she takes his money without turning around.

"Keep the change," Buster says matter-of-factly, and then he is gone. Just like that. In and out of her life in twenty minutes flat, unaware of what he's left in his wake.

There's a ten-dollar tip for her, more than generous. The biggest one she will get all day.

Sometimes, when Dee's feeling at her worst, she takes out her books and reads the blurbs displayed on the back, reads them over and over again, committing them to memory. "'An often amusing, yet disturbingly sad, commentary of our times,'" she says in a whisper. "'Coopersmith's striking metaphors beautifully express the fragility and absurdity of human relationships . . . This volume is a keeper.'"

A woman in a raincoat imprinted all over with that annoying, ubiquitous Louis Vuitton insignia raps on the passenger-side window.

This is who I am, Dee wants to tell her. *An inventor of striking metaphors.* "Where to?" she says instead, and starts the meter running again.

29

SUSAN

The third time Susan and Dee meet for coffee at Starbucks, Dee hands her a copy of one of her books. "I don't know if you're a reader or not," Dee says shyly, tentatively. "Some people aren't . . ."

"I read all the time," Susan says. "Thank you." She flips the book over to its back cover, takes a quick look. "Impressive," she says.

"Whatever," says Dee, but Susan can see that she is pleased.

At the counter, a little boy, about five or so, begins to yell at a dark-skinned-woman who is clearly his nanny. "I want junk food!" he shrieks, open-mouthed. "I'm hun-gree! I want JUNK food! Now!"

Dee smiles. "Lovely."

"I don't have much patience for other people's children," says Susan.

"And your own?"

"I'm afraid I'm not very adept there either," Susan admits.

Dee blows on her decaf latté, mixes it with a raw wood stirrer, pushes the cardboard cup away from her. She fools with the fringes of the black woolen scarf draped around her neck. She looks everywhere but at Susan.

"Do I make you nervous?" Susan asks her.

"Not at all."

"I'm not very good at making people feel comfortable. I just don't have a knack for that sort of thing. People find me, well, a little stiff, I suspect."

Dee nods; she's not going to argue with that.

"What I'd like to be is . . . more relaxed. But I'm just not made that way."

"I understand," Dee says. She looks disappointed.

"You know, after I got back from Budapest and Michael told me he'd been accepted at Harvard, I had . . ." Susan stops. She can't bring herself to finish the sentence, finish the thought. "Never mind," she says.

"No, tell me," Dee says. "Don't be afraid to tell me anything."

"Are you sure?" Susan says.

"Positive."

"Well, after Michael told me the good news about Harvard, I had this urge to get up from my seat at the kitchen table and put my arms around him. He was standing at the other end of the kitchen, sectioning a grapefruit, and at first I thought he'd come to me, come closer, but he stayed where he was at the counter and I stayed where I was at the table and the moment came and went."

Dee nods again. "Every family is different," she says carefully. "My own mother couldn't bring herself to say 'happy birthday' to me."

"Was she a Jehovah's Witness?"

"Excuse me?"

"Isn't it the Jehovah's Witnesses who don't celebrate birthdays?"

Laughing, Dee says, "That wasn't the reason, I assure you. She was a very stubborn woman, that's all. Stubborn and hardworking. But the right words didn't come easily to her, though I'm sure she wished they had."

"I don't have a daughter of my own," says Susan, "but I'm guessing that they're easier to love. Than sons. What I mean is that they allow you to love them, you don't need their permission to cast your arm across their shoulder or take their face in your hands."

"Permission?" Dee says. "Since when do you need permission from your children to love them?"

"If you had a son, you'd understand." Absently, Susan takes a sip from Dee's cup. "If you had a son like Michael."

"If I had a son like Michael, I don't know what I would do," Dee murmurs.

"I do the best I can," says Susan. "As I'm sure you would." Sipping at Dee's latté again, she's aware of something that isn't to her liking—a mixture of vanilla and caramel, she thinks. "This must be yours," she says. "Forgive me."

"It's just a cup of coffee," Dee says. "No need for forgiveness."

Susan rubs her bronze-colored lipstick-print into the cardboard rim of Dee's cup, rubs it and rubs it, until it's almost gone. "Let me buy you another one," she offers.

"Don't be silly," Dee tells her. "Maybe next time, okay?"

Susan likes the idea of next time; it surprises her that Dee might actually want to talk with her again. She's not used to this, to confiding to someone the kinds of things she would normally think of as strictly private. And next time she will know better than to wear her mink coat, which she saw Dee eyeing with distaste when she first walked in. And yet . . . though she herself may not deserve much, she still deserves to be warm on a cold day, doesn't she?

30

LAZY

She should have dealt with Prince Jimmy a week ago but did not, for no particular reason except that it's just one more unpleasant task she would love to simply ignore. And here's the plagiarizing prince now, spiffily dressed once again in blazer and tie, as if Griffin were one of those conservative boys' schools where jeans and sneakers are banned and jackets and ties the only option. (She can just hear the roar of protest that would erupt if she ever tried to get her students out of their jeans and sweatpants and micro-minis and into a nice traditional prep school uniform.)

"Have a seat, Jimmy," she says warily.

"Thank you, Headmistress."

She wishes he weren't so handsome in his blazer, wishes he didn't speak the Queen's English in that accent she finds so alluring, wishes his father weren't worth billions. And billions. She wishes, too, that he would refrain from calling her "Headmistress" in that slightly servile way.

"I've prayed for your dear mother and hope she has been restored to good health," he reports. And there's that disarming smile that makes it easy for her to believe, if only for an instant, that he might very well have offered up a prayer or two in Arabic on Charlotte's behalf.

The moment passes. *Cut the bullshit, Your Highness. 'Fess up, apologize, and we'll see if we can't shave off a few years from your sentence.* "Look, Jimmy," she begins, "we both know the meaning of the word 'plagiarism,' do we not?" No response from the prince, not a word, not a flicker of life in him. Is he playing dead? Out comes her dictionary from the bookcase. "'Plagiarism: to steal and pass off the ideas or words of another as one's own.'" *Comprenez-vous, monsieur?* She slams the book shut, startling him out of his catatonic state.

"The word is unfamiliar to me, Headmistress. For which I apologize."

So he's no longer playing dead, he's just playing dumb. "I'm afraid that's simply not credible," she says, in a voice she hopes is suitably icy.

"Where I come from, there is no such word."

"Where you come from is Eton, am I correct?"

"Even so, I've not heard the word before and only now do I understand its meaning."

Lazy's blood is boiling but she will not allow herself to lose her temper; she will, instead, grind her teeth down to a fine powder. "It's within my authority to expel you, Jimmy," she says. "Please don't make me do that. Please just acknowledge your guilt, accept an F for the class, and we can move on."

"An F is unacceptable," he says coolly. "My father will be very unhappy with that. Who knows what he might do."

Lazy's palms have turned slippery with sweat. She imagines a bomb detonated in her office, a bomb powerful enough to annihilate the entire building and everyone in it. No survivors, not a one. She imagines the enormous front page headline in the *New York Times:*

POSH UPPER EAST SIDE SCHOOL VICTIM OF ARAB TERRORIST ATTACK MORE THAN 900 FEARED DEAD

Headmistress Was In Dispute With Saudi Prince Over Failing Grade

I don't negotiate with terrorists, is that understood? "How about a D?" she suggests. A humiliating grade but without the sting of utter failure.

"I'll take a C plus."

"D plus. And that's my final offer," Lazy says.

Stretching out his royal legs, getting comfortable, Jimmy crosses his ankles and knocks the side of his left shoe against his right, again and again.

"C minus. And that's my final offer," says Lazy. She can live with a C minus, she thinks. A lousy grade, lousy enough to incite any number of outraged parents in the past to call her office and make their dissatisfaction known.

"I cannot, Headmistress, accept anything lower than a C. My father will be much displeased."

His father the billionaire will be much displeased? A gentleman's C, then. But still a shitty grade by Griffin standards. "Done," Lazy says. *Sold to the highest bidder—the young man in the blue blazer, gray flannel pants, and smarmy smile.*

Shamefaced, she cannot look him in the eye as she shakes his hand. (Certainly she will *never* be able to look Ms. Rushton, his accuser, in the eye ever again. She'll postpone breaking the news to her about that C for as long as possible.)

Not her finest hour. Not even when you consider the more than nine hundred deaths she may have averted. Including her own.

Say what you will about twenty-two years of marriage to a man who can no longer surprise you in ways either large or small, the guy is a terrific cook. And there's something almost seductive about the dining room table now, set with pink rattan placemats and their good dishes painted with smudges of violet and pink and pale green around the rim. Tucking into a homemade dinner of gazpacho and grilled jumbo shrimp, and a bottle of Chablis instead of their usual seltzer, Lazy smiles at Richard over their candlelit table. If only he weren't dressed in flip-flops and a baggy cardigan, if only he had a measure of Doug McNamee's WASP charm and good looks . . . If only he weren't so good to her, so attentive at every turn, she might be able to stop feeling so fucking guilty. What's wrong with her, anyway? Isn't she too smart to be so superficial? Or at least smart enough to recognize that most women would be grateful to have a man like Richard in their lives? Perhaps the blame for all of this rests once again with her hormones, that ever-diminishing supply of estrogen. Maybe that's why she's turned dim-witted and selfish and self-absorbed, indifferent to her husband's sweet soul and turned on instead by the sight of Doug, naked except for his Brooks Brothers tweed jacket and a rep-striped tie knotted loosely around his neck. She hasn't had her period since Halloween, nearly three months ago. As if she were some kind of quickly withering crone whose life is swiftly and inexorably coming to a close. Sometimes she stands wistfully, believe it or not, in front of the tampon section of the drugstore, as if her body might get the message and start shifting its gears, setting the right things in motion again. Not likely. Her affair with Doug is the anodyne, numbing the undeniable sting of aging. It's all so transparently clear to her! And so wrongheaded! It's beneath her, isn't it, screwing the best-looking guy on the faculty behind the locked doors of her office, her private bathroom, on the floor, on her desk, or pressed against a bookcase stuffed with leather-bound classics. She's the good girl turned bad. A slutty, slatternly Baby Boomer! Having, guess what, the time of her life!

"Going to see your mother this weekend?" Richard asks. There's a tiny piece of purple lint caught in his eyebrow; Lazy leans across the table to extract it.

"Don't I go every weekend?"

"Just checking. And I ought to go with you this time, don't you think? I haven't gone in a while."

"I could use the company," says Lazy. "Thank you."

"Hard not to feel bummed out when you go there, huh? But just as hard not to feel sorry for her, I guess. Especially after the abortive, um . . . suicide attempt."

"Right on both counts. On the positive side, she told me she joined the Hardee-Har-Har Club on the advice of the therapist she's been seeing at Fairhaven."

"The what club?" Richard says.

"You heard me. They meet in the TV lounge every Thursday and tell jokes to each other." Lazy begins to laugh. "They had a guest speaker this week. I figured he was an amateur comedian or something, but it turns out, get this, he's a Certified Laugh Leader."

"A Certified Laugh Leader!" says Richard delightedly.

"Is that sad or is that sad!" Laughing so hard now she begins to wheeze, Lazy's eyes fill with tears.

"Really sad!" Richard agrees happily. "Pitiful!"

"You are sooo lucky your parents are dead and not members of the Hardee-Har-Har Club!" Lazy shrieks.

"God, yes! Sooo lucky!" Richard says, and pounds on the table with both fists.

The bottle of Chablis they've emptied between them tips over and rolls off the edge of the table, and this, too, strikes them as sidesplitting. Aching with laughter and just the slightest bit sloshed, Lazy isn't so far gone that she can't recognize the look and feel of a pretty good marriage when it's staring her right in the face.

31

JULIANNE

Michael hasn't picked up his cell phone all night, nor has he responded to a single one of her e-mail messages, and so Julianne does something she hasn't done in ages—she calls the Averys' apartment. Even though it is after eleven o'clock and she knows that his mother will, no question about it, be furious. But Julianne's so worried, she doesn't care how vehemently Mrs. Avery may attack her. She just has to know that Michael is all right.

"Sorry to be calling so late," she begins. Sitting at the edge of her bed, she's a little breathless, her heart pumping a little too hard. She's afraid of something but she doesn't know what.

"Julianne," Mrs. Avery says, and her voice is flat, affectless, deadened. "Michael's not home."

"He's at a friend's house?" Julianne says hopefully. Lamely.

"Not exactly."

She doesn't sound anything like the cold bitch she's supposed to be, the cold bitch she is. She sounds weary, half dead. And perhaps even sad, though this is probably just Julianne misreading the smallest sigh from her. "What's going on?" she asks. Waiting for Mrs. Avery to volunteer some information, Julianne pokes at her cuticles with her thumbnail.

"Listen to me, Julianne, and try to understand that I had no choice. My son is a profoundly angry young man. Out of control; I don't know how else to describe it."

Tiny pearls of blood outline the cuticles of two fingers now and Julianne licks them away with the tip of her tongue. There's a buzzing in her ears as she yells at Michael's mother. "What did you do to him? Tell me what you did!" she orders. As if she were talking to her own mother, someone she can occasionally push around in this way. And then she waits for Mrs. Avery to say, *How dare you speak to me like that!*

But instead Michael's mother says, very quietly, "You, of all people, will understand."

"Understand what?" Julianne says. The woman is frightening her; Julianne feels light-headed and off-balance and in her ears the buzzing only grows louder. She curls up on her bed with her eyes shut.

"All right, listen to me, he flew into a rage over something I said and the next thing I know he's attacking Boyfriend's clothes with a kitchen knife. He sliced through a pair of silk pajamas and then a pair of overalls, and he literally destroyed a leather jumpsuit. Destroyed!" Michael's mother says brokenly. "I spent so much time and effort creating these beautiful things and he went to my closet and attacked them like a savage, and then I was afraid he was going to come after me with that knife so I called the police. One minute he was like a wild animal, pacing with a knife in his fist, and the next minute he's sitting on the floor of my bedroom with his head in his hands. And then the police came and they handcuffed him. And you know, Julianne, well, you *do* know. This kind of thing isn't for me; it's more than I can take. Maybe if my husband were home, but he's in Singapore again and when I finally got him on the phone, he told me I did the right thing by not pressing charges, which I could have, of course, I could have said Michael lunged at me with the knife and they would have carted him off to jail. But instead I hired a car to come and take him back to Evergreen. And that's where he's staying for a while until we can get this all sorted out."

Julianne has thrown the phone away and her hands are clapped over her ears. She tries to pretend she hasn't heard a word, but what she has heard most clearly of all is the metallic click of hand-cuffs snapping shut across the tender skin covering the pale underside of Michael's wrists. He is her poor, poor, angry baby, out of control, wild as an animal his mother said, but *she*, Julianne, knows better, because unlike his mother, *she* genuinely loves him, loves the silkiness of his hair, the vivid blue of his eyes, the keenness of his intellect. He belongs at Harvard, far from Evergreen, and even farther from his weak and selfish mother who can't seem to love him enough. But *she* loves him more than enough. And cannot imagine a time when this simple fact will no longer describe what and who she is—the one person on earth who will never turn away from him.

32

SUSAN

Dee has been unable to find a parking space for her cab anywhere near the Majestic, the massive, block-long building on Central Park West where Susan lives. And, in any case, this is her work time, which she just can't afford to squander, she says as Susan comes flying, coatless, out of the Majestic and into the cab's front seat. This is why, Dee explains apologetically, instead of having coffee, she would rather drive around and keep the meter running. "If you don't mind," she says.

Shaking her head, Susan says, "Thank you for agreeing to see me on such short notice," sounding, she realizes, rather like a grateful patient talking to an overbooked, much-sought-after doctor.

"Julianne told me," Dee says. She stares straight ahead at the congested midday traffic just outside the park. "You must have been beside yourself." She does seem sympathetic, but not as sympathetic as Susan had hoped she would be.

And so Susan says, "Please don't judge me too harshly."

"For what?" says Dee.

"For being the mother of a boy like that."

Slamming her palms on the horn as a Hummer in the left lane cuts her off, Dee murmurs, "Asshole."

Susan starts to say something about the ordinary kitchen knife gripped in Michael's hand, about Boyfriend cowering pathetically under her bed as Michael paced and shrieked, paced and shrieked, Susan herself too cowardly to do anything but reach for the phone to call the police. But then she stops mid-sentence, suspecting that none of this will get Dee in her corner but will, instead, only serve to render *her* pitiful in Dee's eyes. Or, perhaps, contemptible. And she doesn't know which would be worse, Dee's pity or her contempt.

"Where's your coat?" Dee asks her, though Dee herself is dressed in a thick woolen cardigan and sheepskin gloves, but no coat. "It's February," she says. "You can't go out like that this time of year."

"Well," Susan explains, "the doorman buzzed me to say you were downstairs and I was already in the lobby when I realized I'd forgotten it. And I didn't want to keep you waiting, of course."

"I would have waited," Dee says, "trust me."

"I do trust you."

"Excellent," Dee says. Central Park West soon becomes Frederick Douglass Boulevard; they are in the center of Harlem, whether Susan likes it or not. In the well-heated Ford Crown Victoria, she shivers now. "Listen," says Dee, and struggles to pull a cream-colored business card from the back pocket of her jeans. "I swear by this guy."

Susan takes the card, which says, "Daniel Kaye, M.D." And, underneath, "Psychiatry." She lays the card on the dashboard, face down. "I appreciate the gesture," she tells Dee, "but I'm afraid I'm not a believer. Not for myself, anyway."

"But have you ever seriously considered it? Because therapy can, you know, be a very good thing in a person's life."

"The concept simply doesn't appeal to me," Susan says, stiffening. "All that breast-beating, the mea culpas week after week, to a stranger who sits there nodding his head and taking notes. I just couldn't. Nor has it worked very well for my son, apparently."

"It's not *all* breast-beating," Dee says. "It can be howls of indignation and lots of other good stuff, too." She turns her head to smile at Susan, but Susan doesn't smile back. "And there's only so many mea culpas a person can offer up, don't you think? You can't allow yourself to feel personally responsible for *everything* that's gone wrong."

"You'd be surprised," says Susan. She tells Dee she'd like to go home now, and Dee makes the first U-turn she can, switching on the radio, letting Susan know that she'd rather listen to Prokofiev's "Lieutenant Kijé" than the sound of Susan's obstinacy.

"At least take Dr. Kaye's card with you," Dee insists when she drops her off in front of the Majestic, but Susan can't even do that.

It's only after she's upstairs and an adoring Boyfriend has settled into her lap that she realizes she's forgotten to pay Dee what she owes her for the ride.

33

LAZY

Doug's face is buried in her neck, the smooth expanse of his naked back pinned beneath her crossed arms. She squeezes his bottom, wipes away the sweat at the base of his spine.

"You're pressing against my windpipe," she tells him. "I can't breathe, dear heart."

He mumbles something unintelligible into her neck.

"What?" she says. Warm liquid is trailing down her inner thigh; maybe it's saliva. She needs a shower desperately and can't wait to get off this couch and get home.

"Clarissa," Doug says, and hauls himself up to a sitting position.

Lazy frowns. She doesn't want to hear word one about his skinny blue-blood wife.

"She has breast cancer."

"WHAT?"

Reaching down now, he cups Lazy's breast in his hand. "It's the tiniest of tumors, thank God, but she'll need chemo and radiation nevertheless," he reports. "And five years on Tamoxifen."

"DON'T TOUCH ME!" Lazy leaps off the couch. Arm draped across the width of her to conceal her breasts, she's relieved to find her panties in plain sight on the desk along with her turtleneck.

"What's gotten into you, honeybunny?" Doug asks. "Take it easy."

"What's gotten into me?" she says, stepping into her panties. "You and I are over, I think. We absolutely have to end it."

"But why? What's wrong?"

"What kind of person do you think I am? There's no way on earth I'm having an affair with a man whose wife has cancer. No way!" The puzzled look on Doug's face makes her want to slug him.

"Don't worry about Clarissa; she's going to be fine," Doug assures her. "The doctor seems truly optimistic."

Lazy gives it another shot. "It's unseemly; it's about as low as you can go."

"What?"

"Am I speaking a foreign language? She *needs* you, for Christ's sake. Don't you think you owe it to her to be at her side every step of the way?"

"I *know* that. Of course I know that. But that doesn't mean you and I can't continue to see each other."

"And 'see' would be a euphemism for 'fuck'? Shame on you!" Lazy yanks the turtleneck sweater over her head. "And where's my bra, goddamnit?"

"Honeybunny," Doug says, "I can't get through this without you. Clarissa needs me but I need *you*."

"You need me to help you get through your wife's chemo and radiation?"

Doug hangs his big blond head. "I know it sounds bad . . . deeply selfish and whatnot, but do you have any idea how much I look forward to being with you? It's in the back of my mind all day long, Monday through Friday, the possibility that you and I might get to make love. I mean, what could be more exciting than that for people like us?"

She knows what he means, that neither of them will ever be an Academy Award winner or a real estate mogul, a Pulitzer Prize winner or a painter with a show at the Whitney; unlike so many of those in the Griffin universe, the two of them are a couple of working stiffs whose comings and goings and accomplishments will never be documented in the *New York Times*. And when they die, their survivors will have to pay for one of those itty-bitty obituaries in the paper, the kind you need a magnifying glass to read. And it's a safe bet that Senator Hillary Rodham Clinton will not be in attendance at their funerals. In a world of chauffeur-driven somebodies, they're nobodies clutching MetroCards.

So, yes, she knows all about the excitement he's referring to, the thrill of a secret life and all that illicit sex. The thing is, she tells him now, though she may be an adulteress, at least she's one with a moral compass. And a marriage she actually cares about.

Doug is saying yes yes yes, he understands every bit of it. He has a PhD from Princeton and an IQ of 156, and there's very little he doesn't understand. But can't Lazy reconsider? Can't she try to put aside her thoughts of Clarissa and Richard and just focus on *him*, a man who needs her? A man who's in love with her, even if he's never admitted it, not even to himself, until this very moment.

Lazy looks at him, astounded. "Don't say that to me," she says. "Not now." She begins to cry.

"I love you," he repeats. "If I could leave Clarissa now, I would. And when she's better, I will. I promise you."

"Richard is such a good husband," Lazy says, and cries harder. "Such a good man. And besides, I love him."

"But I'm the one you're *in* love with," Doug points out, "aren't I?"

And the truth shall make you free. Or make your life utterly miserable.

34

JULIANNE

Other than Morgan, no one at Griffin knows where Michael is, and she thinks Julianne is nuts for cutting school to visit him at Evergreen today. Julianne has burned him some CDs and bought him his favorite magazines— the *New Yorker, Harper's,* and the *Atlantic*—all of which are in a canvas bag next to her seat on a Metro-North train headed for Stamford. She's never cut school before, not even once. But last night, when Michael called from a pay phone in the lobby of Evergreen, he begged her to come. And how could she refuse him? He's only allowed two visitors a week; in the ten days he's been there, his mother has shown up exactly once. She may not be quite the bitch Julianne always thought she was, but she's a very strange mother indeed. The kind of woman who probably never should have been a mother at all, Julianne has concluded.

All around her, people are talking on their cell phones—men and women in business suits, working-class people in ski jackets and sweatpants, a couple of well-dressed elderly women looking oddly preppy with velvet headbands in their silver hair, probably off to meet their friends in Greenwich or Westport. Why can't they all just shut up? Why do they have to keep chatting away like that, casually sharing with Julianne the stupid details of their mundane lives? Across the aisle a middle-aged woman is nodding her head vigorously. "Well, too bad there's nothing you can take for a sinking heart," she says into her phone. "Now that's what I'd like to see on the back of an Advil bottle: 'For temporary relief of minor aches and pains associated with the common cold, headache, menstrual cramps, and sinking hearts.' Yeah yeah, what are ya gonna do? Your hands are tied, right?"

Michael in handcuffs. An image she wishes she couldn't envision so vividly. If she'd been there that night he'd trashed Boyfriend's wardrobe, she would have spoken to him in just the right way, calmed him in a matter of minutes, even gotten him to apologize to his mother. But without her, he goes from bad to worse, and Mrs. Avery, afraid of her own son, has to wimp out and call the cops. Who knows what he's capable of? His anger is fierce and inexplicable; Julianne has no idea what it must feel like to be overtaken by something so appalling, something almost demonic, she thinks. It's his nightmare but hers, too. Her friends think nothing of telling her to turn her back on him. *Just walk away,* Morgan advises. *Get out of there. This is SO not worth it.* And then there's Julianne's mother: *I am begging you. Pleading with you. It's like you're deaf, and blind, too. You're a smart girl, but when it comes to this particular subject, this particular boy, your brains, your good judgment, your power of reason, all of that goes by the wayside.* Well, Julianne's not the first person in the world to have been rendered dumb by love. Nor will she be the last. And knowing this is a comfort to her.

The train is stopping at 125th Street now and a handful of people come aboard. Julianne has spread herself out on a seat meant for three, using the other two cushions for her coat and the bag filled with things for Michael. Staking her claim to these three seats is her none too subtle way of warding off strangers, but the one heading toward her now has chosen to ignore the message.

Holding a see-through bag from Subway, the woman says, "All right if I sit down?"

"Sure," says Julianne. As if she has a choice.

Hard to tell how old the woman is as she unwraps her sandwich in her lap. She has long, graying hair in a braid to her waist, but her face is young-looking, like Julianne's mother. Rings on every finger, even her thumbs. Thin gold bracelets on one wrist, a thick silver cuff around the other. Her hands look young, too. "Sorry about this," she says, and bites into her sub. Salami, maybe, and raw onion mixed in with that fringe of lettuce.

Julianne puts her hand over her mouth and nose and turns away. It's eleven o'clock in the morning, just too early to be in such proximity to a salami sandwich.

The woman, whose name is Riley, has told her life story by the time they reach Stamford fifty minutes later. She doesn't ask Julianne a thing about herself; she doesn't care if Julianne is really listening or not—she just has a need to talk. Endlessly. But it's all right, Julianne doesn't object. Except for the lingering odor of salami and onion, it's not a problem. Listening to Riley's monologue takes her mind off Michael for a while and actually she's grateful for that. As the train pulls into the Stamford station, Riley says, "You know, I should have gone to the senior prom with Patrick Siciliano. He invited me but I turned him down because I just knew Marty Meyerson was going to call and ask me, which he did. And then a couple of years later, Patrick had the back of his head blown off in Vietnam. At the funeral I went up to his mother and told her I'd made a mistake, I shouldn't have turned Patrick down like that. And you know what she said? 'Shoulda woulda coulda.' And I didn't even answer her, I just sort of slunk away. I'd have to count that as the worst moment of my life."

Shoulda woulda coulda. Julianne doesn't like the sound of it; it makes her stomach feel uneasy. In fact, she's been awakening nearly every morning with a burning in her stomach, and sometimes it hurts so much she cries quietly as she eases herself out of bed and into the shower. It hurts in the morning and after every meal and she may even have to go to the doctor if it gets any worse. But she has decided it will get better, and maybe, for that reason alone, it will.

"Nice meeting you," Riley says, watching as Julianne grabs her things and rushes down the aisle toward the open doors.

The cab ride to Evergreen is nine dollars plus tip added on to a round-trip train ticket and the magazines for Michael. And the cigarettes he asked for. An expensive day for her. Her mother gives her money all the time, and there's a monthly check from her father—$150 spending money. Still, it's not enough. A job wouldn't be a bad idea; she knows she should at least consider it. But with Michael, a heavy load of schoolwork, and other school-related stuff, there's not much time left in her day, is there?

She's shocked at the way Michael looks when he meets her in the lobby. Bloated, unhealthy, his face puffed out and pasty. Must be all the medication they're force-feeding him, she figures.

Their arms are around each other in an instant, as if it's been months. Years, even.

"I love you so much," Michael says. Then, "Did you bring me cigarettes?"

"A pack of Marlboro Lights," she says. "And the magazines and some CDs." She pauses. "Oh, and Morgan said she really hopes you're feeling better and back at school soon," she lies.

"Yeah right. Whatever. Let's go up to the lounge so I can smoke."

"This looks like a nice place," she remarks on the way up in the elevator. "Clean. And it doesn't have that icky hospital smell."

"It's not a hospital," he says. "It's a loony bin for rich people."

"Don't call it a loony bin."

"A nuthouse, then," Michael says.

He smokes a cigarette and when he's finished she sits facing him on his lap on a chaise longue. It's a big carpeted room with a jukebox, a pool table, and a huge TV, like someone's den, she thinks. "Where is everyone?" she says. But then she notices a guy in a white uniform standing guard at a window, looking out at the late-winter snow.

"Having their heads shrunk, I guess. Or weaving potholders or something. Or staring into space, contemplating the vastness of the universe and their totally insignificant role in it."

Is she supposed to laugh? She doesn't know. "So, is there a doctor here who can help you?" Picking up his hand, she plays with his fingers. Even they look swollen, she observes.

"Help me what?"

Control his anger? Keep his distance from sharp knives? His fists from colliding with walls? To move from one day to the next without fucking up in ways that make her weep and are probably tearing holes in her stomach? "Help you to feel better," she says.

"I know what would make me feel better," he says, and flashes a delighted smile, the kind she doesn't often get from him these days. His hand descends into the V of the cashmere sweater she borrowed from Morgan, then dips under her bra.

The guy in the white uniform is shooting some pool and paying no attention to them. Maybe he's off-duty; maybe he just doesn't give a shit.

"Let me show you where the ladies' room is," Michael says. "You do have to use the ladies' room, don't you?"

"Now that you mention it, I guess I do."

It's a nice clean bathroom, spotless, with a granite countertop surrounding a matching sink, and a small wicker basket filled with paper towels, little pastel-colored balls of soap, and some Jergen's lotion to soften your hands. And there's a condom in her wallet.

The wall she braces herself against is black ceramic tile and there's not a mark on it—it's pristine. Despite the cashmere sweater, the tile is cold against her back.

Make no mistake: she's not the kind of person who has sex standing up in bathrooms, public *or* private. But as she used to say before someone corrected her recently, *Beggars can't be choosy.* And if the guy she loves is happy (as he so rarely is), then she's happy, too, swear to God.

35

LAZY

The letter arrives in her mailbox at school in an unadorned envelope, without stamp or postmark, on the morning of April 1. There's no date, no salutation, no signature, just a modest white sheet of 8½×11-inch paper with a few sentences typed on it:

FYI, there's not a person in this school who doesn't know that you and your "friend" Douglas McNamee have been fucking each other's brains out. You're a disgrace to that "caring, responsible community" you're always refer- ring to and WE WILL BRING YOU DOWN, BITCH. Just wait and see.

P.S. The wages of sin is death.
(THE HOLY BIBLE, Romans 6:23)

"The wages of sin *are* death," Lazy says in a whisper. Her hands are trembling so violently she can barely light that forbid- den cigarette in her private bathroom. The nicotine makes her heart beat even faster and then she begins to hyperventilate. She's going to die like trailer trash on the cold tiles of a bathroom floor, reeking of cigarette smoke, on April Fool's Day, of all days. April Fool's Day? *April Fool's Day!* A joke! Albeit a singularly malicious and contemptible one. She's flooded with lovely, lovely relief but only for an instant. Because this is her wake-up call. Because even if she and Doug and her job and her marriage aren't in imminent danger, she's been forewarned. *WE WILL BRING YOU DOWN, BITCH.* If these jokers don't, perhaps someone else will—and sometime soon. But is it really possible that her indiscretion (as she prefers to think of it) with Doug is public knowledge? That the two of them might have slipped even once and been seen by a single pair of curious, unsympathetic eyes? Even if this were true, where's the proof? Could someone have installed a surveillance camera in her office and bathroom? *Don't be ridiculous!* And yet someone cared enough to slip that poison-pen letter into her mailbox . . . a student, a parent, a faculty member? She fires up another cigarette, then uses the flame from her lighter to destroy the letter as she holds it over the toilet. Just like in the movies! The letter is soon gone, reduced to ashes, so why isn't she feeling better? She needs to speak to Doug, to hear him say that she, that they, have nothing to fear. But why would he say something so idiotic when they both know they have everything to fear. Everything!

Barely able to put one foot successfully in front of the other, Lazy makes her way to the outer office and summons her assistant Brooke, whom her instincts have always told her she can trust.

"It smells like an ashtray in here," Brooke observes, settling on the couch as Lazy begins to pace.

"Not on the couch!"

"Not on the couch?"

"Don't sit on the couch."

"Why not?"

"Just sit down someplace else. Please."

"Can I sit at your desk? I've always wanted to do that, actually."

"Feel free," says Lazy. "And look, there's something I have to ask you."

"Ask away," Brooke says, swiveling casually in Lazy's chair now.

"Have you heard any gossip about me lately?"

"What kind of gossip?"

"You know . . . something of a deeply personal nature . . ."

"Well," Brooke begins, and accelerates her swiveling, "there are rumors and there are rumors. All of them stupid."

"For example?"

"Look, I really really *really* don't want to talk about this," Brooke says. She spins herself around in a full circle, and when the chair finally comes to a stop, complains, "You wouldn't *believe* how dizzy I feel."

"Oh, for crying out loud," Lazy says, "am I having an affair with Doug McNamee or not? Just tell me already."

"Hearsay," Brooke says dismissively. "I might ever believe it. And even if it *were* true, so what? Who *cares*? I mean, *I* slept with the guy a couple of times this year, no biggie. And so did Cynthia Silman in the drama department, and Mademoiselle Robbe-Grillet in the French department, and Señorita Maldonado in the Span—"

"Enough!" Lazy cries. She thinks she is going to collapse and grabs hold of the edge of her desk. And then Brooke is leading her to the couch, where they sit, side by side, Brooke holding Lazy's hands in her own, apologizing tenderly and sweetly for telling her what she assumed Lazy had known all along.

"I mean, he's a whachamacallit, a serial adulterer, right? But of course a hunky one, obviously."

"He's a bastard," says Lazy. "And clearly I'm the biggest jackass who ever lived." She wonders if it's possible to die of mortification because she can't imagine living beyond this moment; she can feel, already, the life draining from her and wants to shriek, like the Wicked Witch of the West, *I'm melllltinnnng!* And all that will be left of her will be a puddle for Doug to step in on his way home to his poor sick wife, who probably would be shocked to learn she's married not to a man but to pond scum.

"Please don't tell me you're in love with him," Brooke says. "Or that *he's* in love with *you*."

I love you, Lazy hears him saying. *If I could leave Clarissa now I would. And when she's better, I will. I promise you.* "He promised me," she murmurs.

"Whatever it was, he didn't mean it," Brooke insists. "He likes to screw around, but I actually think in his own weird way he loves his wife. Listen, think of it as pretty good sex with a great-looking guy and that's all. Like I said, no biggie."

"And when, exactly, was this?" Lazy forces herself to ask. "The couple of times you slept with him?"

"Oh, let's see, right before Christmas, I guess. And you were already . . ." Brooke looks away. "I'm sorry, I honestly didn't know. If I had, I wouldn't have . . . you know."

"For the record, Doug and I have been together for nearly a year and a half now," Lazy says, "but *you* have nothing to apologize for. I, on the other hand, am old enough to know better. Or so you'd think." The wages of sin are most likely a pink slip and a divorce, she figures. Not to mention a complete loss of dignity. Though maybe, if she's very, very lucky, the Fates will let her off with a slap on the wrist. And a second chance.

Like hell they will.

36

JULIANNE

The three of them—Julianne, Morgan, and Daisy Camarano-Rosenthal—are upstairs in Morgan's bedroom, just hanging. Morgan goes to her closet and pulls out a couple of pairs of jeans that, she claims, she doesn't care about anymore, and tosses them to Julianne. "Try these on," she says. "They'll probably be a little long on you, but otherwise they should be great."

"Are they a size zero?" Julianne asks.

"Um, I don't know, maybe a size one. Try them on, sweetie."

"Are you sure?"

"I want you to have them," Morgan says. "They're Juicy Couture and Habitual; I got them at Barneys last year."

"And you're done with them already?" Julianne says doubtfully.

"Yeah, sure, I've got like thirty pairs."

"They look fabulous on you," Daisy tells Julianne as she zips up the first pair. "Fabulous!"

"And you're so skinny," Morgan says. "Look at that stomach of yours!"

"It's like hardly even there," Daisy says, impressed. "I wish I had a stomach like that."

"So you'll take them?" Morgan asks Julianne. "And the other pair, too?"

She gives Julianne her clothes whenever she gets bored with them, but not too often, because, Julianne senses, Morgan doesn't want her to feel like some charity case. When, of course, she isn't. Not like a housekeeper living in the Bronx with eight kids and grandchildren and no husband. Julianne is just like almost everyone else at Griffin, minus the big apartment and the country house and the vacations.

"Thanks," she says. The next moment she has joined Morgan and Daisy on the carpet where they are sitting with their knees drawn up to their chins, watching her. "I love you for being *such* a good friend," she tells Morgan.

"Speaking of which," Morgan says, and takes a breath. Then she announces that she and Daisy are staging an intervention to try to convince her that she can't continue this relationship with Michael for even one more day.

"Fine," says Julianne, "let's hear it." Because what has she got to lose by listening?

"Okay, great, look, I'm your best friend," Morgan says, "and it's my job to show you the light, even if you don't really want to see it. Honestly, I understand what it is that's so cool about Michael, but his looks and brains take a back seat to the obvious fact that he's, well, I hate to say it, seriously fucked up. And it's not as if you're married—if you were, that would be a whole other story. Then you would *have* to stay with him; you'd have an obligation to, in my opinion. In sickness and in health, till death do us part, et cetera et cetera et cetera. But that is so not the case here. Boyfriends come and go in a person's life; generally speaking, there's always another one out there for you, especially if you're as petite and pretty as you are, Jules. Which I've told you like a thousand times already. The one thing I haven't told you, though"— Morgan takes another long breath and Daisy nods at her—"is that no one even really *likes* Michael. And it has nothing whatsoever to do with the fact that he's mentally ill, which isn't, of course, his fault at all. It has to do with the fact that he can be so horrid to you. Verbally abusive, I mean. And totally clueless when it comes to recognizing how unselfish you are, *always* putting him first.

Come to think of it, what you guys have got is something like an abusive marriage. Except that you don't have to run to some women's shelter in the middle of the night to escape from him, all you have to do is pick yourself up and go home. Not a huge deal—simple, really. But you just don't get it, do you, sweetie? There's none so blind as those that will not see, right?"

"He's *so* high maintenance," Daisy adds. "Don't you want things to be easier, sweetie? Don't you want to be happy?"

"Happy?" Julianne repeats, as if it were a word she were unfamiliar with, a word whose meaning went right over her head. And then, all at once, she's crying, sobbing, really, with her little narrow shoulders shaking, her head bent, her little baby-sized hands clasping each other. She's so tiny and so stricken, Morgan says she only wants to put Julianne in her lap and rock her back and forth and make everything better for her, make her life different than what it is, and has been, for what seems like forever.

Now Morgan and Daisy are crying, too, and none of them can stop. Because they know it's hopeless, that nothing is going to change, that Julianne just won't leave him and that all they can hope for is that he leaves her first. "Which," Morgan predicts, "will never happen. Because what he's found in you he'll never, ever, find anywhere else. And even Michael, clueless as he is, can see that."

37

LAZY

For the past few days, Lazy has taken great pains to avoid running into Doug, whom she would dearly love to tear limb from limb. But before she kills him, she needs to talk with him calmly and so has given herself an official ninety-six-hour cooling-off period, which, in exactly ten minutes, will have come to an end. Her plan is to be dispassionate and aloof. To matter-of-factly let him know that he is an execrable lowlife, an utterly repellent creature, little more than human garbage, really. And that she would fire his sorry ass in a heartbeat if only she didn't believe her own position as headmistress to be at risk.

He saunters into her office during his first free period, in accordance with her written request. Closing the door behind him, he approaches her eagerly, tilting his head for a quick kiss.

"Are you out of your mind?" Lazy says, and shoves him away with both hands.

"What?"

"Just sit down and keep quiet, please," she orders, pointing to a captain's chair emblazoned with Griffin's coat of arms. "Sit!"

"I don't understand, honeybunny."

"That makes two of us. And let me assure you, I'm no longer your honeybunny. If, in fact, I ever was."

"You're not? You weren't?"

Settling herself behind her desk, which always makes her feel more professional, Lazy says, "Okay, listen, Doug, I know all about Chantal Robbe-Grillet and Elena Maldonado and Cynthia what's-her-name in the drama department, not to mention my own little Brooke, so don't waste your breath trying to convince either of us that love has anything to do with you and me. And, may I say for the record that, oddly enough, I find you a thoroughly wretched human being."

Doug is ashen-faced; his washed-out blue eyes bulge with terror. "This isn't going to cost me my job, is it? Because Clarissa is covered under my health plan and now that she's seriously ill, I can't—"

"Don't you DARE pretend that what you're worried about is poor Clarissa!" Lazy is sure her blood pressure has gone right through the roof, that her face is flushed a deep, ugly crimson. Where's that cool, dispassionate self of hers she thought she could count on? Where's that cruelly diminished dignity she wants so desperately to yank back in place? Doesn't she have any breathing exercises to fall back on . . . a soothing mantra she can chant . . . If only she were a practicing Hindu or had joined one of those Yoga classes at the Y . . . What about simply shutting her eyes and saying "Ommmmmmmm" for a while? Even *she* can do that. She gives it a shot for about thirty seconds and then goes for her pack of cigarettes hidden away in her desk drawer. What are they going to do, can the headmistress for lighting up during school hours? Go ahead and let them!

"You can't do that, you can't smoke in here," Doug tells her, the very first time he's tried to stop her. "What if someone sees you?"

Gratefully inhaling her first Newport of the day, Lazy is, against all expectation, suddenly filled with pity for the dejected guy she sees collapsed in his seat across from her. He really is a first-class fool, she reflects. And emotionally defective, as well. To think she was enraged by his cheatin', lyin' ways when actually she should be thankful that she has been able to recognize, at last, just how unworthy he is of her affection. Suddenly she feels buoyant, capable of floating past him and right out of the room, through Griffin's front gate, way up Madison Avenue and back again. She no longer wants to kill the contemptible prick, she decides, or even to belittle him further with a couple of well-chosen adjectives and nouns that would serve nicely. Why waste energy and time disparaging him when she can pity him instead? *You can pity someone but can you regret him?* she wonders. The rules of grammar say no but she says otherwise. *I regret you, Doug. And every single goddamn moment spent in your company.*

"Pardon me?" he says, cupping a hand around his ear.

"That," says Lazy, "is between you and your Maker."

"What? Come on, Lazy, talk to me. Please? Okay, look, just listen to me then. I haven't slept with anyone else since the day I told you I loved you. That was what, well over a month ago, right, and I've been faithful to you ever since. One hundred percent, I swear. And before that, well, it never occurred to me that we had an exclusive relationship. If you'd told me that was what you wanted, I would have been fine with it."

Sure sure sure.

"I just wish you'd said something, Lazy. So just tell me what I can do to rectify things. Tell me. Please?"

It's gratifying to hear the desperation in his voice, never mind that she doesn't believe a word he utters. And she really ought to warn him about the poison-pen letter, shouldn't she? It's the decent thing to do, certainly . . . but really, why bother?

"You and me are history," she says, shaking her head.

"Um, that would be 'you and I,'" says Doug.

38

DEE

With Sonia the cat clamped between her knees in readiness for a manicure, Dee croons, "Let Mommy have your paw, baby, come on, come onnnn . . ." But Sonia's patience wears thin after only two snips of the clippers; hissing her displeasure, she flees and heads straight for the living room curtains, which she scales with an effortlessness Dee finds impressive.

"Naughty!" she hollers an instant later. "Get down from there!"

She answers the phone with her eyes still on Sonia, who is a mere two inches from the ceiling and has now begun her descent.

"He's here!" Will yells into Dee's ear. Her ex's voice is jubilant, there's no mistaking it.

"What?" Dee says.

"The baby!"

"Laura had the baby?"

"Julianne has a brother!"

Half-brother, she thinks, but does not bother to correct him. "Congratulations, Will." She says she is happy for him, and perhaps, at this moment, she is. A little, anyway. Or at least she is happy for Laura, who's finally given birth after all those miscarriages. If it hadn't been Laura, would it have been someone else, some other woman who caught Will's eye and brought their marriage down in flames? Dee has never asked; what good would it do her now to hear Will's answer? She's never had even a glimpse of Laura, but Julianne has met her and given a description, though not to Dee's satisfaction. *A lawyer, I don't know, nice, I guess . . . not so pretty, just ordinary . . . brown hair, brown eyes, maybe hazel, I don't remember . . . what do you want me to say? She's just kind of a regular person, okay? Someone you might not even remember meeting if you'd only seen her once.* Hard not to feel a pang when she heard that. Because, in some perverse way, Dee had wanted her rival—her nemesis—to be someone remarkable. Otherwise, wasn't it as if Will had been so disappointed with Dee and their life together that almost anyone would do in her place?

"Eight pounds eleven ounces," Will is saying. "Twenty-one inches long."

She'll have to buy them a baby gift, she supposes, a gift from her and from Julianne. Something like the musical mobile that had hung from Julianne's crib, Beatrix Potter figures that spun gently to Brahm's "Lullabye."

"A big guy with lots of dark hair," Will boasts.

If she were still married to him, *he* would be the one to give the cat her monthly manicure. One less battle Dee would have had to fight on her own.

"A son," Will sighs. A sigh filled with such contentment, you'd think he'd never, in the fifty years he's inhabited this earth, wanted anything more.

Six years they've been divorced, but that sigh is just too much for Dee and she has to hang up.

Six years and she can still hear him saying, at the bitter end of their marriage, *Face it, your lousy novels have been read and enjoyed by four or five people of all ages.*

And of all the ways he has hurt her and will hurt her still, this seems the cruelest.

39

JULIANNE

S o her father's girlfriend has finally had her baby, and they've invited Julianne to fly down to Houston to meet her new half-brother. Julianne is a little confused by the invitation, one of the few she's received from her father since he moved to Texas four years ago. But her mother, surprisingly, has been urging her to go.

"Why not?" she tells Julianne. "It's about time you saw your father, right? Look, no matter what *I* happen to think of him, he's still your father and it would be crazy for me to deny that. To deny you the opportunity to see him. And aren't you curious to meet the baby? He's your brother, for God's sake."

"Half-brother," says Julianne. "And a baby's a baby. Big deal. He'll probably be asleep the whole time I'm there."

"So you'll spend time with your father. It won't kill you and you may even enjoy yourself. And . . ."

"And what?"

"And a weekend away from Michael can't be the worst thing in the world for you. In fact, it may be the best thing in the world for you."

"Thanks a lot," Julianne snaps, but only because it is her policy never to disparage Michael in front of anyone, especially her mother, who has all the ammunition she needs to destroy him on the witness stand. It is Julianne's responsibility, she believes, to be one thousand percent loyal to him: if he can't count on her, who *can* he count on? Surely not his mother, who had the cops all over him not too long ago, and surely not his friends, because when you get right down to it, he doesn't really have any. Not really. So that leaves Julianne, his one and only defender, supporter, protector. Apologist. Multi-tasking girlfriend.

"Will you go to Houston?" her mother prods. "It's not the rest of your life, pussycat; it's only Friday to Sunday."

"All right all right all right," Julianne says, sounding like Michael, she thinks.

"Great! Go call them back. They're waiting to hear from you."

"*You* call them back."

"You're seventeen years old and you can't call your own father?"

"That's right," Julianne says.

She watches, fascinated, as Ian, the Averys' cook, stands in his chef's uniform over the wok in their kitchen preparing dinner for two—for her and for Michael, that is. His parents are at the opera, but Mrs. Avery instructed Ian to go ahead and cook whatever Michael and Julianne wanted. And so Julianne asked, a bit self-consciously, for Chinese food, chicken with ginger and string beans in a brown sauce. Ian, a guy in his late twenties who isn't a big talker, simply said, "No problem," and immediately went to the Sub-Zero for a package of chicken, which he attacked with a scary but authentic-looking cleaver.

"So you'll let us know when dinner's ready," Michael says, and takes Julianne by the hand.

"Wait," she says, still absorbed in watching Ian wield the cleaver so deftly. His big white hat seems pretentious and show-offy here in the Averys' kitchen, and she wonders if Ian thinks so, too. And speaking of pretentious, what do they need a cook for anyway? It's not like Mrs. Avery even has a job, not like *her* mother, who drives around the city half the day looking for fares and edits manuscripts at night. Think how grateful her mother would be to come home and find a chef all dressed up like Ian on duty in her kitchen every night, just waiting to make dinner for her. And who would clean up the kitchen afterward as well. Dee herself makes a total of five dishes: cornflake chicken from a recipe on the back of a cereal box; angel hair and sundried tomatoes in garlic oil; veggie burgers; tuna salad with shredded carrots, and a peppery macaroni that's baked in the oven with a layer of cheddar on top. That's her repertoire, Monday through Friday. She's no virtuosa in the kitchen but she's good enough, Julianne thinks. She'd like to see Michael's mother fend for herself in the kitchen. Fend for herself *period*. Without her husband's money, she'd be nowhere. She doesn't even sleep with the guy, according to Michael, who swears he hasn't heard a peep out of their bedroom in years. Plus she used to have a serious problem with painkillers until Michael's father sent her away to some rehab place, a ranch in Arizona, to clean up her act. This was when Michael was in second grade, but he still remembers how his mother had just disappeared one day. Just like that. Gone. For what Michael thought was years, but which he later discovered was actually only a couple of months. Funny how this family of his has a habit of sending each other away. Some family! Not to be believed. Honestly.

"Do you like working here?" she asks Ian, and approaches him at the stove.

A deliciously scented steam rises from the wok as he tosses in the contents of a small bowl of minced garlic and ginger. "Sure," he says, "why not?"

Because, she thinks, Michael's mother must be impossible to work for—icy, critical, hard to please. "Oh, I don't know," she says.

"Couldn't you two have this conversation another time?" Michael says, and it's not a question, or even a request; it's an order. "Let's go in my room for a while."

"Dinner in five minutes or so," Ian says, maneuvering what he calls the "wok chans"—his cooking shovels—with a grace Julianne has to admire.

Michael's bedroom is twice the size of Julianne's and, for the first time, just as disorderly, she's startled to see. Books everywhere—piled high on the nightstand, on top of the dresser, even on the TV set. Half a dozen pairs of sneakers litter the floor, along with pajama bottoms, boxers, balled-up T-shirts, and a couple of ashtrays that need to be emptied. Peeking into his bathroom, she can see that it's carpeted with dirty towels, more pajamas, and underwear. "What, is Pearl on vacation or something?" she asks him. "What's up with this?"

"My mother suddenly decided I should be responsible for keeping all my shit in order."

"You're kidding."

"Well, since there won't be anyone to clean up my room for me when I'm in college next year, she figures I might as well get used to it now. Pearl's not allowed in here anymore."

"Harsh!" says Julianne, but she's smiling at the very idea of Michael—or any of her friends, for that matter—actually being responsible for keeping their rooms neat. Or clearing the table after dinner, or even putting a single fork into the dishwasher. They're like married men, she thinks, with the kind of wives who have nothing better to do than pick up after them all day. Except that they're only teenagers—with housekeepers who get paid to do what a wife does for free. Julianne is the first to admit she's a total slob but, unlike her friends, she has no expectations that anyone will be her handmaiden. Certainly not her mother, who deserves better than to have to wade through Julianne's crap. Julianne doesn't have to be told this—she simply knows it. "At least we could put all the clothes into the hamper or something," she suggests to Michael. She kicks up a dusty black T-shirt and catches it. "It'll take a minute."

"Forget it. I've got a Dylan CD I want you to hear." Turning his back, he goes through his vast CD collection, hundreds of albums alphabetically arranged on custom-made shelves.

She comes up behind him and circles his waist, rubbing the side of her face against the softness of his denim shirt.

"Be right with you, just a sec, okay?"

"Turns out I'm going to Houston next weekend," she says into his shirt, and then she backs away, just two small steps.

Dropping into place the CD he's holding so carefully between his fingers, he whirls around to face her. "What do you mean?"

"I just want to see my father and the new baby. My mother's taking me to the airport next Friday after school and I'll be back Sunday night," she says, afraid to look at him, as if she's just delivered shocking, disastrous news.

"Your father? If this the same father who cares about you so much he hasn't seen you in, what, a couple of years?"

"He cares about me," Julianne says in a tiny voice. "He pays for part of my tuition at Griffin and for a lot of other things, too. We're just not . . . close, that's all. But maybe things could be a little different now. I mean they might be, I don't know."

"You're pathetic," Michael tells her.

She forces herself to look at him, to see the way his face has tightened, the way his front teeth are digging angrily into his lower lip. "Don't say that," she says. "You don't have to be so mean."

"Reality check," says Michael. "Your father barely knows you're alive. If you think he actually cares about you, you're delusional. Obviously *I'm* the one who cares about you, Jules. I'm the one who can't go even a single day without seeing you. When I was in Evergreen, I could stand everything except not seeing you. So please, *please,* don't go to Houston."

She's enfolded in his arms now, patting his back, praying praying *praying* that there won't be any tears, that the Depakote he's supposed to be taking to keep him on an even keel, to keep the circuitry in his brain properly wired, is doing its job. Because it's the tears she can't take. The sight of them used to be wrenching, but no more; that was a while ago. Only Dr. Schuster, her shrink, knows the truth, which is that those tears of his make her want to seize him by the shoulders and say, *Straighten up and be a man!* It's entirely unfair of her but she can't help it—she's repelled by those tears. This illness he has is so cruel, as cruel as anything she knows, and she has all the sympathy in the world for him but sometimes she doesn't. Sometimes she feels like she's been emptied of all the patience and compassion—and even love—that it takes just to have a simple conversation with him. And now is one of those times. She can feel how his tears have dampened her shoulder as she pushes him gently away, resenting his stricken face, his pink-rimmed eyes staring at her so beseechingly.

"I have to go home," she murmurs.

He wants to know if she still loves him.

Yes, goddamnit. "Of course I do," she says.

"Then you won't go to Houston."

"I have to go home now," Julianne says. "Right this minute."

"Just promise me you won't go to Houston."

"I can't."

"Can't what?"

"Can't promise you that right now. I have to think about it, okay?" She has backed herself into the doorway, can already see herself striding purposefully down the marble hallway and out of here.

"Fuck," Michael says, and there go his fists into the bedroom door. "Fuck fuck fuck fuck fuck fuck fuck." Each punctuated by the thump of a fist.

There's a hole in the door now the size of a tennis ball and blood across his knuckles and tears leaking from his eyes and the words "temper tantrum" come to her for the first time.

And now she's the one who's losing it, who's lost it, really, as she shrieks, "Why can't you just stay on your meds! *What* is so hard about that?" But she knows the answer and thinks, who is *she* to tell him that the sleepiness, the dizziness, the nausea, that sometimes overtake him, are worth the trade? In the end, she has no right to tell him that this is the choice she would make if she were Michael, living in his skin every moment of every day.

She leaves him slumped against the door, ignoring the arms outstretched in her direction, the broken voice calling her name. Down the hallway she runs into Ian but she brushes rudely past him thinking, for once, only of herself and hearing a chorus of sopranos—her mother's and Dr. Schuster's mixed in with her friends—cheering her on. As if she were some jock on the track team and not just the dazed and weary girlfriend who's had it up to *here*.

40

DEE

I just don't see," Susan Avery is saying, "why it is that in addition to your editorial work you still have to drive a cab. Surely there's something better out there for you—a single well-paying job that you might actually enjoy." She is seated with Dee at a table for two at what they have come to think of as "their" Starbucks, the one on Columbus and Seventy-sixth, a few minutes from the Averys' apartment. She and Dee are taking turns picking at a shared lemon-poppy-seed muffin and haven't made much progress on it.

"I'm forty-nine years old," Dee admits, "and I've spent most of my working life as a novelist. Who's going to hire me with a résumé like *that*?"

"It's not as if you're an actress in Hollywood, for God's sake. So what if you're forty-nine. I don't understand."

Why *would* she understand? How could she possibly? The woman hasn't worked in decades, Dee calculates. And, in all likelihood, she never will again. She's married to a wealthy man who, apparently, asks very little of her. Even if they're no longer in love—as Michael seems to think is the case, according to Julianne—this husband of hers certainly wouldn't suggest that she quit hanging around the apartment and go out and make herself useful. No, Susan can do whatever the hell she wants, all day, every day. She can sew a satin tuxedo or a pair of velvet overalls for her pooch, she can stand over her own personal chef in his official white uniform and watch as he cooks up some penne with broccoli rabe for her lunch or sautés some wild mushrooms to accompany the baby lamb chops for dinner. She can stay up till dawn watching three movies in a row on her plasma TV, or read all 1,455 pages of *War and Peace* in a single week, if she wishes, without worrying about having to earn a living, about the laundry that's been piling up day after day, or a bathroom floor that needs washing, or a credit card bill that might just call attention to an alarming total at the very bottom of the page.

"So what's it like?" she asks Susan.

"Pardon me?"

What's it like to be you? she wants to ask, but of course, she realizes now, she can't. You can't ask a question like that, not unless you're Barbara Walters interviewing one of those celebrities who's only too eager to spill his guts before an unseen audience of millions. And anyway, of all the people Dee has ever known, Susan is the least likely to spill those WASPy guts of hers. Under any circumstance whatsoever.

"Never mind," Dee says, and breaks off a tiny piece of muffin. Just to signal that this particular part of their conversation has come to a dead end.

"Are you all right?" Susan says. "You seem . . . distracted."

There are two tiny poppy seeds caught between Susan's front teeth; Dee contemplates whether to bring this fact to her attention, but decides that Susan would probably be mortified. Better to let her discover them on her own and allow her to be mortified in private in front of her bathroom mirror.

"Well, I got a call from my ex telling me his girlfriend gave birth to their first child," Dee offers, and is unprepared for the tremor in her voice, for the tears that have, in an instant, sprung to her eyes. "Eight pounds eleven ounces," she says. "Twenty-one inches long."

"Like you give a shit," Susan says mildly, and actually reaches across the table to touch Dee's shoulder.

Dee doesn't know which is more startling, the sound of that rude little word on Susan's lips or that entirely unexpected pat on the shoulder. Frankly, she wouldn't have thought Susan capable of either, but look how wrong she was!

"I don't?" says Dee. She wipes her eyes with a rough brown napkin made of recycled paper.

"You're better than that," Susan reminds her.

"I am?" Dee sniffles. "Well, maybe I am. I went out and bought little whatshisname a baby gift, a silver spoon from Tiffany with his initials engraved on it. It's the most useless thing I could think of."

"Good for you!" says Susan.

And in a moment Dee never could have imagined, she and Susan are leaning toward the middle of the table now to high-five each other, like two buoyant teenagers.

Best of all, she thinks, Michael's name hasn't come up yet.

Not even once.

41

LAZY

azy spots her mother in her newly assigned seat (her third in five months) in Fairhaven's dining room. It's 4:30, the early-bird-dinner seating, and all the women at the table except Charlotte are wearing the full-length plastic aprons currently in vogue at Fairhaven. Like babies in bibs, Lazy notes sadly, but Charlotte, to her credit, has insisted there's no way on earth she'll ever put one of them on. (*What am I, an infant?* she'd told Lazy in disgust. *So I spill a little bit of food here and there. That's what the dry cleaners are for, right?*)

"Did I or did I not tell you my lovely daughter was coming to see me tonight!" Charlotte crows triumphantly, as both Lazy and dinner arrive—baked chicken, a perfectly molded scoop of rice, and some bleached-looking sliced baby carrots. "Sit down with us and eat."

"Ah, the obligatory Sunday visit," says Bambi Levene, Charlotte's current best friend, though one whom she always describes as "a tub of lard." A description that isn't far from the truth, Lazy has to admit.

Filling the empty chair next to her mother, Lazy says, "It's a little too early for me to have dinner, but thank you for the invitation. How about if I just keep you company."

"*My* lovely daughter brought the dog with her last time," Bambi says. "An affenpinscher, they call it, with bushy eyebrows and a mustache. He tried to bite me and that, let me tell you, I didn't appreciate at all."

"Well," says Charlotte, "it's a dog-eat-dog world out there."

"You can't argue with that," Bambi agrees. "And if you're not going to eat that rice, Charlotte, I'd like to have it."

"Help yourself, it's your funeral."

"Mom!" says Lazy, and as Bambi reaches over and transfers the rice from Charlotte's plate to her own, the fat that droops from her upper arm quivers like flesh-colored pudding and nearly side-swipes Charlotte's face. "Don't talk to her like that," Lazy scolds. *No wonder her seat's been moved three times!*

"It's too much food for her," Charlotte says disapprovingly. "She's obese and she's going to die before the rest of us, believe you me."

"You talk too much, you know that?" says a woman named Renée Messina, someone Charlotte has complained about though Lazy can't remember precisely why. Her stomach rumbles gently, reminding Lazy that she hasn't eaten since breakfast. But the thought of tasting even a mouthful of the overcooked, anemic-looking food on her mother's plate is vaguely sickening to her. She'll wait for her favorite candy bar, a Milky Way Midnight, at the neighborhood 7-Eleven, even if she faints from hunger first.

"I had my hair done at eight this morning because you were coming to see me today," Charlotte says. "Do you think it looks nice?"

"Very ni—"

"You're always fishing for compliments," Renée chides.

"Well, Lazy hardly ever tells me I look nice. So I don't know *what* to think." Nathan, the waiter, appears with a plate of white bread and pats of butter. "I had my hair done today in honor of my daughter's visit," Charlotte tells him. "How do I look?"

"It's a beautiful hairdo," says Nathan, who has a well-polished shaved head. "But not as nice as mine," he teases.

Reaching into her purse, Charlotte grabs a couple of dollar bills and tries to give them to him.

"Mom," Lazy says quietly. "Don't."

"You know I'm not allowed to take that from you," Nathan says, "but thanks just the same."

"I don't care about those dumb rules; just go on and take it," Charlotte insists.

"Why don't you save it for next Christmas. I'm allowed to take it then."

"Next Christmas? I could be dead by next Christmas."

"No no no, you'll be right here, sitting at lucky table number seven with these lovely friends of yours, just like you are now."

"There's a depressing thought for you," Bambi says, and winks, as if she's said something amusing.

Thinking of Charlotte's perfunctory whack at suicide just a few months ago, Lazy looks at her worriedly, but her mother is rising from her seat, saying there's somewhere she has to be. "Somewhere *important*," she hints mysteriously.

"So what are we doing here?" Lazy asks, as they settle into one of the vinyl banquettes that line the walls of the lobby. She surveys the sorry collection of old ladies all around them, some of whom are tended to by their paid companions in white rayon uniforms and many of whom have metal walkers or canes by their sides. There are men, too, but they're outnumbered by the women four to one, and most of them, according to Charlotte, aren't very sociable, preferring to sit quietly at arts and crafts and bingo, and even "volleyball," which is played seated in folding chairs with a balloon that the teams tap lightly with their fingertips or punch with the undersides of their fragile, breakable wrists.

"Played any volleyball lately?" says Lazy, when Charlotte doesn't respond to her first question. "Mom? Are you listening to me?"

"Well, I'm listening with half an ear. And volleyball's a big bore but a necessary evil; I play it every day. Because, I tell myself, you've got to keep moving, got to keep yourself awake and functioning or you'll end up like a zombie, staring at the four walls of your apartment, your mouth hanging open, your mind rusting away like some piece of junk in the salvage yard. But you know, sometimes I sit right here in the lobby and I doze off because the conversation around me is such a bore, or because I just don't have the stamina to stay awake. A disgrace, really, snoozing in public for no good reason at all. Sometimes Bambi catches me in the act and tells me to snap out of it."

There's a depressing thought for you, Lazy hears Bambi saying. And could anyone argue with that?

"Yoo-hoo, Henry!" Charlotte suddenly calls out, waving in an exaggerated, overly vigorous manner to a slight figure moving spryly toward them. "I didn't see you at dinner."

"Well, I didn't have much of an appetite. I'm more than a little homesick, I think." Henry's cheeks are rosy, like a child who's been racing around recklessly in the heat or the cold. "And who's *this* young lady?" he asks.

"Doctor Henry Shine, this is my daughter, Kathryn."

After they've shaken hands, Lazy gives her seat away to Henry Shine, who's elfin, all of five feet tall, she guesses. And probably pushing ninety.

"Of course you're homesick. After all, there's no place like home, right, Kathryn?" Charlotte says, locking eyes with Lazy.

Lazy knows her mother is thinking longingly of her former home in Fort Lauderdale, which after the death of Lazy's father, Charlotte had left behind in a daze, along with her beloved baby grand and books and extra sets of dishes and plenty of other things she wouldn't have room for at Fairhaven. Lazy had been duly alarmed by her mother's behavior that weekend she'd flown down to Florida to pack her up. She remembers Charlotte sitting there in the middle of the living room on a lone folding chair, unable to speak or move, to lift even a finger to help, to answer yes or no when Lazy pointed to lamps and mirrors and framed photographs, asking *Do you want this? Do you need it? Do you have a sentimental attachment to it? Talk to me!* Charlotte hadn't known what she thought about anything that awful weekend Lazy took her life apart piece by piece, moving swiftly and impatiently through the untidy rooms of her mother's condo; Charlotte could only say that her mind was a mishmash of anxious thoughts, all of them terrible. Which made perfect sense, Lazy reflects, when you consider the shock of having your life turned inside out like that, poor Charlotte losing her husband and her home in the space of only a few months. Lazy wishes she'd been more patient then, that she could learn to be more patient now. Especially on the phone. Her mother ends every call with a declaration of love for her, and most of the time, Lazy, on automatic pilot, says "Me, too." When she doesn't, her mother will wait a beat and ask plaintively, "Don't you love me, too?" And Lazy will force herself to say, "Of course I do," but in that slightly exasperated way that she knows Charlotte hears loud and clear. *Love.* A very confusing subject for her these days. Not something Lazy wants to discuss. Or ponder. She just wants to pretend it's irrelevant. When of course she knows it's at the center of everything. Everything! Like money. All the way back in the first century, the Romans had a handle on things. *Money alone sets all the world in motion,* as one of them, according to Pliny the Elder, said two thousand years ago. Close but not precisely accurate: *Love and money set all the world . . .* Don't get her started. She's not going to think about it. Or about Doug. Or Richard.

"Nettie Rivera died?" Charlotte is saying. "A nice lady, too bad. But you can't really allow yourself to get too attached to these people here; they're taken away in ambulances in the middle of the night, the middle of the afternoon, anytime at all. Sometimes they go into some kind of special intensive-care ward at the nursing home and then to their graves; sometimes they take the short cut straight to the cemetery."

"She had such a nice singing voice, that Nettie, a very sweet soprano," Henry says. "Not that I know this personally since of course I'm only here a month now."

"Well, every death gets posted on the little bulletin board next to the elevators and you can go to the memorial service in the chapel/TV lounge. But you can't take it personally because if you did you'd never be able to get out of bed in the morning."

"You should have yourself assigned to my table, Charlotte, before they put someone else in Nettie's seat," Henry advises. "I'd hate to see you miss out on an opportunity like that."

"I would *adore* being at your table," says Charlotte, and an instant later Henry is leaning forward to smooch her cheek.

"And now I'll be on my way," he says. "A pleasure to meet you, Kathryn."

Smiling as she watches him walk off toward the bank of elevators, Lazy says, "So, is that your boyfriend I just met? What happened to the hundred-and-one-year-old guy?"

"Mister Tannenbaum? Still going strong but fortunately he found himself a new lady friend. And just look at those yentas over there talking about me," Charlotte hisses. "One kiss and I'll never live it down."

"He seems very sweet."

"Henry's an educated man, a podiatrist. The yentas think we're a couple because we sit together at Movie Night. A few times he fell asleep with his head on my shoulder, and I'll tell you truthfully I didn't have the heart to give him that little nudge that would have woken him up. And I have to say it was nice having him there leaning against me like that, even if it *was* purely accidental and I could have been anyone at all, just another body seated conveniently next to his, if you know what I mean."

"You, Mom, could never be just anyone at all," Lazy says. "Trust me."

"So I don't know if he's my boyfriend yet but he's something."

Want to hear about *my* boyfriend? Lazy almost says. *Exboyfriend*. She's *this* close to confiding in her mother, the one person who will always love her, no matter how poorly she may have behaved. And she *has*, without a doubt, behaved poorly indeed.

She thinks back to her days in high school, over twenty-five years ago, when she and her mother would sit at the kitchen table late at night smoking cigarettes while Lazy talked on and on about whatever was on her mind—books she was reading; certain boys who made her heart race; even sex, which Charlotte could discuss with a startling frankness, looking Lazy straight in the eye as she revealed that she had, believe it or not, slept with Lazy's father before their marriage. In the fifties, when you were supposed to be wearing your little white cotton gloves and guarding your virtue 24/7. *Way to go, Charlotte!* What a cool mother she'd had all those years ago! And what would Charlotte say now, hearing that Lazy has been unfaithful, not once, but over and over again, to a husband who has never treated her with anything other than affection and respect? Both of which she no longer deserves.

"Mom?" Lazy begins, but then falls silent as Charlotte turns toward her.

42

JULIANNE

A lovely April night, 67 degrees with a slight breeze that ruf-
fles Julianne's hair like the affectionate hand of a mother
or father—if you happen to have the sort of mother or father who is so inclined. Julianne is with Morgan and Luke, the three
of them killing time in the café in Barnes & Noble on Eighty-Sixth
Street; they've been drinking Snapple and leafing through books
and magazines for over an hour, an activity the store seems to en-
courage. At 10:45 the café is jammed with people reading while
they eat and drink; the store doesn't mind if you spill a drop of coffee or soda or drizzle a few cookie crumbs onto whatever book or
magazine you're reading; all you have to do when you're finished
with it is leave it on the table and walk away. There are people working on laptops, piles of open books on their tables, people licking
crumbs from their fingers as they turn the pages of paperbacks and
more expensive books they will never buy. You could, if you wanted
to, devour an entire book from cover to cover right here in the café
and no one working in the store would bother to tell you to get up
and pay for it. It would drive her mother crazy, Julianne thinks, to
see someone dripping even a single bead of water on any one of her
books. As Dee has told her, those books are her children, though
she has never said this in a way that would make Julianne resentful
or jealous. Only in a way that makes her mother sound wistful.

She's actually going to buy a couple of things tonight, the
newest John Grisham paperback along with *The Collected Stories*

of Flannery O'Connor, which her English teacher recommended recently.

Picking up the Grisham book from the table, she has to smile, remembering the time, four years ago, when she was dying for a TV and VCR in her bedroom. Her mother told her she could have the TV and the VCR, too, but first she'd have to read fifty novels, all of which had to be approved by Dee. It didn't seem to be a bad deal—Julianne loved to read, after all—although it turned out that what Dee had in mind was literature—"Books of real merit, no garbage," her mother decreed. Obediently, Julianne made her way through some Updike and Cheever, John Irving, John Gardner, Tom Wolfe, Thomas Wolfe, Virginia Woolf, Roth, Bellow, Russell Banks, Robert Coover, Joyce Carol Oates, and plenty of other writers on whom her mother bestowed her official stamp of approval. It took Julianne nearly a year and by the end she was feeling a little restless, a little lazy. She arrived home one day with some Grisham book, whose title she can't recall anymore, and her mother scowled at the sight of it. "Is this literature, pussycat?" she said. And then struck a bargain with Julianne, since she was so close to the finish line. She could read the Grisham but only if, when she came to the last page, Julianne could explain exactly why it didn't fall under the rubric of "literature." She did as she was told and, while she read, highlighted one passage after another that she recognized as sentimental and poorly written, dutifully taking note of all the characters that seemed like nothing more than ciphers and the dialogue that seemed so painfully stilted. And so the TV and VCR were hers, though she was only permitted ninety minutes of daily viewing time. She remembers how proud she felt but also how her friends had all reacted pretty much the same way: "Your mother is so totally weird!" In retrospect, maybe her friends were onto something there.

"Let's get going," she suggests to Morgan. "The store's about to close anyway."

Luke collects his small pile of car magazines to bring up to the register. "Still haven't decided yet," he says. "Maybe the BMW Z4. Or maybe the Mercedes SLK. They're both two-seat convertibles but the BMW's a cooler car, I guess." His parents are buying him a car for graduation and he can choose anything he wants as long as it's under fifty grand. "Don't you think the BMW's cool?" he asks, showing the girls three different pictures in *Road & Track* as they wait in line to pay.

"Oh, definitely," says Morgan loyally, though Julianne knows that cars don't do it for her. Like Julianne, Morgan doesn't have her license yet and hasn't even taken Drivers' Ed. Just the thought of having to pass the road test makes Morgan a little sweaty, Julianne knows. And since Dee can't even afford a car, what would be the point of Drivers' Ed for Julianne?

Outside, they walk west on Eighty-sixth, which is more crowded than usual because of the weather. Stopping to look at the costumes in the window of a party goods store, they see Jimmy, the Saudi Arabian prince, bouncing toward them. Julianne has heard rumors that he's the go-to guy for any drug you might want, that he drives a Ferrari, and that one of his uncles was beheaded in a palace coup. She doesn't believe any of it, only thinks that Jimmy must be lonely so far from home.

"Hey," Luke says.

"Guys," Jimmy greets them. He's dressed in a black leather zip-up bomber jacket and black jeans; oddly, his right arm is hidden up to the elbow under his open jacket.

"What up?" says Luke. "Gonna take me for a ride in your Ferrari someday?"

"How about now?"

"You're kidding," Luke says.

"Actually, I am."

"Maybe some afternoon after school?"

"Maybe," Jimmy says, and smiles. He slides his arm smoothly out from under his jacket; there's a small silver revolver in his hand and he's already pointing it at Luke and then at Morgan and finally Julianne. "If you guys would please get into the doorway over there and turn around so no one will pay any attention to you. Not that anyone would care."

"Whoa, is that loaded?" Luke croaks.

Jimmy cocks the trigger and places the nose of the gun behind Luke's ear. "Was Jesus Jewish? Now please do as I ask." Jimmy's smiling again, enjoying this, Julianne sees, and she doesn't get it; could he possibly want their money, their credit cards? He's a prince, the son of a billionaire; what does he need their money for? Maybe Jimmy is a sadist who just wants to torture and kill them; screw the money. He is a native, after all, of an uncivilized country, a country where people are beheaded by swords, stoned to death in public squares for adultery. Wait, maybe that's Afghanistan, maybe she's got her geography confused. She doesn't want to die, that's one thing she's not confused about. She wants to graduate and go on to whatever school she eventually chooses for herself and on the weekends visit Michael at Harvard. He loves her, absolutely, and if she comes out of this unharmed, she will try even harder to make him happier. Or at least less miserable.

"Please don't kill us," she hears herself say just before she turns around.

" 'Please don't kill us, *Your Highness*,' " Jimmy says. "And keep your voice down, please."

"Please don't kill us, Your Highness," Julianne and Morgan and Luke murmur in unison.

"Excellent," Jimmy says. "Good work, guys. And now I will ask you for your wallets and those Barnes & Noble bags."

Reaching into their pockets, they do as they are told. "Here," Julianne says afterward, and forks over her shopping bag.

"Oooh, Mister Grisham," Jimmy says, looking through the bag. "I like him very much. Thank you, Julianne." As if he has just been given a birthday gift from a friend.

"You're welcome," Julianne says automatically.

"And now you guys will count slowly to three hundred while I make my getaway. You will begin counting now. And Luke and Morgan, you will stop holding hands."

They count to twenty-seven before Julianne decides they should stop. All three of them turn and face the street warily; Jimmy is nowhere in sight.

"What the fuck was up with that?" Luke says. "You girls all right?"

Morgan gets out her cell phone to call the police. "I want his royal ass behind bars, don't you?"

Please don't kill us, Your Highness. Did he really get them to say that? Amazing, Julianne thinks. Equally amazing is the fact that Luke smells unmistakably like piss, like one of those homeless guys dozing under a layer of flattened cardboard boxes in a subway stairwell. He has peed in his pants, she realizes, and must be praying that in the darkness she and Morgan haven't noticed. Like that's even a possibility. Poor Morgan, who must be nearly as mortified as Luke.

The two of them abandon Julianne there on Eighty-Sixth Street, hurrying off with a mumbled excuse that's just about inaudible. Later she will hear from Morgan that even Luke's socks were wet. And that he threw them away in a plastic bag as soon as he got home. Along with his jeans and boxers. And even his Nikes, though they were almost brand new. Julianne hates Prince Jimmy for all of this but she, along with her friends, will decline to press charges. Better just not to think about any of it. Because don't they have enough on their minds already?

43

LAZY

Lazy has been skulking around school like a fugitive these past few weeks, and, indeed, she feels like one. She wonders, obsessively, if the students are gossiping madly about her, if the author of the poison-pen letter is right in front of her eyes, a student or teacher walking the halls like everyone else, biding his or her time until the perfect moment to deliver the knockout punch that will be her undoing. She contemplates a formal meeting with Chantal Robbe-Grillet, Elena Maldonado, Cynthia Silman, and Brooke, and the possibility that together the four of them might lodge a complaint of sexual harassment against Doug . . . but they're all young, single women, free to sleep with anyone they please, and if Doug has tossed them aside after a couple of "dates," well, it's probably no big deal to them . . . what is she *thinking*? She's the long-married headmistress who's been sleeping with a married subordinate, one whose wife is currently undergoing treatment for breast cancer, of all horrible things! How flagrant does *that* sound! The smartest thing she can do, obviously, is keep her distance from Doug, along with anyone he's screwed during the current academic year (with the exception of Brooke, of course). One thing, at least, that's gone well this year is the college game: as predicted, Griffin will send almost fifty percent of its senior class to the Ivies, including Chase Greenglass, whose parents took Lazy's advice and doubled their $100,000 gift to their alma mater. And thank goodness for that—if they hadn't, who knows what slightly less prestigious school poor Chase would have been forced to attend? And what weeping and teeth-gnashing and garment-rending Lazy herself would have borne witness to as she tried her best to convince the Greenglasses that enrolling their daughter in a non-Ivy school was not, in fact, the cataclysm they imagined it to be. Every year at this time there are a handful of sobbing mothers and outraged fathers who bypass Kat in College Counseling and make a beeline for Lazy with sorrowful tales of their children being denied admission to the schools of their choice or, perhaps, cruelly wait listed at Princeton, Yale, or Harvard, sometimes all three schools at once. One morning this week, her day began with the Barnetts, both investment bankers, who blew into her office on their way to work, Mr. Barnett already seething, his wife's bloodshot eyes and pink-tipped nose testament to the weeping she finally had under control. In her hand she clasped a Tod's alligator bag Lazy had seen in *New York* magazine for the breathtaking sum of nine thousand dollars, and which, her instincts informed her, would turn up at Griffin sooner or later. Studying the woebegone Mrs. Barnett in her elegant pale gray suit and pearls, she wondered if there was a special circle of hell for those who bought nine-thousand-dollar handbags without a second thought.

"Wait listed!" Mr. Barnett began. "Don't tell me that out of all those thousands of applicants admitted, every one of them is more deserving than Blake! Not possible! Not! And if I see any of those Griffin kids who are heading to Cambridge or New Haven or Princeton next fall instead of my son, I'll rip their goddamn heads off!"

"Take it easy, Josh," his wife said timidly. Unlike her husband, who had refused to sit down, she, at least, was seated, clutching her pricey alligator bag protectively against her chest.

"What do you think, Lazy, I've spent $23,000 a year to send Blake to Griffin just to have him end up at Dartmouth in godforsaken

Hanover, New Hampshire? No way! So you better pull every string available to you to make certain that my son moves off at least one of those wait lists and up to New Haven or Cambridge next September!"

May I remind you, Mr. Barnett, that you and your wife are both graduates of none other than the State University of New York at Albany and yet you managed to do just fine for yourselves nevertheless? Isn't that your chauffeur out there cooling his heels in front of your Bentley? "Please, Mr. Barnett, try to relax," Lazy urged. "Would you like my assistant to get you a cold drink?"

"I cannot and will not relax until I have your assurance that you and Kat Hemenway will figure out how to fix this thing."

This thing? Matching her palms together, Lazy lowered her chin onto the tips of her thumbs. "Blake is a terrific kid," she told the Barnetts. "Excellent grades and SATs, summers in Thailand and Costa Rica building houses for the homeless . . . what could be more impressive? Dartmouth was suitably impressed and offered him admission, and I can't help but think that if Blake were my son, I would be delighted with this outcome." Smiling hopefully, she continued, "It's a wonderful school, Mr. Barnett, an Ivy League school." *What more do you people want, for Christ's sake?*

Except for Mrs. Barnett's sobbing, the room was silent, but only for an instant. "Don't you get it?" Mr. Barnett said. And then stamped his foot on Lazy's Persian rug. "It may be an Ivy League school, but my son DESERVES BETTER AND SO DO I!" he roared.

"You're going to have a heart attack, Josh!" Mrs. Barnett warned him. "Get a grip, will you!"

Embarrassed for both of them, Lazy fooled with her engagement ring, spinning it around her finger, giving the Barnetts time to collect themselves.

"I'm sorry, Lazy," Mrs. Barnett said at last, "but this is a particularly sensitive issue for us. Josh's niece, his sister's daughter, was accepted early at Harvard and, as I'm sure you can well understand, Josh has been having a very hard time . . ."

"And Blake?" said Lazy.

"Blake?"

Your son? "Would Blake be happy going to Dartmouth?"

"That's neither here nor there," Mr. Barnett said irritably. He glanced at his watch. "I've got to get to work. And so do you, Marcia."

"I'll be in touch," Lazy said. She'd never heard of anyone offering a six-figure gift to get his kid off the wait list, but perhaps it had been done. And successfully. She'd have to check with Kat about that.

"Thank you," Mrs. Barnett mouthed to Lazy as her husband walked out. "Thanks."

The instant they left, Lazy went into her private bathroom and enjoyed three drags of a cigarette. "God give me strength," she heard herself murmur. *Where the hell had that come from?* She'd never uttered words like that in her life. And when Brooke flies in now with the latest newsbreak, talking so fast one word slides indistinctly into the next, Lazy is already considering the possibility that this high-powered job of hers is driving her ever closer to the brink.

"Please don't tell me I understood you correctly," she begs Brooke. "Please don't tell me Prince Jimmy robbed three people at gunpoint last night."

"Not three random people, three Griffin students!" Brooke reports. "Right in front of Barnes & Noble on Eighty-Sixth Street."

Shrouding her face in her hands, Lazy says, "Did he hurt them?"

"No no, all he did was take their wallets and whatever was in their Barnes & Noble bags. It was Julianne Coopersmith, Morgan Goldfine, and Luke Zucker-Johnsen, and of course they recognized him and called the cops, who went to his apartment and arrested him."

"He robs three of his classmates and then goes directly home so the police don't have to waste their time looking all over town for him?"

"Yeah, how stupid is that?" Brooke is snorting with laughter. "I mean, really, if you're going to commit a crime, do it right! The least he could have done was run away to New Jersey or something. And if you're going to mug people, shouldn't they be strangers?"

Lazy peeks out at Brooke through her fingers. "Could you stop laughing, please? This is terrible publicity for the school."

"Yeah, but it's still pretty funny."

"Not to me," Lazy says. "And I presume Jimmy's handler Mister al-Salan posted bail for him?"

"Presumably. I saw the Prince coming out of the student lounge a little while ago."

"And how did he look?"

"Fine. Handsome. Princely. I don't know, how did you expect him to look?"

"Conscience-stricken, penitent, embarrassed . . ." Lazy says, surprised at just how good it feels to acknowledge just how bad she feels. And has been feeling for weeks now.

"I think it's so cute that you're such an optimist," Brooke says, gently removing Lazy's hands from her face. "Expecting him to be conscience-stricken and all that. He's a prince richer than God. Oh, and plus he's got a full-time handler. What does he need a conscience for?"

"To keep him from robbing his classmates at gunpoint? And from plagiarizing English papers off the Internet?"

Brooke snickers. "Get real!" she says.

"All right, check his schedule and go find him. I might as well get this over with."

"Yeah, good luck with that."

Remembering the half-dozen or so expulsions during her tenure, all but one drug-related, Lazy feels her stomach clenching.

In some cases, she'd liked and even admired the offenders in question and hated to have to give them the boot. Smart kids who'd behaved foolishly but who would, in time, she'd guessed, get their act together. As, in fact, they eventually had. But Prince Jimmy is in a class by himself, a royal sleazeball, distinctly lacking in all the right qualities, or in even *one single* right quality. Exhibiting an extreme failure of character she should have taken notice of. Lazy seems to have a bad habit of being swayed by the superficial charms of good-looking men. And would like to kick herself for it.

Here's the Prince now, and she's pleased to note that he doesn't look nearly as fetching as he usually does. He hasn't shaved in a while and he's dressed in homeboy duds—ludicrously baggy jeans and big ugly sneakers with untied laces. He's just a thug, albeit a thug armed with a lovely, elegant accent.

"Do you know why you're here, Jimmy?" she asks lamely.

"Here in your office? Or here in this embattled world of ours?"

"You're yanking my chain, Jimmy, and I don't like it," Lazy says. "So cut it out right now and answer the question, please."

"This 'yanking my chain' is an idiomatic expression meaning what?"

"Meaning stop being such a smartass."

"No worries. I will stop that immediately and tell you what you want to know. Which is that I did what the police and my fellow students say I did. But the gun, of course, had no bullets in it, and it was never my intention to harm anyone."

"What possible reason could you have for pulling a crazy stunt like that? Tell me the truth, Jimmy, no b.s."

"No b.s.?"

"No bullshit?"

Jimmy smiles and has no trouble looking squarely at her. "I can only say, Headmistress, that I found myself frightfully bored, and that the opportunity presented itself to me and I decided to run with it."

"Bored?" Lazy says. "Bored?" she repeats quietly, holding back the scream she would love to let loose now.

"Yes, restless and bored. And in need of adventure."

"Why not read a good book?"

"I was doing just that, reading one of the books I'd taken from Julianne, when the police interrupted me."

"This antidote to boredom and restlessness might very well have landed you in jail for a while, did that thought ever occur to you?"

"I thought only that I had to leave the apartment and the watchful eye of Ahmed—Mister al-Salan—and spread my wings, as it were. And I have heard today that my classmates will not be pressing charges. To quote William Shakespeare, if I may, all's well that ends well."

"Except that I have to expel you." Lazy watches in surprise as his face crumples, as if he's truly wounded by the prospect of having to leave Griffin. And here she would have guessed that, for whatever reason, expulsion was his objective all along, from the very first day he arrived.

"Please don't, Headmistress," he's saying. "I want very much to stay. And also to express my regret for what has come to seem like foolhardy behavior."

Damned if her resolve isn't wavering! It's the Queen's English, she thinks, and the way it somehow lends dignity to every word Prince Jimmy speaks, no matter how perverse his behavior. "No," Lazy hears herself say. "I can't be dissuaded, not this time. I suspect you're not a bad kid, Abdullah—"

"*Prince* Abdullah."

"—but you've got to play by the rules like everyone else at Griffin." *Play by the rules? Is she kidding? Who is she if not Queen of the Hypocrites, dissembler extraordinaire?* Hit by a particularly brutal hot flash and an attack of self-loathing all at once, she dismisses Prince Abdullah/Jimmy with a feeble wave of her arm.

"My father—"

"Your father can do as he likes, *Abdullah,* but I stand by my decision." And if he sends in a suicide bomber to blow up the building, well, at least she'll have the satisfaction of knowing she'd gone down with her principles intact.

44

JULIANNE

ollowing several fruitless hours of cruising the racks at
Bloomingdale's one Saturday, Julianne and Morgan decide
to go for a latté and a muffin. Walking into a crowded Starbucks on the corner of Fifty-Seventh and Lex, they see Julianne's
mother parked at the counter in the window with Susan Avery,
the two of them deep in conversation. "How bizarre is *that*?" Julianne whispers to Morgan. She notes that neither of the two
mothers looks happy—no big surprise—but she understands
from the way they are talking, both of them leaning in toward
each other over the narrow counter, that there is an intimacy between them, that they are exchanging private thoughts like old
friends. Julianne is both horrified and intrigued, dying to hear
what they are talking about, but she's not going to confront them;
it's just too awkward in a public place like this, and she has to pull
her thoughts together first. And she can't imagine why Michael's
mother is wearing a wrist watch suspended from a gold chain
around her neck. "She's such a freak!" Julianne hisses, nudging
Morgan. Then, "We have to get out of here."

Outside, Morgan immediately calls Daisy and leaves word on
her voice mail, saying, "You have to call back right away, the *minute*
you get this message. You can't believe who we saw together!"

Julianne thinks about Michael, who would surely flip out if he
knew about the two mothers. Michael, who somehow had convinced her not to go to Houston to visit her father and the new

baby. Her father had already paid for the plane tickets, but at the last minute Julianne couldn't manage to go to the airport and get on that plane. She's such a soft touch when it comes to Michael—no matter what he wants, she just can't find it in herself to say no to him. And now her father is stuck with the plane tickets and can't get his money back. He's furious and so disappointed, and who can blame him? And what's really bad news is that she *truly* wanted to go and check out the scene with her father's new family, but Michael had to have his way. Hearing all of this, Morgan had told her that she, personally, didn't think that whatever needed fixing in that mysterious brain of Michael's was ever going to be fixed. *Hate to say it, but I don't exactly have high hopes for his future. I mean, I'm no psychic, but I can't see even a glimmer of light at the end of that particular tunnel. All I see is pitch-black darkness and you disappearing into the darkness with him. And, as your best friend, it just kills me, sweetie.*

Julianne attributes this deeply pessimistic view of Michael's future to something else entirely; the truth is, Morgan has been freaking out lately, struggling to accept the fact that she's headed to the University of Chicago next year. And not Yale. Morgan's father claimed he was sick at the thought of her being 770 miles away from home, as if the two of them were accustomed to spending so much time together and would seriously miss each other. *Yeah right, I don't think so,* Morgan told Julianne. Consumed by his grief, lost in his work, he is, Julianne knows, a ghostly presence in Morgan's life.

She and Morgan are unable to grab a cab from Starbuck's back to Morgan's apartment and end up on the subway platform instead. As they wait for the Number 4 train to show up, an Asian guy in a tuxedo plays something haunting and familiar on his violin, and Morgan goes crazy trying to remember what it is. And then Julianne realizes it's the theme song from *Schindler's List*.

Morgan deposits a twenty-dollar bill into the violin case sitting open on the filthy floor. The musician is very professional and continues playing, though of course he nods his head and smiles at Morgan, not even knowing it's a twenty she's given him. "So what do you think?" she says, returning to Julianne's side.

"About what?"

"About this poor guy in a tuxedo trying to earn a living in the subway, playing this sad, sad music to all these unappreciative, disinterested people just waiting for the train, not giving a shit about what a talented violinist he is, or even about the Holocaust, in which you and I might have been killed. Exterminated, as it were. Like my grandmother's entire family—first cousins, second cousins, you name it, every last one of them doomed. Grandma Lil was like our age when she was liberated from Auschwitz, the only survivor of her family. Amazing, right?"

And when the Number 4 eventually pulls in, Julianne steps into the car, but Morgan hangs back; it looks to Julianne as if she can't get herself to board the train, which isn't headed for a concentration camp in Poland, after all, but only for Eighty-Sixth Street. Julianne looks over her shoulder at her, yelling at Morgan to hurry up, but Morgan tells her to go ahead without her. "What's wrong?" Julianne calls out, and then the doors close.

"So what was going on with you?" Julianne asks later, when Morgan finally catches up with her outside the Eighty-Sixth Street station. "Why didn't you get on the train with me?"

"It was the whole, sickening, Jews-in-the-cattle-car thing, I guess," Morgan tells her. And then explains that she'd imagined herself on a train to Auschwitz. With her mother beside her, the two of them clasping each other's hands as they hurtled toward their deaths.

"Huh," says Julianne, and wonders if, for Morgan, everything in the world will always be connected to her mother. And if, for herself, every bit of it will somehow be connected to Michael.

45

DEE

"If you're going to give me the silent treatment," Dee says to Julianne at the breakfast table, "the least you can do is tell me why you're so pissed off."

Julianne looks up from the folder she is paging through—one stamped with the words "Join Us to Celebrate Your Admission to Sarah Lawrence"—then casts her eyes down again, mumbling something Dee can't decipher.

"Excuse me?" Standing uninvited behind her daughter now, she gathers Julianne's hair into a ponytail, lets it drop, begins to braid it.

"Will you *stop*!" Julianne says. "You are so unbelievably annoying."

"Old news," says Dee. "Tell me something I don't already know." She's about to say, for the fourth or fifth time, how thrilled she is that Julianne will be going to school so close to home next year, but why would Julianne want to hear that? *Close to home and far from Michael; what more could a mother hope for?*

"You're hovering," Julianne complains. She swivels around for a look at Dee. "And why are you smiling?"

"Sorry," Dee says, her tone of voice making it evident that she's not.

"Well, you should be."

"Sorry? For what?" No longer hovering, Dee has stepped into the kitchen, where she is busy unloading the dishwasher. The cat joins her, hopping inside the dishwasher's open door.

"Okay, look," Julianne says, and tosses aside the Sarah Lawrence folder, "sorry for hanging out at Starbucks with someone you shouldn't be hanging with." She locks eyes with Dee. "I saw you there yesterday, all right?"

Busted, Dee thinks, but quickly recovers. "So according to you, I can't hang, I can't hover, I can't even smile, is that correct?" She is embarrassed, though, as if she's been discovered in the act of something dishonest and shameful, shoplifting a couple of tubes of lipstick from the drugstore, perhaps. "Get out of the dishwasher, Sonia," she instructs the cat, who stares at her uncomprehendingly before licking the tip of a butter knife.

Julianne approaches, hoists Sonia into her arms. "She's kind of a horrible person. Why would you even want to *be* with her?" she says, rubbing her face in the cat's belly. "Are you guys friends or something?"

"She's not horrible," Dee says. "And things aren't easy for her." *I don't have a daughter of my own but I'm guessing that they're easier to love.*

"So you feel sorry for her? What kind of creepy friendship is that? And what do you guys even talk about?"

"I have sympathy for her," Dee says. "I empathize with her. And that feeling is reciprocated." An unspoken name is suspended there in the air between them, but neither Dee nor her daughter reaches for it.

"She's pretty much the worst mother who ever lived," Julianne pronounces, and Dee is already shaking her head from side to side, letting her know that in this Julianne is mistaken. *So you see that he's a boy one could love.* Wasn't it Susan Avery who wrote this to her only a few months ago? Clearly not the worst mother who ever lived. Because, Dee speculates, there might be others in Susan's shoes who would not be able to love him at all.

46

JULIANNE

Julianne and Morgan are babysitting for Luke's sister Ashley, the three-year-old genius. Luke himself is having all four of his wisdom teeth yanked this afternoon and his mother is accompanying him, as any mother (even a famous feminist writer like Luke's) would. It's the weekend and no other babysitters are available: Ashley's nanny is off duty today and Luke's father is playing golf somewhere in Westchester. Julianne doesn't understand why his father couldn't simply cancel his golf date, but Morgan only shrugged at the question, and here they are in Luke's garden apartment, trying to come up with ways to entertain the midget whiz kid. Though she looks ordinary enough, Julianne thinks, dressed in little lavender jeans and a tiny-sized, purple-and-white Amherst College T-shirt. And Luke's apartment looks as it always has to her—spookily neat and orderly, especially for a teenage boy. No socks or belts or underwear draped along the bed or floor, no papers, large or small, scattered across his desk, not a computer disk or CD or DVD out of place. His kitchen is all granite and stainless steel and utterly pristine, the bathroom appointed in marble and, of course, immaculate. *Crazy for a seventeen-year-old to have all that to himself,* Julianne knows her mother would say. And to be honest, her mother isn't wrong.

"Why is the TV on mute?" Ashley says. "I'm going to turn it off. But first I have to tinkle."

"Do you need help?" Julianne asks.

"I'm a big girl, *silly*. I'm a school girl." Grabbing a fistful of her T-shirt, Ashley says, "I'm a college girl!"

"She probably does need help," Morgan says. "I guess we should take her."

"No problem," says Julianne, though she doesn't know the first thing about taking a three-year-old to the bathroom or anyplace else. She considers the fifteen-year age difference between Luke and his sister and how strange it is that they haven't grown up together. Ten years from now, when Luke could very well be married with a child of his own, Ashley will be a mere seventh grader busy with her algebra homework. Unless, of course, she truly is a genius, in which case she might already be in graduate school studying quantum physics at the age of thirteen.

She looks at Morgan's hand, so sweetly attached to Ashley's en route to the bathroom. Being in love with Luke has resurrected her, Julianne knows. According to Morgan, it's what propels her out of bed in the morning and keeps her going all day long, like some amazing drug flowing endlessly through her veins. In the two years it took her mother to die, Morgan was dying a little, too. Losing hope every day even as she pretended that Elizabeth was getting better when she so clearly was not, when she was only growing weaker and weaker, too weak, eventually, to brush her own teeth and had to have Morgan do it for her. But Morgan, after months of steady improvement, is doing well now, and it's such a relief to Julianne, who has enough on her plate as it is.

"So you need us to stay here with you while you, um, tinkle?" Morgan asks. She and Julianne watch as Ashley sheds her Velcroed sneakers, her anklets, jeans, and Hello Kitty panties before arranging herself on the toilet wearing only a T-shirt.

"Yes," says Ashley gravely. "In case I fall in."

Julianne parks herself at the edge of the bathtub; Morgan remains at Ashley's side. "So where are you going to college next year, little girl?" Julianne teases.

"You silly! I can't go to college!" Ashley shrills exuberantly. "I'm a CHILD, stupidhead!"

This is the genius she's heard so much about? "Please don't call me a stupidhead," Julianne says, smiling. "I'm actually the opposite of stupid."

"I don't think so," says Ashley. "But I know, let's play the opposite game," she suggests. "I'll teach you girls. Okay, what's the opposite of . . . light?"

Julianne pretends to think for a moment. "Dark."

"Very good," Ashley says. "Now your turn."

"What's the opposite of . . . win?"

"Lose, but this is too easy," Ashley complains. "Use your brain, girls."

"All right, what's the opposite of guilty?" Morgan says.

"Not guilty, your honor! And guess what?"

"What?" Morgan laughs.

"If you watch too much TV, you'll go blind and your hair will fall out," Ashley informs her.

"Sounds about right," says Julianne.

"Want me to read to you?" Ashley says. "Gimme a magazine," she orders, pointing to a Lucite basket on the floor containing two meticulous piles, one of the *New Yorker*, the other of *New York*.

"Tinkle first, read to us later," Morgan says as she hands Ashley a magazine.

" 'Dining at Le Bernardin may cost you an arm and a leg, but Eric Ripert, its brilliant chef, creates the sort of masterpieces you won't soon—' "

"Oh my God!" On her knees now, Morgan embraces Ashley.

Julianne's arms are covered in goose bumps; she and Morgan are in the presence of greatness and know it. But why is Morgan crying, she wonders.

"Toilet paper, please," says Ashley politely.

Julianne has to release her from Morgan's too-tight embrace, has to lead Morgan out of the bathroom and back into the living room, where she settles her against a loveseat. And runs immediately afterward to get Ashley into her clothes and sneakers. Bending to help her, she sees herself in her own apartment, frantically knotting the laces of Michael's sneakers as her mother walks through the door, hears Michael sobbing, *I lost my wallet.*

Stop, Julianne tells herself in Luke's beautiful white marble bathroom. *Stop stop stop stop.*

"Morgan's a crybaby," Ashley remarks, but without much interest.

Hurrying to the living room with Ashley in tow, Julianne sees that Morgan is flat on her back on the loveseat now, her arms crossed behind her neck, her eyes staring at the ceiling. That classic pose in the movies whenever an actor is in his shrink's office, Julianne notes. And then Morgan starts to tell her about something called "complicated grief," which she learned all about on the Internet, she says.

"It's like if I was spending too much of my time thinking about my mother and feeling like my life was totally useless without her, that wouldn't be considered normal, 'uncomplicated' grief. Like grief could ever be uncomplicated! Give me a break! Like you're supposed to stop loving a person or thinking about them just because they happen to have vanished. Permanently. That's bullshit! Not to mention impossible."

Julianne knows something of grief herself, though if you were to measure hers against Morgan's of course she knows that Morgan's would hold a lot more weight. She understands that Morgan has suffered a momentary relapse. Which can happen to anyone. But she's got her Zoloft and Dr. Schuster's number in her Palm Pilot and will, Julianne foresees, make a full recovery. She doesn't need a degree from medical school or even a PhD in psychology to figure that one out.

"I'm bored," Ashley says. "Will SOMEBODY play with me?"

"Here, read the obituaries," Morgan says, and hands her the newspaper.

47

LAZY

To: All high school students and their parents
From: Kathryn Hoffman

Dear Students and Parents:
It is my unfortunate duty to report that two members of the class of 2004 were discovered flagrante delicto *in a faculty restroom on the seventh floor engaging in an act of oral sex during school hours. This sort of highly inappropriate behavior cannot, and will not, be tolerated, and the two students involved have already been disciplined; only weeks short of graduation, they have been expelled, and letters to that effect have been sent to the colleges they had hoped to attend next fall.*

We are an elite independent school with the highest academic standards, and those high standards extend as well to the way we conduct ourselves every day in the halls and classrooms of this building. The appalling breach in the rules of conduct committed by these two seniors reflects poorly on all of us, and it is thus my hope that this disgraceful incident will not be discussed among you as if it were a trivial matter to be joked about but will instead be recalled as an offense punishable by expulsion. And please remember, as always, that we at the Griffin School are a caring, responsible community, a family, if you will. And

*this is one family that does not condone sexual relations in
its lavatories.*

    Sincerely,
    Kathryn Hoffman
    Headmistress

You hypocritical self-righteous censorious loser! Lazy tells herself. And means every word of it. Her hands are shaking so violently she's had to retype the letter on her computer three times to
get rid of all the typos. Standing by now as Brooke runs off a hundred copies on the Xerox machine, Lazy can only think, *why why
why?* Of the four hundred students in the high school, why did it
have to be Palmer Hughes, daughter of Emma, who was willing to
offer her personal services to Jason Armstrong (whose father had
written the music and lyrics to several smash Broadway hits raking
in millions a couple of decades ago)?

    "Did you *really* have to expel them?" Brooke says. "I mean, it
wasn't a homicide, it was only a blow job. And they can't be the
first—only the first to have gotten caught, right?"

    Treading with infinite care, Lazy says, "I know. And believe
me, Emma Hughes and her husband have already threatened to
sue me personally, along with the school, if Princeton rescinds
its offer to Palmer. And the Armstrongs were none too thrilled
either, especially since, as they've reminded me several times, it
was their money that paid for the suite of new music rooms. But
look, this kind of behavior, harmless though it may be, can't
be—"

    "Tolerated. I know, you said it right here in your letter."

    "Don't look at me like that, Brooke."

    "Okay, listen, I'm no saint either. One time, Doug and I—"

    "I *don't* want to hear about it. Not one tiny detail."

    "He's such a sleaze. You know he slept around at the last
school he was at, don't you? He and Clarissa were both forced to
leave and his wife divorced him. And then he married Clarissa."

"*What?*" says Lazy. "Clarissa was the reason his first marriage broke up? And you know this how?"

"Oh, my mother has a friend who taught at the same school, somewhere in New Jersey, I think." Brooke shrugs. "Look, I *told* you he was a serial adulterer. Why are you so surprised?"

"Could this man be any worse?" Lazy cries, and throws herself across the Xerox machine. "Could I possibly have fallen for anyone more contemptible, more revolting, more repugnant?"

"Is that a rhetorical question or do you really want an answer?"

"What do *you* think?"

"I think," Brooke says, "that you should get off the Xerox machine and help me put address labels on all these envelopes so we can get them out of here."

"And then what?"

"Want a Xanax?" Foraging in her bag, Brooke comes up with a plastic prescription bottle. "Take one and you'll feel a lot better."

"I don't do drugs."

Brooke is laughing at her. "It's not like I'm offering you coke or Ecstasy. And this is even better than a cigarette. You want a little short-term relief from your anxiety?"

God, yes! She's all keyed-up, shaky, sweaty, her palms damp and sticky. All that and heartsick too. She considers the ways, beyond the obvious, in which she has failed her husband—by not running to embrace him when he comes home from work every night; by not kissing him on the lips or anywhere else when he turns toward her in bed to say goodnight; by allowing him to see how annoyed she is when he wakes up at four or five A.M. and turns toward her for more than a kiss; by not paying close attention when he talks about his med school students and his workday; by refusing to walk with him around the Central Park Reservoir every Sunday morning, no matter how many times he's asked her to keep him company; by refusing to answer the phone when their Caller ID informs her it's his obnoxious brother the pediatric heart surgeon on the other end . . . she could spend hours, days, weeks, cataloging her failures, large, small, and smaller, as a wife, a lover, a companion. Doesn't Richard deserve better from her after more than two decades of loving her so attentively? So faithfully? If that Xanax can do the trick Brooke claims it can, she's going to pop one and then head home and sit down with Richard and let him know just how far from grace she's fallen.

Before someone else does it for her. Which she's convinced someone will, sooner rather than later. And isn't a full confession followed by expiation the right way to go? How could it possibly be the wrong way if it instinctively feels like the right way?

"Gimme," she tells Brooke, and sticks out a clammy hand.

Richard has a couple of cardigan sweaters in his wardrobe: one an oatmeal-colored cashmere, a gift from Lazy that she bought at Bergdorf's, the other a linty black cotton that Richard purchased himself at Today's Man for $19.99 and which he changes into immediately after arriving home tonight. On his feet are those army-green flip-flops he's had since the end of the last century. His feet are long and narrow, the toes lined up in size order except for the one next to the big toe, which is longer than Lazy thinks it should be and extends past the big toe by a quarter of an inch on each foot. She stares at these two unfortunate toes in dismay, as always, and then at Richard's sturdy, well-shaped legs, which, like his head, no longer sport much hair; in fact, these legs of his almost look as if they've been waxed. *So pretend he's a bodybuilder,* she tells herself, though measuring in at 5′ 9″ and 155 pounds, he's no such thing.

"Aren't you going to put some pants on?" she asks, stretching out on her stomach all the way across their bed.

"Gotta pee first." He shuts the door behind him but not completely, and the sound of his piss hitting the water seems magnified, too loud for Lazy's ears; like a child, she clamps her hands over them until she hears the toilet flush. "Want to order in Vietnamese tonight?" Richard calls from the doorway of the walk-in closet where he's getting into his pants. "I'm in the mood for that chicken with lemongrass, and the Banh Hoi, that's the angel hair, okay? Hand me the phone and I'll order it."

Stab him in the heart *before* dinner or *after*? An excruciating choice either way. *Sickening.* Perhaps she should let him eat first; surely he won't have much of an appetite after she's sung her song. But the magic pill she's swallowed may be wearing off soon and then she'll be too jittery again to arrange her thoughts properly. Not that they're perfectly aligned now, far from it . . . what she feels like, she imagines, is a neophyte doctor, just beginning his internship, who's been assigned to break the grimmest sort of news to a patient.

"The phone?" Richard says.

"What?"

"Can you hand it to me?"

At least his jeans are on and his poor smooth legs are covered up and out of sight now. "Comeer and talk to me first," she says.

"What do you want to talk about? Let's order the Curry Ga instead of the lemongrass chicken, but I'll tell them not to make it too spicy, all right?"

Rising to her feet now, Lazy looks past him to a framed photograph on the wall—of their son Matt, nine months old in the picture and poised on all fours, his face lifted to reveal a few teeth and a smile full of saliva; Richard's hand is resting at the back of the baby's neck, and *his* smiling face, too, is presented to the camera, the sweetly adoring face of a young father, twenty-four years old, not very much older, really, than Matt is today. A twenty-four year-old father with a full head of reddish brown hair and a wife who loved him too much to even daydream of betraying him. It was she who'd taken the photograph, she who would eventually emerge from the darkness of that postpartum time when her despondence and lassitude were like a lingering virus she just couldn't shake. Nohow. Could not for the life of her figure out how she would ever engage in the world again. It was Richard who searched hard to find her a trustworthy student who baby-sat for five dollars an hour so that Lazy would be able to ease back into her dissertation and, later, snare an adjunct teaching position at Brooklyn College; there she was, finally living at full tilt again. Thanks to Richard, who fought her depression with his own cheerful generosity, his kindly patience, and nudged her gently back into the early nineteenth century where her thesis on Jane Austen waited. In her imagination, it's the heart and soul of both the smiling young man in the photograph and the middle-aged guy hungry for dinner now that she's going to wound so deeply in the next moment. Would the younger Richard be more forgiving? Or more enraged by jealousy, more likely to go after Doug with a glittering sharp instrument? Which one of them would fall into a shocked silence? Which one would bray at her harshly? What does it matter anyway? She's the transgressor and she's the one who's got it coming.

The Xanax must have run its course; her pulse has accelerated, her throat feels scorched. She licks her lips and says her husband's name.

"What?" he says. He's still in the closet doorway, threading a cracked leather belt through the loops of his oldest Levi's.

"It's just that I love you so much," she tells him, her eyes instantly filling.

"Great, Iloveyoutoo," he says, "but I'm hungry, okay?"

"But here's the thing," she says, and lays it out for him, the whole vile, loathsome story of how she came to find herself enthralled by the dubious charms of Doug McNamee, who, she reassures Richard, is nothing more than a contemptible piece of human garbage, having cheated on his first wife with the woman who became his second wife, who, in turn, he betrayed with God knows how many women, well, five that Lazy knows of, and . . . She implores him to forgive her, apologizes two dozen different ways, then goes back to begging again.

"Stop!" Richard interrupts, in a deep voice not his own. He takes a step toward her into the room, thinks better of it and moves backward into the closet, supporting himself with both arms against the door frame. And looking out at her with an expression of such pain and hostility that Lazy feels herself wither inside and out. "Do you think," he says, "that I have the slightest interest right now in hearing how sorry you are or exactly how many women your boyfriend has screwed?"

"He was never really my boyfriend," Lazy explains. "And I—"

"*You?*" Richard says. "*You* have crushed me. It's like I've been mowed down by an SUV. But for some mysterious reason my heart's still beating."

She's desperate to embrace him, to offer solace, to allay his grief, but senses that's the last thing he wants from her.

And then, to her astonishment, he goes to the phone and orders his Banh Hoi and Curry Ga. "You need to be gone by the time my dinner gets here," he says evenly.

"Gone?" She doesn't understand what he could possibly mean.

He's in the closet again, rummaging around for a suitcase, a good-sized one, which he flings in her direction.

"But where will I go?"

"Haven't got a clue," says Richard. "About that, or, apparently, anything else." He opens the top drawer of her dresser, tosses out careless handfuls of bras and panties, a couple of silk slips and camisoles, most of which land on the floor. "We've loved each other for almost a quarter of a century," he says.

This sounds auspicious; she nods encouragingly. "Ever since college, you've been the love of my life," she says.

"And now I'd like to strangle you." Richard seems surprised to hear this, shocked, really. He holds up his hands, showing her his palms. "Not that I would ever allow myself to hurt you."

"Of course not." She can see that his hands are trembling slightly; they're the hands that have caressed her, aroused her, zipped her dresses, latched her pearls, yet, at this moment, she's afraid of them.

"Would you like me to help you pack?" he offers. "Just to speed things along here."

"No thank you," she says.

She will go and stay with her mother for a while, she decides.

A fate worse, perhaps, even than death.

48

JULIANNE

In the student lounge, recently renovated and furnished with a couple of couches and plenty of comfy armchairs, Julianne arranges herself in Michael's lap. He's diligently at work peeling an orange, and across the room, someone else is feasting on a tray of sushi, never mind the large, neatly lettered sign posted on the wall that says:

> ABSOLUTELY NO FOOD ALLOWED!
> IF YOU'VE GOT THE MUNCHIES,
> GET THYSELF TO THE LUNCHROOM!
> **By order of the Student Council**

Underneath, someone has ordered "Go Fuck Thyself!" It is rumored that in the old days, maybe thirty years ago, you could actually smoke in here, but no one really believes it. These days, the bathrooms are where people smoke cigarettes and do a few lines of coke, and where the bingers-and-purgers go to puke their guts out. And apparently where those in the mood for a quickie blow job hang out, like the ridiculous Palmer Hughes and her equally ridiculous boyfriend, Jason Armstrong. Julianne isn't sorry to see them go, or Jimmy the Prince, either. They're bad news, all of them, and stupid beyond belief, despite the fact that the three of them will probably end up, respectively, at Princeton, Georgetown, and Oxford, even though they've been officially expelled.

Or so Julianne has heard. She is, frankly, more than a little tired of this place, of this tiny gilded corner of the world and its mostly smart but clueless inhabitants. She loves her friends, still loves Michael, but it's time for a change of scenery. She'll be at Sarah Lawrence next year and has hopes that there she'll flower into the poet she's always known herself to be. Though she's never shown her poem-filled notebooks, dating all the way back to childhood, to anyone at all. Anne Sexton and Sylvia Plath, those are her kind of poets, not that she has the slightest interest in killing herself; it's just their bleakness she admires.

"Want some?" Michael says, and feeds her a lukewarm slice of orange.

She reaches for her bag on the floor and extracts an envelope of photographs. "Want to see what my brother looks like?"

Michael hesitates. "I shouldn't have stopped you from going to Houston. Still a little mad at me, deep down?"

This is as near to an apology as she is ever going to get from him, she realizes; studying his ugly, scabbed-over knuckles, she shakes her head, letting him know she accepts the apology. "Not mad. And not much to say about a sleeping newborn, is there?"

"He looks like a miniature Dwight Eisenhower," Michael offers.

"What?"

"Or a tiny skinhead."

"Right." She takes one of Michael's hands, slides her fingertip along the bumps of rusty-looking scabs. "You're lucky you didn't break anything this time."

"Lucky," he agrees. Then, "What's his name?"

"Harry. You know, just like David Letterman's baby," she says defensively.

"Did I say anything?"

He's laughing, but she doesn't mind. She's thankful just to hear him laugh, even at the expense of her brother, who, she has to concede, does resemble a miniature skinhead, minus the piercings and tattoos, of course. When Morgan and Luke show up, she's relieved at the sight of them and slips off Michael's lap. She hugs Morgan gratefully, as if they hadn't just seen each other two periods ago in Philosophy.

"Hey dude, do you owe me five bucks or something?" Michael calls out.

"Actually," Luke corrects him, "you owe *me* five bucks. From lunch at Burger King, remember?"

"Okay, whatever," Michael says. "No problem." Going for his wallet, he hands Luke a crumpled five.

Luke examines it worriedly. Squatting on the carpet now, he smoothes the bill against his thigh with the flat of his hand. Again and again.

"What, are you afraid it's counterfeit?"

Morgan glances up from the couch where Julianne has spread an array of snapshots of Harry.

"It's not counterfeit, but it's no good," Luke complains. "Can I have another one?"

"What do you mean, it's no good?"

"Just give him another one, Michael," Morgan says sharply.

Michael is pissed off, Julianne sees, but he returns to his wallet and forks over another five. She sighs; *disaster averted.*

But this second bill fails Luke's inspection as well. He tugs at all four of its corners, runs two fingers across Abraham Lincoln's receding hairline, strokes the president's bearded chin. "I'm sorry," he says finally. "If I could just have one more."

"What is your problem, dude?" Michael says. "Why isn't my money good enough for you?"

"It's not that," Luke says. He reconsiders. "You know what, take back your money and let's just forget it. Let's just say I bought you lunch."

"I don't *want* you buying me lunch."

"Well, *I* don't want your wrinkled-up bills in my wallet, okay?"

Morgan has made her way to Luke's side. "It's better for him if they're brand-new, you know, like, nice and crisp," she explains.

"It's just easier that way." She takes Luke's arm. "Since the mugging, it's . . ." Her voice fades away.

"Since the mugging," Julianne echoes. "Oh, right. Sure." She shoots Morgan a sympathetic look, a look meant to say, *You don't have to explain anything to me.* Because it's all perfectly understandable. And Luke is a sweetie, not a selfish bone in his body, not like Michael, who, face it, sometimes seems like the epitome of self-absorption. But obviously that comes from a lifetime spent with his weirdo parents. Though Luke's are no prize either, come to think of it. Asking him to move downstairs by himself when they have that huge townhouse of theirs—how unbelievably insensitive could people be toward their own son? No wonder he's an obsessive-compulsive who can't even deal with a crumply five-dollar bill. Presumably the world is filled with normal, ordinary adults who get by without seven-figure salaries and multiple, palatial homes, who love their children openly and warmly and have no problem saying the right words out loud. Except for her mother, though, why is it she doesn't seem to know anyone like that?

The sick fuck, she thinks she hears someone saying under his breath. Referring to Luke, presumably. But Michael is busy fitting the rejected bills back into his wallet, the guy who was eating the tray of sushi is dozing across one of the couches. And Luke and Morgan are checking out the pictures of baby Harry.

Maybe it's just her imagination.

49

LAZY

Though she's had dinner alone every night for the past few weeks at the Garden of Eat-In, a coffee shop not far from Fairhaven, Lazy knows she will never get used to this, to sitting at a table for two with the *New York Times* open beside her, quietly eating her grilled chicken Caesar salad, exchanging words with no one except a severe-looking waitress with pockmocked skin, to whom she gives her order, says thank you, and little else. There are other people dining solo tonight as well, but how many of them are veterans of a twenty-two-year-marriage, she wonders. How many of them can count on two fingers, as she can (or could, until a couple of weeks ago), the number of occasions she'd eaten alone in a restaurant over the past quarter of a century.

And since when is Caesar salad made with iceberg lettuce, she thinks crossly. Why don't these people in Queens know any better? Haven't they ever heard of romaine? Chewing on a limp and tasteless crouton, she stares at a young woman across the aisle seated with a friend. The woman has lovely, well-groomed, straight blond hair, and is conventionally dressed in a scoop-necked T-shirt and jean jacket, but she's wearing a thick silver septum ring through her nose like a bull.

"There's this sibling rivalry between the Maltese and the Yorkie," the woman's friend is saying. "The therapist has been trying to treat it, but he's not making much progress." She sips at her drink, then asks, "Can I have some of your fries, Denasia?"

Nodding, Denasia pushes her plate forward. "The thing I don't get is how a Maltese and a Yorkie can be siblings if they're not even the same breed."

"Well, it's like even though they're not biological siblings, they're still brothers."

"Like one of them's adopted, you mean?" Denasia says. With a fingertip, she strokes her septum ring, as if to polish it.

"Yeah, that's exactly it."

"So does this therapist make house calls? The reason I'm interested is because I think my sweet little Pepper may have developed some kind of weird aversion to me. He doesn't run to the door anymore when I come home, plus he's peed on my bed way too many times recently."

Could it be that Pepper's mistaken you for a bull? Lazy would like to ask.

"Well, that sucks," the friend says.

What sucks, Lazy thinks, is that she's forty-three years old and has nowhere to crash except the couch in her mother's living room, which doesn't even open into a bed and is hardly fit for a grown woman to sleep on. But a decent hotel is just too pricey, and she doesn't want to burden her friends. (And though Fairhaven normally doesn't allow any residents under the age of fifty-five, in Lazy's case, they've made an exception, knowing she can't possibly want to spend the rest of her life on her mother's couch.) Charlotte, at least, has been entirely sympathetic, refusing to pass judgment, saying only, "I love you with a full heart and that's that." From Richard, Lazy has heard not a peep, and it seems wisest to refrain from annoying him with pleas for mercy. Perhaps in a few days she will feel otherwise, but for the moment she will practice self-restraint and keep her distance from the phone.

On the neon-lit street, she saunters past one small shop after another, most of them with signs in both Korean and English, though English is rarely spoken in this neighborhood except by the young people, she's discovered. Needing a couple of toiletries—her favorite brand of mouthwash and some cotton balls for make-up removal—she steps into 99-cent Dreams, where everything for sale is priced under a dollar. The cramped aisles are stocked with an odd selection of junky toys and knick-knacks, but toward the rear she finds the travel-sized items she's looking for. And also a box of Monet note cards for her mother, and a small bottle of Windex and a roll of paper towels to clean Charlotte's neglected, toothpaste-spattered bathroom mirror.

"And good night," the elderly Korean man behind the register says.

It's barely past nine, and two hours of conversation and TV with her mother are the only activities that beckon until bedtime. Lazy decides to treat herself to a cigarette before going upstairs, and loiters in front of the Fairhaven Residence for Seniors with some of the kitchen help and a security guard on a break, one and all appreciatively sucking an assortment of dangerous poisons into their lungs.

"You are Mrs. Hoffman's girl?" a tall, slender black man all in white says, and lights Lazy's Newport for her.

"That's me," Lazy acknowledges, smiling at the thought of herself as Charlotte's girl. And also because she can't remember the last time anyone has lit a cigarette for her.

"A nice lady, that Mrs. Hoffman, who came into my kitchen to talk to me."

"You're the chef?"

"Yes, I am Leo, and your mother came to show me pictures of you and your son and your brother."

"I don't understand."

"These old people are very very alone, you understand. And so they will talk to anyone, even me."

Lazy imagines Charlotte marching determinedly into the kitchen, pulling out her little vinyl "brag book" full of photo-graphs, persuading Leo to take a leisurely look at her beloved family. As if he doesn't have more profitable ways to spend his time.

"Thank you," she tells him.

"For looking at pictures? You don't thank someone for something so small."

"I do," Lazy says, and stabs her cigarette into the sand-filled metal canister positioned outside the front door. And then signs in at the security desk. The lobby is empty; from down the hallway she can hear the movie being shown in the TV lounge/chapel. She peeks inside; the folding chairs arranged in so many neat rows are vacant except for one all the way in the back, which is occupied by a uniformed attendant laughing it up as the actor Steve Martin talks his way out of a jail cell. *Dirty Rotten Scoundrels,* she thinks, a movie she and Richard saw on a flight to Italy years ago. *Whatever,* as her Griffin students would say.

In the elevator she joins a terribly hunched old woman who seizes the hands of her paid companion and kisses them fervently, again and again. "You stop that, Evelyn!" the companion orders. "No kissing of the hands, do you hear me?" She pulls her hands away, but Evelyn reaches for them once again and bestows her ardent kisses upon them. "Naughty!" the companion says. "Naughty naughty naughty!"

Lazy is close to tears at this effusion of unwanted kisses; she's never seen anything quite so pitiful.

"Every day is the same thing. I tell Evelyn's son and daughter, but they say I must ignore it. How much longer do you think I can ignore it, tell me."

"You have a difficult job," Lazy says quietly, as the woman tucks her hands safely behind her waist, out of Evelyn's reach.

"I give you this job right now and see how you like it. Ten dollars an hour and see if you can last even one hour, okay?"

Shaking her head, Lazy says nothing.

"In Bangladesh I was a wealthy woman with servants. Now all that is gone. My husband left me. And then he died and here I am." She shrugs one shoulder. "Your life is one thing, and then, suddenly, it is something else. Right, Evelyn?" she says, laying her arm affectionately across the old woman's deformed back. Evelyn doesn't respond; her head is fixed in a permanent droop, it seems, a wilted flower dangling from its stalk. She can only look downward, at her small feet in their bleached-white canvas Keds.

"Well, this is my floor," Lazy announces, walking off the elevator and into her mother's apartment with the impeccable posture of a ballerina.

"Hello, Beautiful!" Charlotte says jauntily. She's dressed in her slightly shabby, baby pink housecoat and backless slippers, and is seated on the couch where Lazy will be sleeping tonight. "I'm watching . . . *Three Men and a Baby* . . . *Two Men and a Boy* . . . well, I'm not sure exactly, but you can shut it off if you want."

Lazy doesn't bother to turn off the TV but picks up the remote and channel-surfs indifferently until she's back where she started. "Do you happen to know a woman who lives here named Evelyn?" she asks.

"The little hunchback lady? She's a dear friend of mine though of course I can hardly bear to look at her. She doesn't talk much, to tell you the truth, just hello and good-bye, that sort of thing. I think she has what you might call dementia. But did you know she's an ordained priestess, though of course she doesn't have her own congregation anymore."

"Priestess? What are you talking about? Do you mean she's an ordained minister?"

"Minister, priestess, whatever. And at least she's not bossy and full of herself, like some people I know around here." And then Charlotte is off and running, giving Lazy the lowdown on every deeply flawed person who's snubbed her lately.

As the theme song from the sitcom *Two and a Half Men* plays in the background, Lazy falls asleep with her head on her mother's shoulder, not unlike Henry Shine in the lounge on

Movie Night. And, like Henry, she, too, is more than a little homesick.

She is now convinced she's reached the nadir of her forty-three years on earth, and who would disagree?

She and her husband are estranged, and the fault lies not in the stars but entirely with her.

She and her seventy-seven-year-old mother are roommates.

Menopause may very well be just around the corner.

And for dessert: tonight at 8, Griffin's board of trustees is scheduled to convene for an emergency meeting and she's the guest of honor. Or dishonor, if her instincts serve her correctly.

A Xanax and a pep talk from Brooke, her loyal assistant, two cigarettes smoked on an empty stomach, and she's off. In the elevator that will bring her to the ninth-floor conference room, she checks her lipstick, smoothes the shoulders of her Chanel suit, and curses herself for neglecting to stop off in her private bathroom one last time to pee. Except for her mother and son (who called last week on Mothers' Day though he failed to send a card or flowers), there's no one in all the world who would truly mourn her passing, she decides. Well, maybe Brooke and a couple of old friends from college and grad school, but they'd get over it soon enough. And then there's Richard, whom, despite her love for him, she so cruelly, so stupidly, torpedoed. The next time he speaks to her again for longer than two minutes, the conversation will, no doubt, take place in a lawyer's office.

She hops off at the seventh floor and ducks into a faculty rest room, the infamous site where Emma Hughes' daughter performed her ill-considered act of fellatio. (Ill-considered, and plain old dumb, but not enough to keep the kid out of Princeton.) A quick visit to the toilet stall proves to Lazy that she doesn't have to pee after all, but as long as she's in the bathroom, she might as well take a swig from that mini-bottle of Scope she keeps in the zippered compartment of her purse. A swig of mouthwash—isn't this what alcoholics rely on, desperately hoping to rid themselves of the scent of their sins? *Sin sinful sinner offender transgressor outcast.* If only she could remember something of Brooke's little pep talk. But she can't recall a word of it. And will, consequently, walk into that conference room with shoulders sloping, eyes lowered, her self-confidence in the sub-basement.

Waiting for her in their seats around the seminar table are a host of luminaries and quasi-luminaries, all Griffin parents—a guy from the original cast of *Saturday Night Live* (or SNL, as Lazy knows they like to call it these days); a screenwriter with a former coke habit and suspiciously reddened nostrils (not to mention two Academy Awards, one for best original screenplay, one for best screenplay adapted from another medium); a correspondent from *60 Minutes II*; a correspondent from *48 Hours*; a correspondent from *Dateline NBC*; a Pulitzer Prize–winning critic; a humorist whose book is currently number two on the *Times* hardcover bestseller list; a biographer whose book is number three on their paperback list; the chairman of one of America's largest and most profitable investment banking firms; and, lastly, one housewife worth untold millions who goes by the name of Emma Hughes.

Ten pairs of eyes are staring at Lazy coldly; there's not a sympathetic gaze in the bunch. Is this really possible, that not a single one among them knows what it's like to stray from the path of righteousness? What about, for example, Paul Conway the screenwriter, who's sniffing away this very moment despite the rumor that he'd kicked the habit long ago? What about Josslyn Bluestein, the esteemed literary critic who had an affair with a gay student of hers, and continued the affair even after the student's ex-lover killed himself because of it? And what about, say, Gil

McSweeny, the humorist who's laughing all the way to the bank and screwing everything in sight despite the ALS-afflicted wife lying at home in bed, unable to move or speak? Can't at least one of them find it in his or her heart to offer Lazy even the slightest bit of empathy? Apparently not, judging by all those unequivocally hostile looks trained in her direction.

Emma, the board's president, takes a sip from a sweating bottle of Aquafina—one of a dozen arranged at the center of the beautifully burnished table—clasps her bony, bejeweled hands together, and stares balefully at Lazy. She's looking even more anorexic than usual, Lazy observes, and her regulation tan has a sickened, yellowish cast to it. Hard to tell if it's a touch of hepatitis, a vitamin deficiency due to self-starvation, or simply a spray-on tan session gone wrong.

"It has come to the board's attention," Emma begins, "that our headmistress's character is, I regret to say, not as sterling as we might have expected or hoped. In fact, Kathryn Hoffman has, for the past year and a half, been engaged in an inappropriate . . . Ironically, I'd said once before to Kathryn herself that I found her unfit to lead the school in this new century . . . Her behavior has indeed proved me right . . . not that I take any pleasure whatsoever in bringing this to your attention. . . ."

Lazy fades in and out, choosing to imagine herself floating on her back in the calm, turquoise waters of Saint Maarten, where she and Richard so happily celebrated their twentieth anniversary two years ago. Why bother to listen to the charges being leveled against her when she can effortlessly transport herself to the West Indies, far from Emma Hughes and her stony-hearted board of trustees who have chosen to ignore all of Lazy's hard work and accomplishments during these past nine years of her tenure as headmistress. Never mind the millions in endowments she has helped to secure, the Ivy League acceptance rate that has risen year after year under her leadership, the reputation for academic excellence she has helped to successfully maintain . . . It's only when she hears Doug's name uttered and the catch in Emma's throat, that she snaps to attention. Emma's eyes are glossy with tears, Lazy sees from the other end of the table, and sees as well how blind and dumb she herself had been not to have guessed that Emma, too, was one of those notches in Doug's belt. WE WILL BRING YOU DOWN, BITCH . . . this hardly sounds like Emma (it sounds like one or both of her daughters, come to think of it), but studying her now, Lazy finally gets it. That she and Emma were rivals in a contest Lazy hadn't even been mindful of . . . That Emma is untouchable and cannot be toppled from her throne . . . And where, by the way, is Doug? Isn't he just as guilty as she of conduct unbecoming? Isn't *his* character not what the board might have expected or hoped? Why does he get to stay put in these carpeted, air-conditioned hallways while she gets the dishonorable discharge? Because, she hears Gil the bestselling humorist explaining, all too humorlessly, *I think I speak for every one of us here tonight when I say that as leader of our school, Kathryn, of all people, should have known better than to indulge in a long-term sexual relationship with a subordinate.* (Where, Lazy wonders, is the guy's celebrated sense of humor?)

There's a murmur of assent rising from every corner, a vigorous nodding of heads, the sight of which makes her slightly dizzy. She longs for a cigarette now, like the blindfolded, condemned man standing before the firing squad in a hundred movies. And she longs to put her life into rewind, to travel swiftly backward to that day a year and a half ago when Doug's endless flirting finally turned to something deeper, and, aroused and flattered, she allowed (well, to be honest, actually encouraged) those nimble hands of his to slide under the back of her cashmere turtleneck and unhook her bra. Mistake number one, that unhooking of the bra. If only she'd pronounced the simple word "don't." And done the right thing even when it was all too thrilling to do its opposite.

She's half tuned-out again and hears—though only dimly, as if she were deep under water—the unanimous decision not to renew her contract. But aren't there other, more important things to be renewed? Her marriage, her self-respect, her self-confidence? All of these are in disrepair, but she has a small measure of hope for all of them. Even her marriage, though that may be stretching it.

Isn't there something she'd like to offer the board? Emma is asking her now. *An apology, perhaps?*

Taking her cue from Senator Hillary, last seen this fall live and in person at the Goldfine funeral, Lazy and her Chanel suit sail off without a word.

50

JULIANNE

Michael is dying to see a certain indie band whose music has been described by Internet critics as "brilliant and fierce," and so he and Julianne take the subway all the way down to the Lower East Side on this Friday night in early June. They're both wearing jeans and T's and Birkenstocks, and they're both carrying fake IDs in their wallets—a laminated driver's license for each of them that attests to the fact that they're twenty-one. Without these IDs (snagged in the Village for only fifteen dollars), they can't get in to see the band, which is playing in a club that serves liquor.

"I'm so stoked for this!" Michael says happily. "*So* stoked!"

Julianne isn't. She's a pretty big fan of the indie scene, but this particular band, whose music she's listened to on the Internet, is just a little too fierce for her. But it's fine—she's with Michael on this warm sweet night and everything's good. As they come off the train, she sees a black woman in a floor-length red satin wedding dress, accompanied by her brand-new husband in a white suit, and three tiny flower girls in white satin gowns that skim the sooty, unswept subway floor. The bride is carrying a bouquet of scarlet roses to match her dress; she smiles shyly as Julianne congratulates her. Julianne thinks the bride deserves better than the subway on her wedding night, but the woman seems okay with it. "Good luck!" Julianne adds, and then she and Michael are heading up the stairs.

One thing Julianne *is* stoked for is the summer, only weeks away now. The summer before college. She can hear herself saying, years from now, *The summer before college, okay, that was when* . . . Sure, even when she's forty or fifty, she'll still be referring to this summer as the summer before college. She and Morgan already have jobs lined up—which they got through Luke's mother, the big feminist—providing women safe escort to abortion clinics around the city. It's something Julianne and Morgan feel strongly about. Michael feels strongly about working in a bookstore and that's understandable, too.

It's a five-minute walk to the club and they hold hands along the way. A line has formed outside the door; a dozen or so people are waiting to have their IDs checked before they go in. When they get to the head of the line, Julianne sees that the person in charge is a big guy in a sweat-stained T-shirt that announces, in huge, shouting letters, "I FUCKED YOUR GIRLFRIEND." Great. It's meant to be funny, she supposes, but to her there's something threatening about it and she feels a chill run through her.

"IDs," the man tells them, sounding bored.

They hand them over, no big deal. They've done this a million times before. Julianne isn't worried; they're high-quality fakes, with the official seal of the State of Delaware embossed on them, and they've never failed to do the trick. The street is a little dark, despite all the busy restaurants and clubs, and the guy in the obnoxious T-shirt steps back into the light to examine the IDs more closely. And then he stares at Julianne suspiciously.

"No way you're twenty-one, honey," he says, not unkindly. "What are you really, fifteen?"

"She's twenty-one," Michael insists, "just like I am." His voice is calm and reasonable; he's not looking for trouble. He just wants to spend the next hour listening to the brilliant, fierce music of this band he's read so much about.

"Look," the guy says, "I don't make the rules, I only enforce them. That's what I'm paid to do, okay? It's nothing personal, all right? You," he says, gesturing with his thumb in Michael's direction, "are in. She's out. And it's not the worst news you'll ever hear, right?"

"This can't be happening," Michael is murmuring, as if an atomic bomb has been dropped, as if the streets are on fire, their lives about to come to an end.

The guy says they're holding up the line.

"This is completely unfair," Michael protests.

Julianne takes his arm and leads him past the entrance to the club. "Look, I know how much you want to do this, and I don't mind going home alone. Go to the concert and we'll hook up later."

"No," Michael says. "Absolutely not. We're both going. As planned. I'll figure out a way to sneak you in, that's all." He fumbles with a cigarette and his grandfather's monogrammed lighter; Julianne has to hold his hands steady so he can get the Marlboro lit.

"I honestly don't mind missing the band," she says. "I was only along for the ride, just to keep you company, really. Are you listening to me?"

He's not listening; to Julianne's horror, he's grinding the lit end of the cigarette into the underside of his bare arm, somewhere between his wrist and elbow. Even before she knocks the Marlboro from his hand, he's crying out in pain. "Ohmygod ohmygod ohmygod," Julianne wheezes. There's a small bottle of Poland Spring in her canvas bag and she spills every ounce of it over his arm, hoping the cool water will help. Her eyes are wide open: she can see where all of this is going. Already she can hear the sound of her voice coaxing, begging, pleading, soothing, wheedling. So it's just one more ruined night in what feels like an endless succession of them.

"Why would you do that to yourself, baby?" she asks him, as if there could possibly be an answer that would make any sense at all. The flesh on his arm has begun to blister; she has to look away.

"Don't you understand?" he weeps. "Don't you understand that I wanted *both* of us to hear the band? *Both* of us, not just me."

She has to get ice for his arm, she decides. "Stay right there," she says, and takes off, sprinting down this small, narrow street until she finds a deli at the end of the block; outside it is an ice-filled stand displaying see-through plastic containers of cut-up cantaloupe, honeydew, and pineapple, bottles of water, containers of strawberries and raspberries. Asking permission from no one, she scoops up handfuls of crushed ice and races back to Michael, ice water streaming from between her fingers. His back against a brick wall, he's rocking slightly on his heels.

"Maybe this will help a little," she says breathlessly, and dribbles ice across his cruelly damaged skin.

He doesn't seem to notice. "That ID was perfect," he says. "That asshole just wanted to fuck things up for me. For us."

"No he didn't," Julianne says. "He was just doing his job."

"Are you *that* stupid?"

"Excuse me?"

"Rules can always be broken. Sometimes they're meant to be broken," Michael explains. "I'm telling you, that guy just wanted to fuck things up for me." His voice is pitched unnaturally high and this is a warning for Julianne to back away, but instead she moves closer.

"You're upset about missing the band, your arm hurts, you need to go home," she says quietly. "How about if we try to catch a cab?"

"How about you shut the fuck up?"

You know who the real asshole is? she thinks to herself, and then, in the next moment, as Michael's hand flies up and strikes the side of her face with such shocking force that her ears actually begin to ring and she has to struggle to keep her balance, she realizes that he's read her mind. Only later does it occur to her that she'd spoken aloud. But no one has ever hit her like that before. *Hit her, period.* Not once in all her life has anyone raised a hand to her. And so she is stupefied, unable to feel anything except her own disbelief. And no matter what Michael says or does, this is the end of the line for her.

He's weeping furiously, apologies mixed in with his tears, *I'm sosososorry*. And Julianne has no doubt that he is. Though he doesn't touch her again, doesn't try to kiss her or her battered cheek. The whole left side of her face is aching, but that's something she'll share with no one.

All at once, Michael has gone truly berserk, ripping handfuls of baby-fine hair from his temples now. It hurts Julianne to watch, but not as much as she might have expected. Other people are watching, too; a small Friday night crowd has gathered, and a guy and his girlfriend, in their thirties, probably, ask if Julianne needs help. They want to know if they should call the police on their cell phone. Or an ambulance, perhaps.

"No thank you," she tells them. "It's fine." Because this is the end of the line for Julianne-and-Michael, and he knows it. This is where she gets off. Without a good-bye, without even the briefest passing glance over her shoulder.

51

SUSAN

After dinner with an old friend from her boarding school days and a movie (a Diane Keaton–Jack Nicholson romantic comedy, which she thoroughly enjoyed), Susan takes a cab back to Central Park West. A doorman in a maroon-and-gold uniform helps her out of the taxi; another doorman ushers her into the building and comically tips his cap. Zipping along the marble hallway in her Ralph Lauren alligator loafers (fifteen hundred dollars and worth every penny, Susan would say if asked, not that anyone has), she greets Francis, the elevator operator, by name, and asks after his children and grandchildren, for no other reason than to be polite. Though she has to admit she's in particularly high spirits this Friday night. It's been a lovely evening, starting with that wonderful softshell crab at Café des Artistes and ending with a movie that hit home, especially the scene where Diane Keaton needed her reading glasses just to find out what time it was when she woke up. The indignities of middle age! Susan has rarely thought to laugh at them, to laugh at herself, but perhaps, she reflects, she should get in the habit of doing so whenever possible.

Flipping light switches in the foyer (*foi yay,* as she had been raised to pronounce it), she goes into the kitchen for some water, which she drinks, gleefully, straight from the bottle, feeling as if she's gotten away with something, violated a cardinal rule of etiquette, perhaps. And no one will be the wiser. She actually laughs out loud! And wipes away, with the palm of her manicured hand, the Perrier that has dripped to her chin. Boyfriend comes out to greet her in his pajamas—the softest, lightest cotton ornamented with red-lipped rubber duckies against a flotilla of bathtubs with wings. "If you aren't the cutest thing I've ever seen!" Susan says, and bends to the floor to lift him into her arms. Carrying him to her bedroom, passing guest rooms, her husband's office, the den, the library, she is pierced, unexpectedly, by something she would have to identify as sheer loneliness. She has, of course, always been a rather solitary creature, savoring her own company, but at this moment, close to midnight, in this vast apartment of hers, she craves the sound of Mickey's distant voice, now across the world in Singapore, a voice that, in her imagination, would be calling simply to say that she is missed. Even if it's a lie, she'd like to hear it; though she presumes he no longer loves her, he can still miss her, can't he? It wasn't always like this, this marriage that isn't much of a marriage. Mickey is deeply, sharply, intelligent and a very rich man as well, two excellent reasons for Susan to have fallen for him. Which she did, so many years ago, just after she left her job as a fact-checker at *Newsweek,* and went to work as a paralegal at a Wall Street firm. This was how she happened to meet Mickey, who was, at the age of thirty-two, already a partner in mergers and acquisitions. She was quite sure, after a few months, that Mickey loved her, and if it wasn't possible for her to fully return that love, at least she felt a genuine, abiding affection for him. What she has missed most during these years since they have drifted quietly apart is the way the two of them used to lie in bed together at the end of the day, chatting with great pleasure about not much of anything—the pretentious name of a law partner's country home, a friend's outrageously bad toupee, a waiter's mispronunciation of "salmagundi." Now, just recently, in fact, they have separate bedrooms, and not many shared pleasures. No great tragedy, but why shouldn't things be better than they are? Why can't they be? There's nothing about their marriage, after all, that is irrevocable. Nothing that is inevitable. Nothing that cannot be changed for the better. How foolish were they both to have allowed things to devolve as they have. They need to ask more of one another, offer more. Surely they're capable of that; how difficult could it be?

She draws Boyfriend's face to hers and kisses the tip of his damp black nose. "Let's get ready for bed," she says as they approach her room. She wonders if Michael will come slinking in at four or five—as he often does on the weekends after a night out with Julianne—and contemplates leaving the foyer light on for him. But she's feeling too lazy to walk all the way back along the gleaming, silver-veined marble corridor. He'll just have to do without that welcoming light, that's all.

The overhead fixture in her bedroom is on, though she could swear she'd flicked it off as usual when she left for the evening. Would bet her life on it, in fact. Entering the room, she goes directly to her bed, yanks back the peach-colored satin comforter, and deposits Boyfriend on her pillow. She steps out of her shoes, pulls off her linen pants and silk T-shirt, unclasps her necklace of shining onyx beads. She drapes the shirt and pants carefully across her bed, returns the necklace to the jewelry box on top of her dresser, ambles in her underwear toward the master bath. The one with the hot tub, and a shower with walls and floor patterned in pebbly aquamarine glass tiles imported from Italy, each one costing nearly a hundred dollars—a price tag that ignited a bitter argument with Mickey, who would have been perfectly content, he said, *with plain old tiles from Home Depot, if you really want to know the truth.* Well, she'd won *that* argument, at least. Though in retrospect, it seems impossible to refute his point. Tiles are tiles; they cannot add anything but the thinnest gloss to your life, they cannot ease your soul or fortify your shaky ego. She was mistaken to have thought otherwise, she sees, and is ashamed now of her foolishness, of having fought so hard for something of so little value, really.

The bathroom is the size of a large bedroom, with luxuriously appointed, burnished fixtures everywhere. She doesn't recall leaving the lights on here, either, come to think of it. Walking beyond the threshold, it takes her only an instant to see that there is someone in the shower, though the water isn't running and there is no hint of steam in the air. "Mickey?" she calls out, stupidly, because of course he's in Singapore, not due home for another five days. "Michael?" She crosses the room swiftly, knocks on the frosted glass. Nothing, no response at all. And this is when her heart comes to a standstill. Wrenching open the glass door, she is compelled to look, though how can she bear to? In a single moment she interprets what she sees; her son's frozen, unreadable face, his wide-open eyes utterly blank, communicating nothing. She cannot tell, looking upon him now, what his life had been like, what it had been all about these past few days, weeks, months. And she cannot know for sure what he was thinking as he knotted the thick rope around his fragile neck and kicked away the three-legged wooden stool beneath him. Kicked away his life.

She, his mother, cannot understand why she is unable to make even the smallest sound. Shouldn't she be screaming her head off? It seems to her that she should, but the sight of her only child suspended there, swaying almost imperceptibly, has rendered her mute, nearly lifeless. She does, however, remember to take her terrycloth robe from the back of the bathroom door and to dress herself in it. She does not want her son, even in death, to see her like this, in her underwear.

Boyfriend has followed her here; absently, she reaches down for him. The expression on his face is intense and alert, vigilant. Holding him in her arms, she walks in circles. She cannot think what to do, though of course there are phone calls to make. Mickey. The police. Someone to cut the rope and lay her son gently on the bathroom floor. The shower door is slightly ajar; she cannot bring herself to shut it, as if Michael needs light and air. Whatever it was he needed tonight, she failed to give him. Instead she was laughing it up in a movie theater on the other side of town. Who will forgive her for this? Certainly she will not forgive herself; certainly she does not deserve her own forgiveness. She is halfway between the shower and the hot tub now, rocking on her bare feet in front of the mirror over the sink, rocking Boyfriend in her arms. And there it is, the note her son has left for her, a sheet of plain white typing paper folded exactly in half, attached carefully to the mirror with a single piece of invisible tape. Written in ballpoint pen, unhurriedly, it appears, in small clear precisely formed letters.

> *Has anyone supposed it lucky to be born?*
> *I hasten to inform him or her, it is just as*
> *lucky to die, and I know it.*
> WALT WHITMAN, *"Song of Myself"*

She should have known it would be Whitman, his favorite poet. Despite herself, despite everything, she cannot stop the upward turn of her mouth into what she supposes must be the most sorrowful of smiles.

52

JULIANNE

By the time Julianne and her mother get over to the Upper West Side, Michael's body has already been taken away. To the morgue, where the cause of death must be determined (as if there were any doubt) before he can be released to the funeral home and prepared for burial. *The body.* The terminology is pitiless, really. Letting Julianne know that the body Michael inhabited for eighteen years is still around, though Michael himself is not. And will not ever be again, no matter how long and hard she weeps, her head in her mother's lap, soaking her jeans, Dee's hands caressing Julianne's hair, her voice saying, with infinite tenderness, *I know, pussycat, IknowIknowIknow.* Her mother can't hide from Julianne the relief she feels; Dee thinks she can, but she can't. If Julianne were her mother—a worried bystander but still a minor player—she'd feel that relief, too. But she is herself, the widow left behind, she thinks. And not to be a drama queen, but every cell in her body is grieving.

Mrs. Avery comes to the door in a bathrobe and bare feet. Julianne has never seen her with her hair uncombed, without makeup and earrings and her armfuls of gold bracelets; she's a mess, she looks old and worn-out. Shattered. Ruined. Just like Julianne herself. You can't look at that face of hers, of Mrs. Avery's, and not feel sorry for her. She falls into Dee's arms in the foyer and sobs bitterly, and Dee is weeping now, too. Seeing Michael's mother in Dee's embrace is a startling sight, even though Julianne had seen them together in Starbucks that time, and even though she knows there's some kind of weird friendship between them. Julianne and Dee were the third phone call Mrs. Avery made. Sort of pathetic, in Julianne's opinion: First her husband. Then the police. Then Dee. Michael's mother wanted to be with them tonight, needed to be, she said. Any port in a storm, that's Julianne's guess. According to Michael, his mother barely had any friends at all. Big surprise.

She was watching *David Letterman* when the call came. Julianne answered the phone in her room, but Mrs. Avery wouldn't talk to her. She asked to speak to Dee instead, and Julianne should have been suspicious right there. When Dee came out from the kitchen to break the news, Julianne kept one eye on *Letterman* and said, *What?* A little annoyed at her mother because they were doing the Top Ten List on the show and Julianne didn't want to miss anything. They'd already had a conversation about the bruise on her cheek (which Julianne explained away, in the laziest manner possible, by saying she'd walked into a wall, a door, she didn't even remember anymore, she said). Not that Dee bought it. *Does this . . . this . . . tragedy have anything to do with the mark on your face?* she asked later, when Julianne stopped howling for three minutes and it seemed as if she might actually be able to put a few sentences together. Julianne didn't answer her; she wasn't in the mood. Her mother put a cold washcloth over Julianne's eyes, which was sweet of her, though it didn't, of course, do any good.

Julianne wanders around the Averys' huge apartment aimlessly now, while the two mothers talk, *sotto voce,* in the living room. She doesn't care what they're saying to each other, who they're blaming for what. The simple truth is, she knows, that Michael would be lying on his bed, propped up on his elbow reading, or listening to a Dylan CD, "Highway 61 Revisited," probably, *this very moment,* if he hadn't hit her. He couldn't bear the thought of what he'd done to her, she's sure of it. But there's something else she's sure of, as well, which is that what happened tonight was inevitable; that eventually some large or small thing would have sent him over the edge. If not tonight, then definitely some other night. And she doesn't need Dr. Schuster or the bene-fit of the passage of time to help her reflect on this; she won't be any smarter or more perceptive six months or a year from now. She knows what she knows—that because of his illness, Michael didn't have what it takes to navigate his way in this world, to move past the things that got under his skin and stayed there, burrowing deeper and deeper, until there was no way out. His intellect was razor-sharp and he could ace an A.P. Calculus test with the same ease that he could analyze a page from Nabokov, but he didn't have the ordinary skills the rest of us have, she thinks—the ability to make light of things, to shrug our shoulders and move on. She should have been better at showing him how it works, how you just unclench your teeth or your fists and let go. She should have been better at this, but she wasn't. She failed him and there's no getting around that.

Going into his room is a mistake, but unsurprisingly, she's drawn to it. Everything in it—even his dusty black flip-flops with their worn-down heels, sitting side by side on the floor, a gnawed pencil and an uncapped stick of deodorant on his desk, a spiral notebook for his Am Civ class with her name written all over the cover—is infused with a poignancy that just kills her.

It crosses her mind that she could be a museum guide giving a tour here. *This is one of the beds we made love in, where he kissed every part of me joyfully, delicately and sweetly, convincing me I wanted nothing more than what I had right here. And this is his paperback copy of* Lady Chatterley's Lover, *one of his favorite books, which he liked to read aloud to me over the phone: "So I believe in the little flame between us. For me now, it's the only thing in the world." And this, ladies and gentlemen, this is the door his knuckles rained blows upon, again and again and again, while yours truly stood by watching uselessly, until at last I had enough and simply walked away.*

In the end, she was not a person he could count on, though she will swear on a stack of bibles *this* high that she did the very best she could.

53

DEE

I t is close to five A.M. before Julianne finally falls asleep in her bed, Dee beside her, wide awake, wired, her mind in overdrive, tearing from here to there and back again. *Nothing good can come of this.* How many times had she repeated this litany of hers to Julianne? Who could not see the wisdom, the usefulness of it, who could only engage in that adolescent eye-rolling and then that look of sorely tried patience broadcasting the same old message: *Give it up!* Well, she hadn't exactly stepped aside as Julianne had wanted, but she hadn't been able to protect her, either, not the way she should have. She never saw it coming, not this, this catastrophe that blindsided her and has left her child ravaged. But she's out of harm's way, at last. Her bruised, purplish cheek a reminder of what *he* was capable of. Though Dee is too ashamed to utter the words out loud to anyone at all, to her Michael's death is a mercy. Indisputably a tragedy, but a mercy, too. Guiltily she allows herself this luxury, this gift, allows herself to turn things around so that she can take away from a boy's calamitous death something like a blessing, something conducive to her daughter's future happiness and welfare. She is, after all, Julianne's mother; she *has* to see it this way. What Susan, the unluckiest of mothers, may feel, beyond a crushing weight of guilt, Dee neither knows nor can bear to contemplate at this moment. But the loss of a child—even an impossibly difficult and tormented one who brought his parents little enough joy—is surely the worst that life can offer. This, too, is indisputable, and Susan must already know it, already feel it. Dee would like to think that she and Susan are genuine friends of a sort, united by mutual worry and concern, and she wonders if their affinity for one another will survive the loss of the boy who had bound them together. Without him, there's no sense of urgency, no need to voice those endless fears of theirs. Yet who can say what they still may need from one another? And she's open to the possibilities.

Struggling to keep watch over her daughter, as bars of frail sunlight appear through the Venetian blinds and Julianne suddenly moans and rolls onto her back, flinging a tiny-wristed arm across her chest, Dee is dangerously near to dozing off. She's been awake for almost twenty-four hours; can't she afford to shut down for intermission, to put this vigil on hold for an hour or two? Why is she guarding her daughter with such singlemindedness? Whom is she trying to impress at six thirty in the morning? It's not as if she's in the running for the Mother-of-the-Year Award; not even close. As she drifts toward a kind of restless, unsatisfying half-sleep, it occurs to her that she has a story to tell. For the first time in a long while, she feels that unmistakable urge, that itch that demands immediate attention. It's not what a mother is born to do, to explore on paper the secret heart of her daughter's life, but it's what *this* mother feels a compulsion to do, God help her. The old transformation-of-life-into-art trick. Which, if she's lucky, may prove healing to both of them, to her and to her dearly loved child. She'll see how it goes. And will guard Julianne with her life.

54

LAZY

Subject: A DEVASTATING LOSS IN OUR FAMILY
Date: 6/7/2004 7:09:23 AM Eastern Standard Time
From: khoffman@griffin.org
To: griffin.org

It is my terribly sad duty to inform you of the tragic death of Michael Avery, an illustrious member of our Senior Class. Michael was one of our brightest stars, and, as many of you know, had been slated to attend Harvard in the fall. Over the weekend, however, he inexplicably chose to take his own life. It is Griffin's great loss and Harvard's as well. To Michael's bereaved parents, Susan and Mickey, we extend our heartfelt condolences. And our assurances that Michael, in all his brilliance, will not be forgotten.

Tomorrow morning at 8:30 there will be an assembly in the auditorium for all high school students. Dr. Muffy Landau, our school psychologist, will be on hand to take questions any of you may have about Michael's suicide specifically or the subject of suicide in general. Those of you who feel a need to meet with Dr. Landau privately are urged to schedule an appointment with her immediately. Please make every effort to take advantage of her expertise.

I have been told by the Averys that there will not be a funeral or memorial service. You may honor Michael's memory by making a contribution to the school in his name.

Kathryn Hoffman
Headmistress

How truly odd it is, Lazy reflects, to feel so unnerved at the simple thought of meeting Richard tonight for dinner. A meeting arranged at her behest, late last night in a call she made while locking herself away in her mother's bathroom in Queens. *No problem,* Richard told her graciously, but he didn't ask what, all of a sudden, was so urgent. And she didn't volunteer to fill him in, though what she might have said was that the events of the past week have taken their miserable toll on her, particularly the death of Michael Avery, which, unlike her dismissal, was shockingly unexpected. She heard today from Brooke, ever the source of vital information, that Michael had been officially diagnosed as bipolar, but how is that knowledge any consolation? Eighteen years old and already a ghost . . . A Griffin student to the bitter end, quoting Walt Whitman in his suicide note. Evidence of a literary sensibility even in his final hour on earth. So *he* may have found peace, perhaps, but what of his parents, marked forever by his needless death. Drifting along the Upper East Side, only blocks from Griffin, unable to think of anything but the Averys, she shivers in the hot wind of this summery night. Compared to the Averys', hers is a life to be envied and she knows it. She has a son alive and well. At Harvard, in fact. Susan Avery would exchange places with her in a heartbeat. True enough, but so what? *She* herself is still a middle-aged screw-up, soon to be officially unemployed, and currently without even a proper bed to call her own.

She and Richard, who haven't seen each other in over a month, have twice spoken briefly on the phone about her pile of mail waiting to be picked up, but until now have ventured no farther than that. And here is her husband, waiting for her in front of the unassuming neighborhood bistro he's chosen for their first dinner together—their first sight of each other—in ages. Peering out at her from under a billed black cap that covers the sparse hair he still has left. He's wearing Nikes and jeans, and—forgive her for noticing—a long-sleeved light blue oxford shirt in need of a quick date with a steam iron. Richard has a new, skimpy beard, rust-brown dusted with gray, that renders him a little unfamiliar. And intriguing.

"Hey," he says, and smiles tentatively.

To her, even this small gesture, this hesitant smile, seems promising, and she moves toward him to skim the palm of her hand uncertainly across his bristly cheek. From this modest beginning, it's possible they will take an infinite number of baby steps and, eventually, find their way home together. At least this is what she imagines.

The beauty of it is, she's free to imagine anything at all.

55

JULIANNE

Next week, or the week after, or the week after that, when Dr. Schuster tries to raise the subject of closure—as of course she will—Julianne will tell the good doctor she is wasting her breath, that for her, Julianne, there is no such thing. There is only this, really: every moment, incandescent or dismal, that she and Michael spent in each other's company, every word they exchanged, every kiss they savored, every bit of it, was only leading to that night. To a rope fastened tight around his neck, three lines from "Song of Myself" taped to a bathroom mirror. Michael letting Walt Whitman do the talking for him because he just couldn't bear to do it himself.

Julianne is done with all of this now. And undone. Left behind in a darkness all her own.

56

MORGAN

J ulianne is about to shut down her computer for the night, but Morgan, who's sleeping over (as she has several times this week since Michael's death), wants to get one last look at her e-mail.

"Be my guest," Julianne says.

Subject: Elizabeth Goldfine
Date: 6/11/2004 10:14:57 PM Eastern Standard Time
From: myfinalemail.com
To: morgansfine@aol.com

Dear Morgan Goldfine,

MyFinalEmail.com is a company that enables its members to convey their last wishes upon their death. We have therefore contacted you at the request of the late Elizabeth Goldfine, whose email to you follows as an attachment. Please accept our sincere sympathies on your loss. And also our apologies. Although this message should have reached you last fall, there was, apparently, some confusion with our server, an unfortunate occurrence for which we at MyFinalEmail.com accept full responsibility. Rest assured that we are a bona fide, legally regis-

tered company, and that the message you will be downloading is
absolutely authentic.

Yours truly,
MyFinalEmail.com

Morgan's hand flies straight to her open mouth; her teeth grasp
the webbing of flesh between her thumb and index finger. She
bites down hard, drawing blood. She understands that she is
awake at Julianne's desk, though really this fact doesn't seem to
fall within the realm of what is possible or probable.

Somehow she manages to get herself up out of her seat and
stagger to the door, which she locks with a purposeful twisting of
her wrist. (As if there's a danger that Julianne's mother might, at
three A.M., come waltzing in to look over her shoulder.) Because
this is between Morgan and her mother; no one else is welcome.
Except, of course, Julianne.

Returning to the computer now, Morgan covers the silver
mouse with her palm, zigzags it idly along the mousepad. Noodling
around as if the mouse were a musical instrument she were playing. Wasting time, prolonging the exquisite agony of anticipation
for another few moments until she gives in and, with a mixture of
the purest joy and terror, downloads her mother's words. And then
backs away from the computer. Because when push comes to
shove, she's just not up to the task at hand and has to have Julianne
read the words aloud to her.

Julianne nods; no worries.

Dearest Morgan,
The first thing I want you to do is stop crying, okay? You will live
your life successfully without me and we both know it. You will find
love and, I hope, a wonderful and satisfying career. And someday,

if you're lucky, you'll have wonderful children as well. You can't possibly understand, at this point in your life anyway, what it feels like, this love I have for you and your brother. Especially now. The thought of leaving you like this, unfinished, is unspeakably painful, the very worst of what is happening to me. (I promised myself I wouldn't descend into self-pity, but maybe just a smidgen of the stuff is good for the soul after all. Hey, I'm a dying woman, why not indulge myself a little, right?) Listen, it has been my greatest pleasure to be your mother. To watch you grow into the smart, discerning, openhearted young woman I know you to be. I can't, obviously, have a hand in your future happiness, or in guiding you along whatever path you choose for yourself. You're on your own, kiddo, for the next seventy years or so, at least when you happen to be in the market for motherly advice. But Daddy is as smart as they come about almost everything—go to him whenever you need some wise counsel. His one big failing is that he'll work 24/7 if you let him. So if you ever feel that he's been neglecting you, you need to let him know it. Don't be afraid to yank him back into your life. Yank hard, if you have to.

Enjoy college! Revel in life! It's all right, though, to miss me a little and to think of me now and again. But don't overdo it in the grief department, okay?

All right, done nagging. Except this: As long as you live, don't ever forget that you had a mother who loved you immeasurably. And who desperately wished she could stick around and watch your life unfold in all its grace.

Love you, kiddo—
Mommy

This is what Morgan has been waiting for since September, right there in 12-point type on Julianne's screen. Her mother has told her to stop crying, but what seventeen-year-old is going to listen to her mother, right?

With her eyes shut, she tries to summon up her mother's distinctively low-pitched voice, one that always seemed to Morgan a little sandpapery, a little gritty—its timbre unforgettable. But she's remembering it imprecisely now; she can't hear it in the way she wants to, with unfailing clarity. Like a voiceover in a movie, heard by the audience after the character has died or flown the coop, never to reappear.

Maybe it will return to her someday, a perfectly captured memory. In the meantime, there's this e-mail, a gift which seems, astonishingly, to have come to her straight from heaven.

57

LAZY

Putting an end to her long, bleak sojourn in Queens, Saint Richard, as Lazy gratefully thinks of him, has seen fit to welcome her back into their Upper East Side apartment. The sleeping arrangements—she in their comfy bed, he on the living room couch—may last for weeks, or even months, Richard warns her tonight.

"The thing is," he says, sounding almost apologetic, "I haven't forgiven you, not yet anyway. It's a process and it's going to take time, maybe a long time, I just don't know. It's like I'm recovering from an illness or an injury, and I'm healing slowly, making the smallest strides each day."

"*I* haven't forgiven myself either, if that's any consolation to you," Lazy says.

Richard nods. "What you did was terrible and stupid, but it doesn't necessarily have to wreck everything between us," he says. And offers her, a bit awkwardly, a good-night kiss on the forehead—far more than she deserves, Lazy knows.

As her final act as headmistress, she is required to show up at graduation today. But, *oh Christ,* how can she? How can she possibly make her way onto the stage of the auditorium at the Metropolitan Museum of Art—where commencement is always held—and offer a few brief remarks to the assembled graduates and their parents. Every last one of whom has surely heard by now all about her unrenewed contract and that *long-term sexual relationship with a subordinate*. An official letter from the board of trustees won't go out until midsummer, but Lazy *knows* they know.

WE WILL BRING YOU DOWN, BITCH!

No hyperbole there (except for the unseemly and highly inappropriate use of the word "bitch"): she has indeed been brought low. If not for Richard's encouraging words this morning before he left for work, Lazy might still be in her pj's now at three in the afternoon, choking on her guilt and a profound sense of failure. Thankfully, there was Richard to ease some of her suffering on Commencement Day, as she prepared herself for what would likely be two of the worst hours of her misbegotten life.

"Go there, make your dignified speech about the importance of a top-drawer education, hand out the diplomas, march in the recessional, and then get the hell out. You'll be absolutely *fine*," he'd assured her at breakfast.

Not that she was able to knock back more than a single spoonful of Raisin Bran.

"I'll be *fine*?"

"And don't forget: 'No one can make you feel inferior without *your* consent.'"

"Says who?"

"Says Eleanor Roosevelt, one smart lady. And indisputably a class act."

Okay then!

The hired photographer has asked the students to arrange themselves on the front steps of the Met this still-bright afternoon at 4:15, and there they are, Lazy sees—those ninety-nine surviving members of Griffin's senior class, outfitted in their newly purchased crimson robes (all of which will later be donated to one of

New York City's worst public high schools where, presumably, they will be put to good use by the disenfranchised). Many of the Griffin girls with rubber flip-flops under their manicured feet, many of the boys in begrimed sneakers. Couldn't they have bothered, on Commencement Day, to put something decent on those privileged feet of theirs? Where are all those Jimmy Choos and Manolo Blahniks Lazy's heard so much chatter about? And, for the boys, what about some handmade Bruno Maglis or nice, soft Ferragamo loafers? It's not as if they can't afford them, for God's sake.

But what does *she* care? She, who, by six o'clock tonight, will no longer be affiliated in even the most tenuous of ways with the exclusive (as the *New York Times* has insistently, annoyingly dubbed it time and again in its illustrious pages) Griffin School.

Everyone, it seems, is staring at her now as she daintily ascends the steps in her highest heels. Including poor, mournful Julianne Coopersmith with her arm slung across the thin shoulders of the motherless Morgan Goldfine, and next to her, the slightly dopey Daisy Camarano-Rosenthal—she, at least, in a pair of pricey black satin Prada slingbacks. All three of them, along with their classmates, staring at Lazy not unkindly but simply in surprise at the very sight of the soon-to-be ex-headmistress, dressed so bravely, so optimistically, in a Chanel suit they know to be reserved for special occasions.

"What's *she* doing here? She must be fucking kidding!" Lazy hears someone say. It's one of those adolescent voices of the sort she's spent the last nine years listening to attentively, a voice that will soon be heard loudest of all in Princeton, New Jersey. Far beyond earshot of Manhattan, thank God.

And then another of those voices says, wisely, "Whatever."

Looking over her shoulder into the distance, Lazy sees Doug McNamee sauntering uptown along Fifth Avenue, hand in hand with his ailing wife, two small figures growing larger and more distinct as they approach.

Whatever, Lazy murmurs to herself, and turns away, having no choice now but to continue up those precipitous stone steps and into the Met. Where she will, one last time, do what has been asked of her. And with as much dignity as she can muster.

After all, who is she to argue with Eleanor Roosevelt?